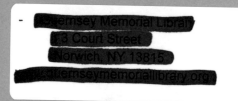

THE SAINTS OF RATTLESNAKE MOUNTAIN

THE
SAINTS
OF
RATTLESNAKE
MOUNTAIN

DON WATERS

UNIVERSITY OF NEVADA PRESS | *Reno & Las Vegas*

University of Nevada Press | Reno, Nevada 89557 USA
www.unpress.nevada.edu
Credits: "The Saints of Rattlesnake Mountain," originally "Estray," published by *The Kenyon Review*. "Last Rites" published by *The Antioch Review*. "Española" published by *The Georgia Review*. "La Luz de Jesús" published by *Idaho Review*. "Full of Days" and "Todos Santos" published by *Southwest Review*. Part 1 "Two Kinds of Temples," originally "Church," published by *H.O.W. Journal* (Helping Orphans Worldwide). "Day of the Dead," "Deborah," and Part 11 "Two Kinds of Temples," originally "La Llorona," published by *ZYZZYVA*.

Cover design and illustrations by Kimberly Glyder
Cover photograph: inacioluc ©shutterstock

LIBRARY OF CONGRESS CATALOGING-IN-PUBLICATION DATA
Names: Waters, Don, 1974- author.
Title: The saints of rattlesnake mountain / Don Waters.
Description: Reno & Las Vegas : University of Nevada Press, [2017]
Identifiers: LCCN 2016048233 (print) | LCCN 2016056131 (e-book) |
    ISBN 978-1-943859-29-0 (cloth : alk. paper) | ISBN 978-0-87417-470-0 (e-book)
Classification: LCC PS3623.A8688 A6 2017 (print) | LCC PS3623.A8688 (e-book) | DDC
    813/.6—dc23
LC record available at https://lccn.loc.gov/2016048233

FIRST PRINTING

Manufactured in the United States of America

CONTENTS

THE SAINTS OF RATTLESNAKE MOUNTAIN

THE SAINTS OF RATTLESNAKE MOUNTAIN

Hard to think such hot open range, some days, was prison. The biggest difference from inside was the sun, that sun, endlessly burning ears and necks and deepening brow lines. Also the voltaic air, air like tonic, and the long, empty, endless stretches. Out here Emmett felt like a loosened molecule without boundary. Another difference was the nature of Emmett's outdoor work, which offered unobstructed views of rocky ridgelines presiding over the nearby facility. The enormity of the mountains and sky and desert apron—all of it—made him startle awake some mornings believing in the possibility of God. Such bigness taunted him, terrified him, hurt his bones, vibrated his muscles and tendons, made him feel more a man, and not a man, and left him wondering what, anymore, being a man in the world meant.

Everything was stilled in the moments before, each man's head haloed by noontime sun. The Judas mare, named Judy by the warden's boys, as an insider's joke, stood patient and unspookable, a straight shot up the run line, several hundred yards above the corral's entrance.

Sun played brightly on the warden's badge. To Emmett the warden looked like a sort of king on top of his horse, built to give speeches, sign orders. He had delicate hands, calm mannerisms, and a handsome, generous, sun-leathered face. The warden's ranch boys flanked him, also on horses, boots pressed firmly into well-oiled stirrups. Gustavo, the farm's guard, straddled the fence's railing, his rifle even and cleaned and horizontal on his lap. Gustavo was squinting, listening, waiting. They all waited. In these final quiet moments Emmett was a witness among witnesses, a sweet ache behind his ruined knee, counting breaths, waiting for the silence to end.

Wind blew southeastern, and sagebrush softly rustled.

+ + +

Adrenaline kicked when the wild band of horses reached the arroyo's summit.

It was downhill from there. The horses were funneled into the steep floodplain and marshaled by a glass-bubble helicopter that buzzed, behind them, like a giant, mechanized mosquito. The pilot terrorized the band with his machine's thwapping downwash, trapping them between blades and the wide open gates at the bottom of the arroyo, where Emmett and Billy clutched the steel gate with trembling fingers, stomachs contorted with fear, both struggling not to vomit as the stampede neared.

Emmett watched, listening to the palpitating violence of the helicopter's backwash, feeling the ground shudder, feeling his old and beaten and tired heart skip.

Coming fast and kicking clods and dirt and rocks, the mustangs were led by a sorrel mare, her head bared high. At the rear of the roundup, protecting his family from the helicopter, from the noise and blades and false wind, ran the band's stallion, a magnificent blue roan.

The Judas horse began galloping in front of the feral band, as a sort of greeter, a leader, a guide. That was her job. She was a well-trained mare. To the corrals they approached.

Sad, aching excitement nearly burst Emmett open. His throat burned. He understood this reduction well: freedom, then chase, then entrapment.

The run line was a naturally formed arroyo strategically tucked between hills, steep hills rich with crumble and scree, hills that discouraged wilds from pulling back, turning around, and bravely doing what the blue roan stallion was now—incredibly—doing:

the horse was running away from the Judas mare, away from the corrals, away from the trap.

Emmett watched the stallion pull his nose high and turn, galloping back up the arroyo in the direction of the helicopter, aiming for it. He'd never before seen such brave foolishness, neither from animal nor man.

"Sonsabitch!" Gustavo yelled, nearly tumbling off the fence. "Look at him run!"

By instinct the other mustangs sprinted alongside Judy and into the corral, slamming against each other, hopping about, stunned. Suddenly, very suddenly, confined. For a short while it was a kick- and blood-fest. Spooked beasts. It happened. They bit, kicked, brayed. Eyeballs, veined red, nearly burst from skulls. Family, and now turning on each other. In the pen, black lips pulled back to reveal blocky teeth as square as dominoes. Emmett and Billy ran behind the gate and pushed it closed, locking them in.

It was done. The helicopter was called off, via radio, vanishing into the day's pale light, and the seven horses settled into nervous pacing, watched over by the warden and the men and the other horses already contained.

Emmett's eyes stung from the smell of the horses' nervous shitting. He smelled fear and watched striated muscles along bodies ripple. Incarceration bred violence. The math on this sort of thing was simple. Emmett knew the symptoms of caged syndrome, the panic, the need to throw elbows, make room, and earn a name. And confusion. To be tamed was a sort of brutal learning.

The gather went well, except for that one horse.

Finally the warden kicked his leg like a ballerina, one fluid movement, and slid down. He held his gal by a green leather bridle, patting her neck along the grain. His horse, not range-bred, was very pretty, Emmett thought, especially her long eyelashes.

"That blue roan," the warden said, looking to the hill, to the stallion that had torn away. "What do you think?"

The warden was mining for opinions.

"He's beautiful," Emmett said, and he meant it.

The escapee stood hilltop, head lowered, surveying the inter-connected metal corrals on the quarter acre of hot, impacted dirt, head swaying side to side, pawing a hoof.

"Sure, beautiful. Rib-thin, but a fighter," the warden said. "You men." His slit eyes trained on Emmett and Billy. "I want you to get him for me. He's worth a steak dinner. And let's hope against anemia. Too many horses on the range have been coming down with it."

The warden wasn't a man of many words. He pinched the brim of his cinnamon-colored Stetson to put some emphasis behind his order. Emmett and Billy exchanged glances. The warden had said what he said, nothing more. Then he began leading his horse away, but Emmett wished the warden hadn't asked. Emmett hadn't seen a more spirited stallion in some time, and he wanted, just once, to see this kind of horse go free.

Emmett tasted iron, from a crack in his lip. "We should proba-bly let that one go off," he called out, watching Billy's mouth react with a flinch.

The warden stopped, turned. "No. I want him. Understood?"

"How do you figure we do that?" Emmett knew what the warden did with horses. "He's got two feet and a thousand pounds on us," he added.

"That horse won't leave his family," the warden said. "He'll probably stay close by. You watch. When he comes in for a sniff, toss some rope round his neck. It's that easy."

The warden saddled up, staring down until Emmett lowered his eyes in submission. He had a place, and the warden wanted to remind him, make sure he knew it, even though he usually treated Emmett with more respect. They had more or less a business rela-tionship. At some point during his incarceration Emmett had ad-mitted to himself that he liked his keeper. The warden treated his ranch boys respectfully, too. Of course, since moving outside the fences, Emmett was also privy to some other things. For instance, the warden thought he knew what was good for every kind of beast. The warden also liked his beasts broken down; had that itch in his veins; liked to have beasts feed from his hand. The warden was like that, touched by hubris. He owned a cattle and sheep and hay ranch and at night, whenever the valley was under a dark, new moon, the warden's impressive spread twinkled like a thriving desert pueblo. The man was in the habit of taking problematic and uncooperative and attitudinal horses to his ranch, where he broke their spirits more by dressing them in silver-studded tapaderos. Every Nevada Day, he paraded them down Carson Street in the capital so that kids could toss candy at them.

When the warden and his boys were far enough away, trotting across furrowed open country and growing smaller in the wide horizon, the farm's guard carefully withdrew a flask from his uniform's breast pocket. Always big on surprises, Gustavo. He was still sitting on the corral's fence. Emmett smiled, watching his kind, delinquent friend throw a deep sip.

"I could take that blue roan bareback," Gustavo was saying. He was holding out the flask in offering, sucking alcohol off his gums, his rifle falling against his shoulder. The pits of his uniform were wet oval patches.

"I'd like to see that," Emmett said. "That stallion's sturdy. Look at him, staring down, unafraid. He's got scars, living outside. Probably making jokes about us right now."

"Still," Gustavo said, the flask dangling in his fingers, "wrap a strap round his flank and I could ride the full eight. Got a gut now like I didn't back then, but hell, I could take one more."

Emmett looked around to make sure they were alone. Billy was in the tack shed on the other side of the pens. When he was sure, Emmett took the flask and swigged.

Already living at Great Basin Correctional was a bachelor band, five of them. It was one hundred and twenty days, minimum, for mustangs. The bachelors had been gathered four months before and ushered through the gentling program, where the warden's boys used resistance-free training techniques, desensitizing them by touching them with ropes and poles. The horses were now, in the parlance of the BLM handbook, "rehabilitated." The green-brokes were good animals, almost gentlemanly, and were more than curious about today's arrivals: three mares, three foals, and a painted colt. The colt's legs, Emmett noticed, were powerful, as steady as pillars.

Sure enough, just as the warden had said, the blue roan did eventually make his way down the arroyo—curious-like, Emmett saw. Sunlight at his back thickened his silhouette and made him appear larger. Emmett and Gustavo passed the flask and watched the smart, skittish horse for a while. The stallion had white hind socks, bluish tint, attentive ears that rose into points, and the large, nervous eyes of a paranoiac. The closer he came, the more his nostrils flared. He was sniffing. He was pacing, gauging his family's predicament. He was outside, they were inside. Emmett reached for the flask again, took a sip, and wondered how to coax out the fear.

"For an ungoverned animal, that's some perfect example," Emmett said to his friend.

+ + +

The work, mainly, was shoveling shit. Tons of shit. Emmett could now pinpoint a horse's diet, knew when they ate, and what, whether hay or mineral pellets. He'd been kneecap deep in stud piles bordering on two years, and he worked hard every day.

The job was also brushing gentled horses, spraying down dirt, and making sure bulldozer tire troughs were clean and full of water. The warden's boys, ranch-trained, real cowboys, desert cowboys, mostly did the training. Some of them had even graduated from farrier school. Trustees helped out, bonding with horses, exchanging trust. Trust was a currency new to many of them.

The days were long outdoors under the sun, sun three hundred days a year, and Emmett had come to know two times of day intimately: the part with the sun and the part without it. His time was spent either shimmering and hot and suffering or in pitch darkness, separated by moments of magenta fireworks at dawn and dusk. Weekends were quiet, two boring days on the farm waiting for Mondays to arrive. During summer months several dusty-haired kids from the nearby town scooted out on ATVs in order to taunt the trustees. Standing at the perimeter gate, trespassing on

Corrections property, the kids liked to yell at them. They yelled high holy, not knowing, if they kept up such nonsense, that someday they'd end up inside, too. No good warning kids destined for the life, anyhow. At least that was Emmett's view. The kids took pleasure yelling down at the trustees. And the trustees allowed it. The trustees welcomed it. Anything to break up the endless days.

Prisoners on the farm lived alongside mustangs, and by showing love, by showing tenderness, by caring for unruly animals undergoing *rehabilitation*, the trustees would *rehabilitate* too. At least that was the theory. A study published somewhere said so, it was on paper, all written down, who knew where? Emmett didn't care. None of that mattered, but Emmett knew some things. The program began in the seventies, arranged by a ranch lady with a spot in her bleeding heart for wild horses and bad men. She also donated rangeland.

Emmett was eight years toward twelve when he was transferred outside. Getting on in years, or wandering into that territory, he posed a negligible threat to anyone but himself. Knee was shit, eyesight a joke. The angry engines of his youth had sufficiently conked out. The warden found in him a perfect candidate. And the governor, a woman, liberal, what columnists in the newspaper thought was a four-year fluke, championed the program by throwing money at it. The governor was quoted somewhere that if she could rehabilitate one man—and one was asking a lot—then it was worth it for Corrections to continue partnering with BLM.

Trustees matriculating into the program lived in donated trailers outside the prison's fence line, on a few acres of level hardpan, which meant, for all intents and purposes, Emmett and Billy, the only current farm inmates, were free men. Free enough. No bars in sight, no cellblocks. Men that ended up working the farm were usually older, like Emmett, or minimum-security hacks, like Billy, who was caught by accident, couldn't afford proper representation, and was sent down the line to pad some junior prosecutor's resume.

For eight years Emmett followed the same scuffed-out green line to the cafeteria for every meal. Another line, turned off-yellow, led back to his cell, which he shared for several years with a bona fide lunatic. Esteban had a knife inked on his backhand. The pointy tip of a blade quivered on his knuckle. He liked to smash cheekbones with it.

Inside, there was something of value: Emmett had discovered the Word again. He welcomed the Word back into his life. On Sundays, as he'd done as a boy, Emmett assisted a priest, who wore blue jeans to services. Emmett rang the altar bell as the priest unveiled the chalice. He carried the wooden processional cross at the beginning of Mass.

One hundred forty-four months. Twelve years for assault in the first degree, from a dispute inside a Mini-Mart, a crime between strangers, of coincidence. It was a dumb argument that turned into a legitimate nightmare. Punches thrown, scar and bone, the whole nine. A hardnosed judge compounded Emmett's sentence. The judge tallied up his previous transgressions. Compared with others, though, his rap sheet was pathetic, just minor-league footnotes: shoplifting, drunk in public. The grand theft auto was a misunderstanding that his lawyer was still trying to clean up. Anyhow, the assault conviction sealed it, and the judge sent Emmett on a long raft ride. Several months in, Emmett floated a lunch tray at another inmate's forehead. Fucker had tried stealing his applesauce during Easter dinner, of all times. Emmett drew more for that offense.

Inside, you set boundaries. You learned the game of shut up and no eye contact and move to the side or else. And you never did favors, because once you did one, the favors never ended—never. Emmett talked little and made superficial friends, except for the priest and some other Catholics. Jimmy in the ten-by-twelve library.

Half a decade passed before his depression lifted. One morning Emmett awoke to the sound of cell locks popping and wasn't bothered. The sound soothed him. Emmett knew his routine. Knew his place in this world. Or a place that accepted him. In prison there was no more pretending. The freedom of not having freedom brought massive amounts of comfort. Men can acclimate to confinement, and confinement suited him. Certain men needed imposed order to live untangled lives. Emmett had gotten used to prison. Perhaps too used to it. But many couldn't bear it, and they trimmed down time by earning GEDs or enrolling in Online Community College or participating in group therapies. Emmett only went to Sunday Mass. Still, his court-appointed lawyer sent letters, made appointments. Parole was sneaking up on him. The woman told Emmett that freedom approached, that freedom was possible. After each meeting he stayed up late, worry filling his stomach with pressure, like bad gas.

The warden, as it happened, had seen something he liked. He selected Emmett from a computer spreadsheet. The warden had plans for him. The warden inked transfer papers. And like that, Emmett found himself outside the perimeter fence, choking on the deeply yellow sun, tears in his red eyes, blinded for weeks by it.

Emmett knew shit-all about pens and horses and dirt. He knew even less about roundups, about living in solitude, stud piles, about any of it. On his first night in the trailer a fat moon hung in a blue-black sky. A knot tightened inside his chest so hard he could hardly breathe, the blood rushing to his temples. He found himself kneeling, an attack triggered by a sudden case of freedom.

So much open space, he often thought—too much space. And in this desert, especially, where a person could see for a hundred miles. Emmett could hardly bear it. The world looked as though it went on forever, it never ended, and therefore, since it was so daunting and limitless, he was unsure where he should stand on it.

+ + +

Always spraying down dirt. The pens needed dampening. Otherwise dust clouds lingered around the farm.

That same day, Emmett watched Billy drag a hose around the pens, thread the hose under and through his legs, near his groin, and insert it, smiling, into a trough. Billy stood there, like some gentle idiot, like he had one long, green prick.

It was easy to forget about Billy sometimes. Sure, the guy joked around—in his dumb way—but said little. He almost, Emmett thought, hovered. Billy was fond of listening to AM talk on an old transistor radio that he lugged around. Billy was a nonviolent, three-year casualty of drug laws. A good kid. A decent kid who wore his hair long and messy, like untended vine, which threaded through his gold aviator glasses, which the warden let him wear. Billy liked standing by himself, upright as a yucca shoot, hose in hand, quietly imitating a fountain.

He liked spraying down the dirt. It was something to do.

Billy was also an attempted suicide, and he was really, truly, the nicest attempted suicide Emmett had ever met. Emmett knew the story. Billy's girlfriend had found him near comatose in his apartment. Then came the ambulance and the cops. Everything fell down around the kid when one cop peeked inside a closet and found boxes of ephedrine, imported from Mexico.

Outdoors, the prisoners and guards and ranch boys moved slowly. Heat did that. There was plenty of sitting around, bullshitting, thinking, ass-scratching, talking about everything. Talking about nothing. Listening to silence. To the wind.

"Weather's turned," Emmett said to Gustavo, following lunch. "The coyotes are visiting at night again."

They were at the tree stump that doubled as their table. Cards lay on it. They were playing five-card draw, but it was slow going. Slow because Gustavo refused to budge on his hand.

"They yip outside the corrals. Scare them horses," Emmett went on. "I'm afraid the horses will start kicking at each other."

Gustavo sat on a beach chair, his belly spilling over his belt. Emmett watched his friend carefully lean forward to unpin his cards from the stump, take an annoying ponderous gander, and pin them down again. A fat black fly danced in the air above their game. Gustavo was thinking too long, refusing to draw a new card. His stall tactic irritated Emmett. Emmett knew the score. He was not going to lose when he was top-heavy with two pretty queens and ready for any combo Gustavo threw.

"Those horses could take down any coyote," Gustavo finally said. He stomped the dirt, showing how.

"But I'm afraid they might turn on each other," Emmett said.

"Spooked, as they tend to get. You're not here at night. I am. I hear the ruckus."

"Well, if you don't tell Billy, I'll leave the rifle a few nights," Gustavo said. "If one gets too close to the pens, plug it. Kill one and the pack won't return. It's bad luck. They're superstitious."

Emmett thought about his friend's offer. He was skeptical. "You'll give me your rifle?" he asked.

"I trust you don't peek at my cards," Gustavo said. "That's a big kind of trust. One of the biggest, in fact."

Gustavo was a mix breed. Nose veined by years of nightly whiskey nipping, he also had a silver incisor in his smile. Got that tooth on discount in Nogales, he once told Emmett. It cost more than his pickup, and Emmett believed it. Gustavo drove a bona fide clunker. Anyhow, his friend was gentle, and funny, not the prison guard type, not the prison guard type at all, and Emmett was glad to call him a friend.

Later, he and his friend watched the blue roan stallion emerge from the hills and circle the corrals. The horse was poking around, and increasingly curious. It hoofed close enough to sniff the wet dirt and touch noses with one of his mares before wandering up the hill again, where he stood watch. The horse could join his family, Emmett knew, if he wanted. The horse was welcome here. But part of Emmett understood what that horse was suffering through. Stress accompanies change. An upcoming hearing would determine his fate. And all this working day and night with mustangs, and bonding with them, would better his chances for early release. Yet it was hard to wrap his mind around the notion.

Emmett had no family, no plans, and nowhere, really, to put up his feet. And ever since leaving the facility, ever since he first stepped outside, into sunlight, he'd managed to lose the Word. He understood how this big world knew how to break the Word down, tear the Word apart. Inside, the Word had given his life direction, solace, and purpose. Outside, it was hard to know where to look. Outside, the chaotic disorder of the natural world mystified him. Outside, hounded by winds that blew hot over his forearms, he was forced to look for the Word among rocks and desert scrub and weeds that just about died struggling from parched soil.

Thinking too much about his release sickened him. He looked around, sudden queasiness moving up his throat. He felt crushed by the immensity of everything, with the desert spread out like a giant, sandy cape that could fold over at any moment and suffocate him. Everyone had a view of the valley's tallest mountain, named Rattlesnake, but whatever was up there also had a view over him. If that mountain didn't stop the sky from going on and on, he could probably see the earth's curvature. Hell, he could probably see a cliff far away where, if he ever left, he could plummet.

He grabbed Gustavo's shoulder.

"Qué pasa?" Gustavo said, steadying him.

Emmett blinked through wet eyes. He watched Billy throw an arc-stream over the pens, drenching one mare, a pretty bay. The horse bristled.

Emmett closed his eyes while the universe expanded beneath his prison-issue tennis shoes.

+ + +

He awoke the next morning to the sound of his door slapping against the trailer. It was hot: desert heat, itchy calves, tongue as abrasive as sandpaper.

Without knocking, Kim had opened the door and let the heat in. She was flicking a packet of Insta-Coffee when Emmett opened his eyes, situating her in the morning light. Kim was big-boned, healthy as a watermelon, a scoop-of-ice-cream-each-night kind of woman. She carried a couch in her ass, and she was lovely, perhaps the loveliest he'd ever known.

"It's nine-thirty and you're sleeping," Kim said to him. "Warden told me to ring his office if this ever happened."

"Cleaning the pens last night," he said. "Up late. You know. Auction weekend coming up."

Kim glanced at a cardboard twelver crumpled in the trash. She declined to comment. Instead she said, "One of the warden's ranch boys phoned. Said there's a new band. They look healthy."

Emmett said, "One's still wandering around in the hills."

Kim slit her eyes. "Gustavo here?"

"Not that I know."

"Billy?"

"Am I under interrogation?"

Kim bent, showing him her lovelies. Very quickly she tucked him back into his shorts. A shiver rolled up his thigh. "I just want to know how much privacy we have," she said. Her short bob was hidden under a baseball cap adorned with the BLM agency patch. The image showed the most perfect river disappearing through perfect trees and perfect mountains. When she smiled, which Emmett thought she should do more, her smiles were forced, as though smiling dredged up unspecified amounts of childhood pain.

Kim grabbed his hand and placed it on her tit. She squeezed his hand with hers.

"Not now," he said.

"Why not?"

"Not right. Morning time."

"So old-fashioned," she said.

The trailer moaned as they stepped outside. Kim gave Billy his chores. The crisp morning needled Emmett's lips. Emmett liked the silence of mornings, the way everything looked new all over. One bachelor, a sorrel greenbroke, watched everything from a pen. He was two years old, star on his muzzle, and on his way out. Warden's men had softened the horse. Emmett had watched the whole time, as the rebel glint in his eyes slowly disappeared, sad as that was to witness.

Emmett had chores on his list. There was an Adopt-a-Horse event scheduled for the coming weekend. Adopt-a-Horse weekends were loud events, and the visiting families depressed him, simply by their existence. Families made Emmett miss the family he didn't have. And always with these families were squealing girls chomping gum and boys electrified by the sight of large hoof stock.

Adoption weekends also lured ranchers from surrounding towns, men looking for deals, and of course it would mean a visit from that small-time cabaret singer from Reno, who lorded over the microphone playing auctioneer, his rapid, high-pitched voice like machine-gun fire.

Adoption weekends were anything but silent.

Plus, Emmett could still not get friendly with how much he and Billy stuck out, like they were human sparklers with their hair on fire. How he was part of the circus, an attraction, the bearded lady. Live prisoner! Everyone stared. Visitors were forbidden to wear blue. Only trustees wore the color. Blue jeans, blue T-shirt, TRUSTEE stenciled on the back, blue baseball cap, also bearing TRUSTEE. Emmett often thought if he were heavier, perhaps rounder in the belly, on auction days he'd resemble a goddamn blueberry.

The Bureau of Land Management kept records. They had government scientists and bureaucrats and who-knows-who on staff in Carson City, and when the figures said the range needed thinning, the warden and his boys got the phone call: time for another gather. Then the horses were mellowed, trained, adopted out. Fifteen thousand mustangs roamed the desert backcountry as guests of the state. Horses over eight years old were rarely adopted. Families wanted studs, foals, not geriatric pets.

So it irritated Emmett when the warden began inviting one local land owner into the auction circle, a man named Meyer, Early Meyer, a man with the same kind of grease-eyed stare as the pedophiles in Unit C, a man who purchased older horses for pennies and quietly turned around and sold them to Mexican slaughterhouses. Early Meyer lied up and down on the adoption forms. Said he worked the horses. Said he kept them as hobby. But everyone knew otherwise, including the warden. Early Meyer hated mustangs because they nibbled down his green fields during summer months.

A dirt road connected the farm to the prison. Beyond that was a paved road connecting the prison to the interstate. All other roads encircling the prison were dirt or tended gravel. In the distance, Gustavo was driving up, a plume of dust rising behind his beat-up truck. He got out with a tray of coffee cups. He carefully set the tray on the tree stump, on top of their card game.

"Sorry yours is cold," he said to Emmett. "I ordered the double, as you like."

Kim walked over, fists on hips. She looked at Emmett sipping his fancy coffee. Then she looked at Gustavo. She shook her head.

"Relax," Gustavo said. "I brought cups for you and Billy, too."

On this day Kim was all business. She folded her sleeves into crisp denim squares and instructed Billy to feed the greenbroke bachelors, Emmett to spray down the pens, and Gustavo to stop standing around and looking the spitting image of a moron.

"Just go over there and throw your shadow over my water bottle. At least you'll be doing something," she said to him.

Kim lugged a blue supply cooler toward the pen that held the new arrivals. The horses backed away. "We're starting with her," she announced, pointing at the dominant mare. "We get her done and the rest will cooperate."

She hooked her boot on the fence and pulled herself up.

They carefully guided the horses, one and then another, into a channel of paneled steel chutes, restraining them in the squeeze chute, which kept them from moving, and where Kim could work on them. She administered worming immunization and drew blood to test for equine anemia. Then she shaved the horses' necks and applied liquid nitrogen freezemark brands. Each horse made noises for that. It wasn't the most ideal situation. Usually they allowed the horses to rest for several days, acclimate to confinement, but anemia was rampant this year and Kim wanted these horses tested.

At the top of the arroyo the blue roan watched Kim work on his family. All afternoon the stallion stood in the same spot, like the day before, and watched them get treatment, get handled. The more his family was bullied, the less the horse on the hill moved. Emmett knew that these horses' lives would change, from living an open-range life to trotting circles on ranches, with over-eager girls braiding their manes. When it was time to treat the painted colt, Emmett spoke up.

"This colt is—I don't know—strong," Emmett said to Kim.

"Maybe we should wait for the warden's boys." He'd had problems with one-year-olds before. Their attitudes.

"Just get him in the chute and we'll be fine," Kim said. She was on a roll, she said, and didn't want to stop.

She failed once, and on her second attempt nearly hustled the horse from the far side of the pen into the chute. The colt was hyper-alert, suspicious. He pranced around mockingly. For a while it went on like this, Kim approaching, the horse darting away.

"They don't pay me enough," Kim said loudly.

Again she failed to direct the colt. She was bent and her hands were low, palms open, as though shoving air around. At last she grabbed a rope and landed a loop around the horse's neck.

"How is that gentling training?" Emmett asked her, watching her tug the horse.

"Save it," Kim responded.

The colt was a fighter, like his dad, and the rope tightened as the horse darted around the pen, the rope pulling in Kim's hands. A purple vein throbbed in her neck. "Stop staring at my tits, idiots, and help me!" she yelled. She locked her strong thighs.

Emmett and Billy both grabbed the rope, and when, after pulling and cursing, the colt was finally inside the squeeze chute, Emmett breathed a sigh of relief. He noticed Billy's aviator sunglasses had come to rest on the damp dirt inside the chute. Billy shut the gate, and then he casually took a knee.

It was one of those moments, Emmett realized later, that would live in him for all his days, arriving at night, before sleep, to terrorize his dreams. Trauma had powerful claws. He would recall the mechanics later, because it happened quickly. On his knees Billy was reaching for his sunglasses, but he was leaning in too far. Emmett took a breath, just one, as he watched Billy, half in the chute, patting the moistened dirt by the colt's rear hooves.

Beast was already full-on spooked. The colt made rapid cooing noises and, without warning, kicked and connected, peeling back the western hemisphere of Billy's face. Layers of skin, fat, bone. The stratum came to rest again, though not taut. Emmett saw white and dark. Blood washed over exposed skull, like water down glass.

Billy went limp.

Emmett stood dumb and blinking and unbelieving and could not accept the idea of a face pulling apart so effortlessly.

"Rags, idiot!" Kim was yelling at him. He finally heard her when sound returned to his mind. Kim was already dragging Billy from the chute by his ankles. She was ordering Gustavo to dial emergency. She yelled at Emmett to get cotton balls and bandages. "Now!"

Cotton balls? Emmett swayed on his feet, nauseated. No such thing on the farm as cotton balls. Emmett ran, following orders, and after the ambulance left, he leaned against Gustavo's truck, ash-faced, numbed-through, licking his brittle lips, touching his face in the side-view mirror and examining it. Emmett was amazed by his skin, the bone structure beneath. He was mesmerized. Simply amazed a face could come apart in such a way.

Gustavo took a hard seat on the tree stump, ruining their card game.

"They'll patch him up," Kim was saying. "They'll patch him up. They'll patch him up."

"How can you patch that up?" Gustavo responded. "His face lifted off his skull."

"There are ways," Kim said, and she also said, as though she knew something specific, "modern medicine."

Gustavo put the bones of his wrists against his temples. "The warden's going to transfer me. Something like this happens on my shift." His eyes were blank, distant. "I never liked working inside. That recycled air. I'll be back to it now." He looked to Emmett for confirmation. "Tell her."

"It was an accident. It could have been avoided. Billy wasn't following procedure," Kim said. "I'll tell the warden Billy wasn't following procedure. What business did he have, anyway, crawling around by that colt's hooves? Was he doing that on purpose?"

Emmett had once witnessed a horse enter the paddock gates too fast and with too much force and crack headfirst into the steel girder, snapping her neck. That poor damn horse's hooves trembled until one of the warden's boys finally stood over her and put her down. What happened on this day was worse.

Emmett looked hillside. He felt chilled by the falling sun. Standing watch over them was the colt's father. The horse stood motionless throughout the late afternoon.

He wanted the horse gone. That horse was bad luck. But he wouldn't goddamn leave. Emmett picked up a rock the size of a golf ball, walked halfway up the arroyo, and threw it. The animal did not move.

+ + +

Kim stayed that night, her first overnighter. Officially it was forbidden, but when Gustavo left there was no one to say otherwise. And judging by that all-in look she gave Emmett, she wanted his hands on her hips. She wanted comfort. They had the sun, and hot dirt, and sometimes they had each other. There could still be found in another's touch brief reprieves in this parched outpost.

They made dinner. With plastic forks, scooping beef mush from cardboard containers, they ate in silence on the tree stump, using it as a dining table in the late sunglow. They lounged in dilapidated beach chairs, watching the sun descend behind penned horses. Emmett couldn't shake the memory of Billy's eyes, how blue Billy's eyes were—so piercing, so light blue.

"You want to know the worst thing about prison," Emmett said, after some time. "Health care. They never gave Billy meds. He smiled every now and then, but," Emmett said, cutting a hand through the air, "silent."

A red ant crawled across Kim's cardboard container.

Later, they undressed. Later, they felt each other's bodies with dry, apprehensive hands. Kim inched down her jeans, covering her smile with her fingers.

"I don't know how to thank you," Emmett said, after. He squeezed her fleshy shoulder. Then stopped squeezing. "Hear that?"

Kim rolled, pressing her warm breasts against his ribs. She ran her fingers over the hair on his shoulder.

"Yelping," Emmett said. "Those coyotes come to terrify the horses. They love scaring them. Wish they'd watched what happened to Billy. Then they'd know."

Kim put a finger on his lips. "Shush."

Later, Kim drifted off, but Emmett couldn't. Sleep was impossible. He was plugged in to some kind of energy force beyond his understanding. His thoughts ran. What had happened to Billy, coyotes, new horses, woman in his single, cramped bed. The adrenaline had yet to dry off. Close to eighty degrees inside the trailer, too. In the middle of the night the moon shone through the window, making a perfect rectangle of white light on the cheap linoleum. Emmett dressed. He sat outside in the beach chair petting Gustavo's rifle, listening to the coyotes circling the farm. Their eyes passed through his flashlight's beam, phantom-like, glowing. He heard the horses acting up whenever the coyotes moved closer.

More than anything Emmett wanted to plug one of the coyotes. He wanted to watch one fall, watch one beast fear for its life, confused by its own death. He liked these horses probably more than he ever liked any living thing, and he couldn't stand for this kind of harassment. He heard the coyotes earlier, sniffing at crumbs outside the trailer. Now he heard them in the darkness, scuffing through brush. He aimed the rifle at the dark. He walked toward the corrals and, standing beside the pen, under the moon's quick light, was the blue roan stallion.

Emmett lowered the rifle. The horse turned its large head from one of his mares and looked at Emmett. And Emmett thought he read sadness. The horse was majestic, God-like, but sad, indeed sad. There was, for the briefest moment, he thought, an understanding between them. Two rare loosened atoms, getting along as best they could.

Emmett banged the butt of the rifle on the dirt, spooking the horse. Its hooves shuddered and clacked as it galloped up the arroyo.

Still, there was the matter of the warden's order. The man wanted that horse. Emmett felt regret ache in his ribs as he poked around the tack shed with a flashlight. He threw a length of rope over his shoulder and hiked up the steep wash, into the dark, half-assing it, questioning his commitment.

The horse was in front of him. Moonlight was in its eyes. The horse led him away from the farm, teasing him, coming into view, disappearing, seeming to play with him. Brush rustled to Emmett's right. He walked on. He heard coyotes yipping near the corrals again. Emmett stopped, breathing heavily, overwhelmed again by the idea of paroling out. He was afraid of darkness, but more: open space. He realized he could, if he wanted, keep going. Disappear into the dark. Keep going forever. No one could stop him. But the bars had him. The bars were so tightly around him now that they could have been his own ribs.

Emmett rushed back in the direction of the farm, guided by the glowing aura of the warden's ranch. The sight of the cool, blocky prison mid-distance calmed him when it came into view on the other side of the hill.

How he missed it. He was shamed by how he missed it. He understood the rules, the procedures. There were small bits of charm to be found inside, too. Was he crazy to think of prison as charming, or was his gauge blown, was he institutionalized? He was charmed, for instance, by the sweat lodge on the grounds for Apache prisoners, who earned cigarettes for teaching people their language so the guards couldn't understand kited messages. Emmett even knew several phrases.

He was ashamed he didn't know how to live in the open anymore, free. Life on the farm and in prison was simple, controlled. Brushing his teeth and tying his shoes had methods. Inside, you were rewarded with TV for good behavior. Attending classes meant more access to computers. And there was a priest every Sunday. Out here, his Bible had lodged under his small bed, but inside an entire life could pass without ever seeing the sun, which wasn't that bad, not that bad at all, not when you knew how deeply that sun could burn.

+ + +

Kim shuffled around loudly the next morning. She made coffee,

Emmett thought, at the same volume as a rocket launch. He pulled on socks dustier than the ground. Kim fumbled with her clothes. She met Gustavo outside.

Emmett overheard the gist through the open window: Billy was alive, still in ICU. The colt had cracked several ribs, but the permanent damage was to his face. He'd live, Emmett overheard Gustavo say, but the stitches would turn him into a rag doll.

Emmett nearly fell down the trailer's stairs when he opened the door and saw the blue roan stallion, a rope around his neck, tied to his family's pen. Emmett, walking closer, rubbed his unshaven neck. The stallion had a white snip running along its nose, markings he hadn't noticed. And its gangly mane draped over its eyes, like a pissed-off teenager. But the horse wasn't struggling. The horse was calm. The horse snickered. One of his mares snickered in response.

"You caught him?" Emmett asked Gustavo, amazed.

"He was looking to get caught," Gustavo said. "I drive up and find him wandering around. He nearly put that rope round his own neck. We're keeping him outside until the boss comes by for a look."

One of the warden's boys, kid by the name of Step, was at the farm too. He was walking around the pens with a clipboard, ticking down a list. Every so often the kid pulled broken crackers from a fanny pack and chewed them, open-mouthed. Finally the kid came over and handed Emmett the day's duty list. Not a surprise: shoveling shit.

Emmett spent the morning, for the millionth time, cleaning the corrals of stomped stud piles, but this morning he had the vinegary aftertaste of Kim on his tongue. The corrals needed cleaning by day's end. And now, without Billy, he was alone in the work, prepping for the upcoming weekend, the families.

Emmett was in no mood for families.

He opened gates, closed gates, moved horses from one pen to another, shifting them like pawns on a chessboard.

+ + +

He was alone that night on the farm. And felt it, too. He felt more alone than ever. When night came, he ambled over to Billy's trailer and flipped on the lights. He even turned the light on above the tiny stove. He left Billy's trailer lit up, as though he still occupied it.

Later, Emmett lay in bed with his head against a lumpy pillow. He listened to the world around him, to the coyotes talking their crazy, yappy language. Their conversations echoed around the valley, and he tried conjuring the nature of their talks: the weather, this heat, that asshole with the gun that chases them off.

He was sleepless. The more he listened to the coyotes, the more he disliked the idea of the blue roan tied up outside the pens. That was a vulnerable situation for any beast. Coyotes were big on harassment. Emmett groaned and threw back the sheet and pulled loose carrots from the mini-fridge. The flashlight opened a tunnel of light as he walked toward the holding pens.

The stallion already had rope burns on his neck from standing tied up all day. The blue roan's family, on the other side, had yet to settle down. They paced.

The stallion was apprehensive. Breathing heavy, and quick, the horse smelled the carrots Emmett scattered on the dirt. At last the horse's neck arched and his lips pulled and grabbed a carrot, chewing. The animal's jaw muscles were powerful. Emmett trained the beam on the horse's long eyelashes. Quickly he set a hand on his muzzle and withdrew.

About fifteen hands. The horse wasn't the tallest, or the handsomest, but mustangs were once conquistador possessions, bred by skilled horsemen for endurance, agility, intelligence. This stallion was healthy, a leader, and Emmett knew he didn't have any business in the world of men. Not after raising such a beautiful family in all this big, confusing freedom. It pained Emmett to imagine the stallion dressed in parade gear, the rest of his life staring at open ranges from behind fences.

None of it was right, Emmett thought. None of it: old man Meyer arriving on auction weekends with his beat-up trailer, gathering the older horses, the leftovers. That wasn't right. And the warden wasn't right for allowing it. Emmett helped rehabilitate the animals and then here comes a hick rancher to escort the eldest among them to death. Goddamn that wasn't right at all. Emmett never signed up for that. And it wasn't right to place Billy in prison, where he didn't belong, just for melting pills for the juice.

Sure, men like Emmett and Esteban and many, many of the others were meant for the confined life. Men like him were sometimes worse than beasts, turned into beasts, concrete in their souls. But this animal before him didn't deserve pens, didn't deserve being roped outside slipshod corrals in the exact dead center middle of nowhere.

Emmett remembered the time Gustavo drove him into town. A crime, of course, to transport prisoners off the farm. Emmett could have squeezed diamonds from coal during that short drive, even though they just motored to town for a six-pack. Gustavo could have lost his job. Emmett thought of another night he walked past the perimeter gate alone, to the borderline, testing limits. He stopped walking fifty yards past the gate, afraid to venture farther. The world was out there.

The stallion was beautiful, as he'd told the warden. This stallion was true.

Emmett could lie. Say the stallion bucked rope during the night and ran off. As it happened, the horse didn't pull or run when he untied him from the pen. It seemed almost like the horse was holding his breath and awaiting instructions. And the horse didn't yank when Emmett led him up the arroyo. As if the horse accepted being led.

Scree fell from looming cliffs, rocks clacking, reminding Emmett of Kim's stumpy fingernails tapping at his window. Emmett guided the horse away from the farm, into the darkness, into the desert. A breeze blew cool against his cracked lips. Carefully, Emmett removed the rope. The blue roan jumped when Emmett smacked his hindquarters.

"Go on," Emmett said. "Get."

The horse stood there, not getting. Not moving. The horse even turned around when Emmett turned around. Emmett snorted, yelled, tossed pebbles, which made the horse run, but as soon as he disappeared, he appeared again. "Get on," Emmett said. "Get yourself another family. Go on. You're free. Now go on."

He tripped several times on his frustrated march back to the farm. Felt each wrong step in his knee. His hip was going too. His knee felt on fire. He used the rifle as a cane, balancing himself, the barrel shoved into the dirt.

Emmett kept watch throughout the night, scanning the blackness for the stallion's eyes in the flashlight's dimming beam. He listened for sounds of hooves on rock. He could hear but couldn't see the stubborn animal. Emmett was offering it freedom and the horse wasn't taking it. Emmett couldn't bear to watch this one broken. The warden would be at the farm in the morning, his gold badge on his belt, horse trailer attached to his tow hitch. Emmett had to get rid of the animal. He knew he couldn't send another down that path. Petting the rifle, he imagined, in his anger, delivering a brain shot. Then waiting for the animal to come to a gentle kneel before inserting another behind his ear.

Around three in the morning, the blue roan appeared at the same spot near the pens where their game had begun. Goddamn, Emmett thought, and spat.

He would not sleep until the horse was run off. A caged life was an awful one for a range-born animal. He wouldn't allow it. Couldn't. He ran at the horse, hands high and yelling and blood filling his tongue, until the horse fled, but the damn thing returned. It went on like this, Emmett growing delirious, furious.

He sat on the card stump as an ember in his heart died.

Emmett turned, snuggling the rifle against his shoulder, raising it. He heard the horse just behind a curtain of black.

+ + +

Kim had been in and out of the pens for hours, bearing witness to what had happened. From inside his trailer, he'd watched her fling open her door and run from her pickup, hands in her dusty hair.

It wasn't the bullets that did it. It wasn't so much his upbringing, what he learned from his neglectful parents. It was the cell and the bars that did it, what that taught him. It was the man on the cross that did it, what He taught him.

He'd opened it up, everything.

Kim had linebacker shoulders. And he had a bad knee. She could easily take him to the dirt. But she didn't come looking. Kim paced around the corrals, confused and shaking. All her hard work, long days and months, returning week after week to tend to mustangs . . . For what? said her wide eyes, her lost expression.

Standing at the window, Emmett watched her.

The gates were open. The rehabilitated bachelors and the blue roan's family were gone, all gone except for the blue roan, that impertinent bastard. The blue roan had stepped inside the pen on its own, as though trading himself for the others. Even the colt was gone. From a distance Emmett saw Kim's fists pump like twin hearts. She was walking toward the blue roan, backing the only horse left into a corner.

Emmett turned from the window, sat on the bed. Soon Gustavo's silhouette filled the empty doorframe, crowding out sunlight. Emmett hadn't slept. His lips felt heavy. For a moment he wondered if he was returning from a dream.

Gustavo stretched an arm against the doorframe and the hinges moaned. Without his ball cap, his black hair resembled patted-down grass. He leaned against the door and tossed a handful of sunflower seeds in his mouth.

"Look at you," Gustavo said, cheek like a chipmunk.

And Emmett did. He quit breathing for a moment and looked at himself: dry elbows, sweat-stained blue shirt, tanned arms, tired knees, not much.

"My tax dollars hard at work on you," Gustavo said. "And you throw opportunity away. I gave my time, my friendship. We had a good thing going. And you don't care."

"The night went all wrong," Emmett said, trying to explain. "The horse wouldn't go."

"We'd planned to drive to Indianapolis. The races. Remember? See the races?" His friend shot him a long, disciplining look. "You had maybe six more months. And now you set the warden's horses free before auction weekend. Lord's shitting bricks up there, man."

"Don't say that," Emmett said. He was already inside a daydream with cramped cells and high cinderblock walls and the smell of bleach and the Book under his beaten pillow. He would no longer be Emmett. For a while longer he would be #37118.

"You ruined your chance at early parole," Gustavo said. "I hope you know that the warden is not looking forward to this conversation. Had me on the phone already, yelling. Kim told him."

Gustavo had brought the standard uniform, folded and washed, the right size. Emmett stood. He would enter the facility and the warden's office like every other prisoner. Gustavo's pickup was full of pallets, dents in the side, still running. Emmett looked out at the gray prison, which appeared tiny and compact compared with the expansive sun-blanched backdrop. Interconnected buildings were surrounded by fence line and three towers and, farther, the flat, yellow valley.

At this time of morning inmates would be in the yard, working the weights, gossiping. That was one thing Emmett disliked. Inmates were evil gossips, worse than grandmothers.

Gustavo had with him a pair of bright shiny cuffs, new. "After you dress, since we're going inside," Gustavo said, almost apologetic. "You know the drill."

Emmett knew. He dressed quickly, and turned, hands at his back. He felt cold comfort as the cuffs loosely hugged his wrists.

The day was warming. It would be bright and hot and clear. He asked Gustavo for help when getting into the pickup.

Emmett watched Kim inside the empty pen. She was keeping the blue roan in the corner, stepping forward, her hand out in offering. He wanted to tell her that he was sorry, even if it wasn't true. Kim was a good woman. The brim of her BLM cap shaded her good, decent face. For a moment she and the horse were lost behind a pile of brush as the truck rolled slowly toward the gate. Concertina wire sparkled under early springtime sun.

He surveyed the now-empty corrals, early light dropping at angles like golden slides through the slats. Something calling itself pride was in his mind. His skin tingled with the feeling.

The blue roan came into view again as the truck sputtered forward.

The horse was cornered, but near the opened gate, and he could make it, if he tried. Emmett's chest was warm, his chest felt full and great, as though the Word was being pulled through his veins, centering inside him. He didn't need convincing. Watching the horse, that wild beast, was testimony enough.

LAST RITES

Billy's mother's wine cellar was in the rear of the second kitchen, down a helix staircase. Every time we went it was like entering a secret cave, expecting to discover in the damp, semi-dark nook special treasure or ordnance. We whispered among green slotted bottles, so many, and on such fine, tall shelves that the place reminded me of the library.

On that day Billy stood at the shelves, carefully considering his choices. Each bottle's long neck accused like a finger. Over the past six months he'd emptied the shelves, one and then another. I watched him fist two bottles with red labels. He gave them to me and pulled out several others.

"This should last a few nights," he said.

Billy's house served to remind me of our different situations. Great creaking wood hallways opened onto chambers and sitting areas and kitchens, two of them. There were antique chairs, scenic paintings, crystal ornaments, but the objects lived in a foreign context, since I lacked the proper vocabulary to name anything. Everything was expensive, I knew. And I also knew when you sat in the plush couch you got lost forever. The house overlooked downtown from the hill and, from long vertical windows along the staircase, we often watched the sun disappearing behind the mountains, soon replaced by artificial casino lights. Downtown Reno summoned with epileptic beacon lighting, blinking on-off, sequentially, mega-photon bulbs programmed to throw light in hypnotic waves.

Ms. Sorrentino was in the middle of her bed. It was a structure so large and ornate that it brought to mind Versailles, or at least the images I'd seen of it on TV. Fussy red and gold pillows were heaped around her, as if she lay on a lavish throne. The room smelled faintly of waxed wood and medicinal ointments. Platinum candelabras held unlit white candles. The woman was unconcerned anymore by her disarming beauty. She was once more than this. Wall-mounted pictures showed her younger, active self: running barefoot on white sand beaches and sitting in hammocks with books. She now wore a bathrobe opened at the neck, and from the doorway I stared at the fleshy line created when she crossed her arms and her breasts met. Her freckled chest was soft and pale and amazing and beaded with sweat. An empty wine glass shivered on the tabletop when Billy set the bottles down.

"I said bring eight," Ms. Sorrentino said to her son.

"No more of the '68," Billy said, pretending not to understand.

"No, eight. *Eight.*" His mother looked at him sadly. Then she said, sauced already, "William, come here."

He stepped back. "We're going out," he told her. "To the movies."

"Stay in. Come here." To me she said, "Come here, both of you, and let me hold you."

I thought about it. I stood in the doorway with clenched fists. I thought about Ms. Sorrentino holding me. Enough light still shone in her eyes, those struggling embers. I'd had many nights with her, nights alone, nights with her in my head, nights wiggling on my own wet sheets, her damp yellow skin warming to my touch as I sucked poisons from her pores.

Ms. Sorrentino was half out of it, as she'd been for as long as I'd been visiting Billy's. Dozens of empty bottles already stood upright on the hardwood floor like an uncertain crowd. She rarely left this room. There was a worn trail on the patterned rug from the bed to the bathroom. Pleated drapes were parted to spy on downtown, just blocks away. Houses along this old cliff row were built with ancient mining money and lived in by who knew who. I did not know these decorated people, only Billy.

Billy uncorked a bottle and poured a quarter glass like a maître'd. His mother bent over the wine as the faithful did the chalice. Billy's eyes slit into hurt as he watched. He grabbed my arm, squeezing hard. "Let's go," he said.

"Don't do anything, kids, I wouldn't," Ms. Sorrentino said, her voice a weakening song.

Ms. Sorrentino sang other songs too, maddening songs and thoughtful songs, fleeting parental warnings to us from that bed as big as a desert mesa.

Our decks were waiting on their tails by the double oak doors. There were prayers that needed to be prayed, and Billy and me, we certainly prayed.

Oh, that summer, how we did pray! Under cauterizing sun, we prayed for each other, and for his mother, and for the open summer months to unfold and keep unfolding. We prayed to hurry things up, to have the mysteries solved, thinking that once we solved them we'd be somewhere.

Remembering those days puts stings of envy in my chest. Now my Sundays are spent mowing the lawn, paying bills, but that was a time when I prayed hard alongside my good friend with the stricken mother—her vanishing beauty! At night we would wipe away church lessons, forgetting what was whispered in the pews, but then, in daylight, we'd pray again and remember.

The smell of burnished wood and resinous incense remain sharp memories in my mind.

+ + +

Of course, we rarely went to the movies, but we did have a father. The dusty alleyway separating St. Mark's from the small stucco rectory was renamed for Father Bowling. A street sign even proclaimed it: Bowling Alley. Our church was an old downtown city church, a sad, falling-down place surrounded by motels that rented rooms by the month. At night casino lights painted the roof's cross in various hallucinatory colors. Over stained glass windows were bars, and from inside, during certain light, the saints looked imprisoned. Brown, shiny Astroturf decorated the outside steps. And spindly desert weeds choked the yard, where some amateur mason, from an earlier time, had sculpted out of concrete and granite a chaotic mound that showcased the Virgin Mary inside a halved porcelain bathtub.

Indoors, St. Mark's was hollow and holy. The pews were wood and the altar was smooth, speckled marble.

We toed our skateboards and made them stand into our fingers. Billy and I carried our decks through the door. Father Bowling was already in the sacristy, fiddling with the sacrarium's piping so that holy and baptismal waters drained outside into his tomato garden. Father Bowling had given us silver crucifix necklaces, and he often swore, telling us that Catholics were the denomination that said Jesus and Christ and Jesus Christ the most, but he was proud that he didn't. He preferred fuck and shit.

"You boys are early for the five o'clock," he said when we wandered in. He was securing the drainage pipe's brass elbow fitting.

"Cops kicked us out of the Purple Coyote's parking garage," Billy told him.

"We need to raise money and build you a park," Father Bowling said. He pressed his palms against his knees to make himself stand. "I'll bring it up in homily on Sunday. You boys shouldn't be skating casino garages."

"It's got good surface," I told him.

Father Bowling wore a proper, black button-down and white clerical collar accentuated by jeans and cowboy boots. He was not young, not old, and a definite Texan, and he made a big production when telling kids his love for them was as vast as the Presidio skies where he was born. He shaved the sides of his head close like a rodeo man and his calloused hands brought to mind a day laborer's. I held to faith like faith was a father, also because the faith was passed down from Mom, but Billy wasn't really raised in it like me. He just started attending catechism classes on his own.

We donned black cassocks and white surplices, waiting for Father Bowling to dump a load in the bathroom. When he emerged, the sacristy smelling desecrated and intestinal, he slapped his stomach proudly. "Hallelujah," Father Bowling said and punched my shoulder.

Weekday masses, you only needed one or two. Billy and I worked together. On Sundays, the big day, you needed four. Jonah and Alex usually joined, and we'd stalk the altar like a gang. This afternoon, at the five o'clock, the church was nearly empty. Just old women with fritzed dandelion hair and lapsed cases praying for dying relatives. Fewer eyes meant less pressure, but on Sundays we served the Lord right.

I carried the processional cross. Billy chose the altar candle because he enjoyed playing with fire. Five o'clock weekday services ran short. We chanted gospel and listened to scripture and escorted wafers and wine to the altar when it was time. My father appeared as a parishioner in a camouflage jacket, but he left before the end, dipping five fingers into the holy water's font on his hustle out. Billy rang the bells when the Eucharist was held up in the oval stage lights.

We both looked up.

Afterward, in the sacristy, Father Bowling asked Billy about the state of his mother. That's how he put it, *the state of your mother.* I thought about Arizona, Mississippi, Tennessee, which one might she be?

Billy refused to respond. I glanced at him.

"You're his friend." Father Bowling turned to me. "Mind telling me how his mother's doing."

I didn't know what to say.

"That's not part of this," Billy said. "That's not right to ask him. I don't come here to have *that* be part of *this.*" He crushed his cassock into a tight ball, punching it into his cubby.

"I'm just wondering," Father Bowling said, "if she might want a priest."

Billy shot me a look, like let's get out of here. He grabbed our decks by the trucks.

"Okay, okay," Father Bowling said. "Okay," he said, patting the air like he was firming it down. "Okay," he said. "Truce." He reached for his back pocket, found a tin of dip, and sailed the tin through the air like a Frisbee. Billy caught it. "You boys need to realize next year is confirmation," he said. "You should start choosing your names."

+ + +

At home the microwave sat atop the ironing board by the front door, a box full of our dishware beneath its branched legs. When I saw the items boxed and waiting, I knew I'd have to sift through my things again, debating over what to sell. I told myself our situation would never approach that one winter, when Mom propped open the oven to warm the place and we stood in line at St. Vincent's for sandwiches wrapped in wax paper. She had a full-time job now at the hospital, and we had a proper two-bedroom—no more sharing that one-bedroom with the bunk bed.

I found Mom in the duplex's basement, listening to a small black and white set. She was pushing boxes around with her junk knee. Mom buried her disappointments behind forced smiles. She quickly showed me one. Her uneven bangs were obvious and homemade, but her hands were strong, smooth from worrying out the wrinkles. The basement smelled damp, of insect decomposition, of mold. The set didn't have a picture, only sound. A commercial for dish soap squawked from it.

"Work the service?" Mom asked me.

"Me and Billy," I said.

"Billy and me," she said. She smiled again. Then her smile folded. "Insurance on the car is due," Mom told me, "and I need that knee surgery."

"Garage sale," I said, "without the garage."

"Maybe you could make lemonade again. Twenty cents a cup."

"I'm too old."

"Listen," she said. "Janie in Sacramento knows someone. Her cousin. He's moving to town. He'll be staying with us for a while."

"A boarder? Again?"

"We need the help," she said.

"And where's he going to sleep?"

The basement overflowed with cardboard boxes containing unread magazines, old bank calendars, and the husks of ancient coupon books. Mom ascribed to the theory of wealth by accumulation. If we owned stuff, whatever kind of stuff, then we were never without stuff, right? There were rat traps in the basement's corners. And dust clouded with each ginger step. "It's not a problem. I'll sleep down here," she said cheerily, "and he'll take my room for as long as he stays."

When we'd moved in, we found a pentagram duct-taped to the linoleum floor of the tiny second floor bedroom—my room. Melted wax sucked at the edge of each star. Mom shrugged it off. She said that it was probably just some hick ritualizing over luck, over gambling, some kind of strange pagan fun, since we lived so close to downtown, near the casinos. Then the right part of her brain spoke up. She talked to Father Bowling after Sunday's mass, and the next day he rumbled over on his fancy motorcycle and tossed around holy water. Then he thumbed a cross into my forehead, for good measure. It was a small room, a standard room, except for slanted ceilings, where you had to bend and then crawl the closer you neared the wall.

I didn't like the idea of a boarder. There were already two boarding houses on our block, big ones, three story numbers, with porches, with couches on the porches with the stuffing bursting through the fabric like magma. Why couldn't this guy live down there, with the other lopsided lives?

"Love you," Mom called out as I stomped back upstairs.

I called Billy. "What are you doing?" I asked him.

"Dipping."

"Save some for me," I said.

"My head is full of stars and I threw up, but I like it," he said.

"I'm coming over."

"No," he said. "Let's meet. My mom's already on her third bottle and she's crying again."

I knew how Ms. Sorrentino sometimes got, dropping in and out of sleep, yelping for her son, crashing and then awakening to drink more. I often wondered about Billy ghosting around the fourth floor of that mansion, touching the textured wallpaper that felt like threads, sitting silently at his grand oak desk and staring at flashing casino lights.

We cruised downtown, our skateboards thundering over cross-hatched sidewalks under the glow of neon. We left our eager shoe imprints across the city's cement. We were fatherless and free.

At night downtown was a graveyard of stunned zombies. Men patted their pockets. Men stared blankly into the empty mouths of their wallets, confused. Teenagers older than us drove past in cars, yelling at younger girls with faces painted like twenty-year-olds. Casinos kept the doors open, and streams of oxygenated, smoky air blasted our necks. Just past the Purple Coyote was Circus Maximus, with its midway for gamblers' kids. We entered, but as we walked over the balloon-patterned carpet, past squirt-gun games, past the bottle-cap toss, we knew we were getting too old. This was no place for us. The lifeless eyes of the midway workers brought to mind car wrecks and landslides, past tragedies stamped to the body. Circus acts were announced at the top of each hour and happened in a central ring, a supersized version of a boxing ring. We lingered around long enough to watch an imprisoned kangaroo with huge, cartoon gloves beat down a man who overacted. I saw my father dressed as a carnival barker, the brim of his hat as even as new cardboard. He begged passersby to throw darts for three quarters. I did not have any.

Dip made my eyes tear. It was incredible how quickly the blood in my head drummed. Tobacco gnawed a jagged pouch between my lip and gums, and gave me cotton ears, and made it feel like there were flies behind my eyes, flapping delicate, powdery wings against neurons.

Somehow it had gotten later, and we were in the river park, sitting on our bench, the sky above us blackening, our skate decks underfoot in explosions of crabgrass. Billy was peering at the city's lights and rubbing his crucifix. I was trying to focus but couldn't.

He said, "Not even July the fourth yet." He spat on the ground, picking specks of tobacco off his tongue. "It's going to be a good, long summer."

"I need to toss," I said. And I did, in the bushes. When I returned to the bench my friend's eyes were closed. And his lips were moving, as though he was scattered in prayer.

There were deep tides coursing inside him, I knew. And he was fisting his crucifix for ballast. We never discussed whether or not we believed in God. I had questions—a lot of questions. Billy, meanwhile, clutched tightly to his faith as a defense against further trauma. For him there wasn't space for questioning. For him faith was essential. For him faith was everything.

My son, he's two years and five months old. We count him by months because each is a milestone. His mother is prettier than ever when she holds him, placing her face to his, her nose to that tiny button. Watching her with him, I sometimes think of Billy's mother and wonder: how does that bond operate under the approaching pressure of disappearance? As the woman wasted away in bed, inside her wine-drunk mind, her boy roamed the streets. What were your thoughts, what were your terrors, you who viewed everything from your platform on the hill?

Time moves fast. My son's body grows like a shoot. There will come a day when he asks about otherworldly things, about the mystery of stars and planets and our place among them. And I don't want to be the type of man who quashes his wonder. Allowing wonder to develop is a gift. To snuff out awe is to crush the nature of the human heart. And I know how the enervating aura of hope and heaven bonded me to my mother, and I can still count the number of ways it carried Billy and me, at least for one final summer at thirteen.

Later that night, cold grilled cheese sandwiches were waiting for me on a paper plate. The plate had wicked-up the grease and the cheese felt like rubber. I ate in silence, alone, on a kitchen table stripped of utensils and place mats. In the basement I heard Mom wrestling her dragons. Our place looked fully scooped out. Only the couch and dining table and picture frames remained. Nearly every photo in the duplex showed my mother, another figure's mysterious outline, and me, at two, at three and five. This third person in my baby photos had been scissored free. So he was just a giant question mark set against each frame's cardboard backing, a ghostly imprint onto which I projected a varying slideshow of faces. Whenever I asked about my father, my mother always said the man couldn't even spell the word. And that's all she said, or ever said, about him. Of course, I disliked these pictures, these reminders. To me, they just landscaped our home in pain.

I dumped trays of ice into a plastic bag and walked the stairs to my room. It was as though the heat of the universe congregated here. The window only lifted six inches. An industrial fan, aimed directly at my bed, shoved around whatever small amount of fresh air that managed to drift in through the window. I removed the bedsheet, poured ice cubes on the mattress, and fitted it back on.

Praying was complicated, organized business: begging for world peace and a chillier room. Begging for a transplant donor for Ms. Sorrentino and for the perfect confirmation name. I opened with Our Father and closed with Hail Mary. On my knees, in prayer formation, I held the crucifix in my open hands instead of the standard palm-meet, which seemed too much like preparing for a dive into water. Christ on the thin cross was a tiny creature, silver and futuristic-looking, his arms up and high and spread. At that scale he looked to be celebrating. If Jesus Christ and his Father and the Holy Ghost were up there, recording my whispers, I wondered if they made a joke when I asked to keep the toaster.

I did not want a boarder, so I prayed against that idea too.

Sleep was impossible until the ice cubes melted, soaking the bed, the fan cooling my nightly sweat.

+ + +

Mom came to the city because of the easy divorces and found they were so easy she bought two more. Along the way came me. There wasn't much to do downtown for underage kids other than skate over broken sidewalks and dip tobacco.

Our early summer plans began with good intentions. Paint stores, back then, didn't imprison spray paint cans inside solitary confinement cages. Perhaps they do now, I sometimes think, because of what Billy and I did as kids.

Anyway, there we were, in the paint store, examining the spray paint selection. Billy and I finally agreed on the black and fluorescent orange. We already had stencils, and tape, but we needed the paint. The idea on the fluorescent orange was, when applied to a black rectangle on a curb, cars trawling neighborhoods would be able to locate addresses easier. And in Billy's neighborhood, each street was certainly dark at night, and quiet, the houses set far from curbs by wide, tended lawns. House numbers were nearly impossible to read, except on curbs.

All day we knocked on doors. Unfriendly faces soured behind black grille screens. Only two people granted us permission. The first, an elderly lady, who leaned against her door for support, and who wore curlers at noontime, didn't realize what she was agreeing on until the job was done. Still, we painted her curb number. We acted like seasoned professionals, and after we finished, she handed us a five-dollar bill and a bruised apple.

The other customer was a car salesman. We'd seen him on television. The man answered the door without any hair. He told us, yes, sure, go ahead, but only because his son was our age and he appreciated initiative.

"When I'm sixteen," Billy said later, while taping stencils to the curb, "I'll never buy a car from that guy. On TV he has a mountain of hair. That's false advertising."

We painted the curb: black background with fluorescent orange house numerals. Our lungs burned from the fumes.

When the car salesman strutted down the walk to inspect our work, our choice of colors, black and orange instead of black and white, he threw his ball cap on the cement, his face heading off in all directions. We watched him tear through our gear bag like a rabid animal, scattering everything around the cul-de-sac. He grabbed the black can from my hand and covered our work with it. Billy looked on calmly.

"He has to go to sleep," Billy said to me.

Later that night the car salesman got it on his white, three-car garage, the biggest address on the block, in bright orange. We were not artists. Our aerosolized scribbles were screams. We spray painted crosses on the handball wall at our park. More than once Billy wrote JESUS SAVES. Father Bowling squinted with interest at our black and orange fingertips. When we ran out of paint, we stole more, and when we finally stepped inside the confessional and told Father Bowling everything, he made us pray twenty Acts of Contrition, fifteen Hail Mary's, five Our Fathers, and told us, "*Knock off the shit.*"

So, we did. We hid the cans in the sacristy, behind boxes of communion wafers that Father Bowling purchased at wholesale discount.

+ + +

Gary arrived in late June, behind the wheel of a Yugo with California plates. It was a foreign car and ugly and compact and not one friend of mine trusted it. By extension I disliked its driver, also Californian. We'd seen plenty of Californians filter over the state border only to fall down like drunken apes outside casino entrances. Californians were worse than rodeo people. At least rodeo people apologized when something got ruined.

Gary stood at the door, his skin meshed blue through the screen. He wore tan slacks, a tucked white shirt, and a brown, braided belt with the end looped neatly into his pocket. His skinny white teeth were long and looked vaguely like fangs.

"I'm, hello, Gary," Gary said to me.

I turned and walked away from the door.

Sometime later my mother heard his incessant knocking from the basement, where she was arranging her cot. Gary carried a shoebox with shampoo bottles poking out while Mom gave him the five-second tour.

"And where will you sleep?" Gary finally asked her.

"I'm happy in the basement," she responded.

Gary nodded and gazed down at me. "My cousin Janie says you're an altar boy."

My crucifix knocked against my chest as I nodded.

"Well good, I attend too. I've tried living with non-Christians but it never works. Anyway, my blackjack dealer's license only took a week. Why I'm here. A job. Anyway, I'm looking forward to meeting the pastor at my new church."

Gary proceeded to tell us about his fifty-cent Christianity, named Christian Science, or Church of Christ Scientist, or something like that, but I didn't think those two words—Christ and Science—should ever be married. Also, I'd seen the Christ Science building before, near the airport, a rectangular aluminum structure that looked more like a barn. Gary went on, but I plugged my ears with questions. Had he never heard of Rome? Had he never seen pictures of the Papal Basilica of St. Peter's? His Jesus was not the same Jesus as mine.

I forked dinner in eight bites, and then I took off while Gary moved in. The sun was vigilant and up. The heat held. Some downtown sidewalks looked blasted by mines. Some looked like thrust faults. I chose routes strategically, following smooth cement that was easier on the wheels.

St. Mark's was the definition of sanctuary. The smudged cushions on the wood pews looked handed down through generations. Shiny indentations in the kneelers reaffirmed how many believed. We knew from Father Bowling that the church did not have air-conditioning, but by some miracle it remained cool, and it was dark, a good place, in other words, to organize my thoughts. I often wonder, these days, the subjects of that searching boy's questions. Were the hinges of my faith already loosening? Did I stare at the fake blood on Christ's palms and ask Him the whereabouts of my father? If not, why not?

Father Bowling appeared from a side door that led to church offices. He was palming a small bundle of manila folders. His Dallas Cowboys T-shirt had barbeque stains on the collar. Father Bowling saw me and wandered over and sat at the end of the pew, saying nothing. Arms outstretched, he leaned back like a vacationer and began knocking his knuckles against the wood. A hollow sound reverberated throughout the high nave. He knocked twice more and looked up, as though following the echoes as each hit the ceiling. He smiled and arched an eyebrow.

I stuffed the five-dollar bill from the spray paint job into the offering box.

At home Gary was showering. I heard a tinny radio bleeding through the door, songs from some Christian pop band. This was something new, and unwelcome. I stopped at the base of the stairwell and listened. The lyrics went something like, "We hold your feet and pray and we await your return," and nonsense like that, but with drumbeats and melodies and synthesizers. I hated it. There was a new poster pinned to the wall in Mom's old room: Jesus was healing a pauper in rags, the man's two white blind eyes looking up. It was pathetic. Gary showered for an hour, and when he emerged from the bathroom, steam billowing out like from a sulfur pit, I was certain he was cleaner than Christ reborn.

+ + +

Like always, we were in the park downtown, where the river forked around an island of grass and trees and joined again on the other side, whole. We were dipping and spitting in the grass and studying *The Incredible Book of Saints*. Across the park I saw my father playing tennis with a blonde woman, his shorts revealing legs sculpted by exercise. He hit the ball nicely. I spit a long teardrop onto a flat rock. Dip fogged my thoughts, made my eyes lose focus again.

"St. Thomas Beckett was assassinated," Billy said. "I like him."

But I was unsure, I told Billy. You wanted a saint that meant something special. I was fixated on St. Vincent de Paul, who served the poor, but I didn't want to be reminded, my whole life, of the life I'd lived. Our saints would look after us, and I wanted more encouragement from mine.

"Ah," Billy said, after a while. He shut the book. "I got it. I know my name."

"What?"

"Never mind."

"Tell me."

Finally he gave up the page number. I flipped through the book.

"You can't have a woman saint," I told him.

"I don't care. I am."

I looked closer at St. Monica. Patron Saint of: Homemakers, Housemakers, Married Women, Widows, Disappointing Children, Alcoholics. Billy's mansion on the cliff presided over the park from a comfortable distance. I wondered if his mother was up there at that moment, her skin as yellow as a wasp's stripe, red wine like lipstick on her mouth and her thin waxy body sweating.

"You should choose another name," I said. "Father Bowling won't allow it."

"We'll see," Billy said. "St. Monica, says here, was St. Augustine's mother. Father Bowling talks about that guy a bunch."

From over the pedestrian bridge walked Paisley Michaels. We knew Paisley from catechism classes. She wore a purple T-shirt and cutoff jean shorts and her judgments were all tightened up around her petit body like a tourniquet—approaching, in other words, with her arms crossed. She was the loudest member of CCD and could name the commandments quickest. Her shadow fell across our scabbed knees.

"You shouldn't be doing that," she said, studying our bulging bottom lips.

Billy spat overdramatically, nailing my grip tape.

"Gross," Paisley said. She looked at our book. "You choosing saint names?"

"Just scanning the competition," Billy said. He didn't meet Paisley's eyes. But I did. What I saw was a young woman. What I saw was a girl who'd once eaten snot, a girl who'd somehow transformed herself into a miracle, with breasts. They held like firm plums under the outline of her T-shirt. And under summer's light, she looked more adorned, more freckled, with longer brown hair, a smaller, more hesitant version of Ms. Sorrentino.

Billy held open the can of dip, sniffing the black granules. Even from a few feet away I could taste it. Dip was sharp, like burnt matches, and it knocked you between the eyes. "Want some?" he asked Paisley.

She shook her head.

"We can get something harder, if you want," he said.

"Oh yeah, *sure,* like what?"

Billy pinched his index finger and thumb together, kissing them and lifting his fingers away, bringing to mind smoke. "There are plants over there, growing on the riverbank. I saw some hippies farming them last week."

"You're lying," Paisley said.

"He is," I said.

To prove us wrong Billy led us to the riverbank. A tangle of bushes grew there. The cup-shaped leaves hung low, bobbing as the flowing water caught. Little brown pods sprouted from the plant's stem. Billy picked several. We carefully inspected the pods in our palms. Billy told us they were drugs.

Later, after Billy skated away from the Mini-Mart, he met us in an alley. He was breathing hard. He patted his pocket. Then smiled. I was surprised at how interested Paisley became as Billy worked his bullshit.

"First . . . ," he said, producing the stolen cigarette papers from his pocket. "You need these." Next he crushed the dry pods on the ground. It took him time to roll anything resembling a cigarette, and when we smoked it, the thing hardly burned. It tasted of sticks, of crabgrass, burnt paper, nothing.

"You feel it?" he asked me, face pinched, holding in his breath.

"No," I said.

He grabbed the false joint and toked furiously. The cherry end burned bright at his attempt. "Oh, yeah," he said. He puffed harder. "I feel it. I definitely feel something."

He held it out for Paisley, and again I was surprised when she accepted.

I felt nothing but energetic shame as I watched Paisley inhale. I was ashamed by our corrupting influence, as she held our book to her chest, her breasts crushed by the pressure of saints.

+ + +

The heat made me itch. The heat drove me to curse God. Part of me blamed the faint outline of the pentagram on the floor. The tape's adhesive was still sticky. Part of me blamed Gary, how he snored like a Viking. Part of me blamed my father. I never blamed Mom. She was the one who stayed.

I walked over moonlight shafts that fell through the blinds in the shape of white ribs. It was after midnight. I walked downstairs. On all sides were frames, were pictures, my mother and me, but my father's face was a guessing game. I carried the ghost of him like Christ bore the cross. Before bed every night I prayed to the truer Father, not as television imagined Him, not as some figure with a flowing beard on a throne, but as a sensation of goodness and hope and salvation. His image, when I shut my eyes, appeared as a sort of golden gauziness.

I opened the door and went outside and sat on the concrete stoop and held my naked chest.

Street pebbles bit into my bare feet. It was late. And there was no one out—just the washy sound of drunk drivers from the nearby boulevard. From the shadows a white cat emerged and walked past me. I made sucking sounds, because cats liked that. Each time I made a suck the cat would stop, swivel its head, and peer at me coolly. It looked like it owned the night world with its slow, purposeful gait. The cat then sat in the middle of the street, looking like a figurine. We surveyed each other. I'd always wanted an animal, a friend, some warm creature to lie beside at night. Soon the headlights of a car approached, ruining our connection. The cat remained in the street, staring at me. Cars did not slow on my city street. Cars accelerated. I stood. Still, the cat sat motionless and watchful. I hissed. But the cat did not move. Finally, I stood and yelled, flailing my arms wildly, and the cat ran away just before headlights bathed me in light.

+ + +

I met a doctor on the steps of Billy's house on the Fourth of July. The sky was red, a sort of atomic color bursting along cloudscapes. It happened.

The door was open and the doctor was writing in a small

black book. He was dressed like a boatman, with deck shoes and rolled-up khakis. I knew he was a doctor by the stethoscope hanging from his neck. I'd never seen an actual doctor at someone's house, but they did that, I knew, for people with two kitchens. He held his face as straight as a man at a card game.

"She's awake and going through picture books upstairs," he said evenly, "if you want to see her."

In the second kitchen Billy was carefully placing wine bottles inside cardboard boxes. He tapped down the top of one. There was a bow affixed to it, some leftover from Christmas, I guessed. Each box was marked in pen. *Monday, Tuesday, Wednesday . . .*

"Dr. Burchfield tells me not to give her this," he said. His eyes dropped on the floor. The fridge was open. The only item inside was a brown head of lettuce. "But my mom wants it, and who am I, you know? She likes wine."

I followed him up the stairs. But I put my hand on the oak railing, and stopped, when I heard sobbing. Sound carried in that cavernous house, especially sobs. Billy went the full way and delivered the box of wine to his mother.

There was a duffle bag at the oak doors, and when Billy bounded down the stairs, taking them two at a time, he grabbed the bag's thick strap.

"July the fourth," he said. He was excited.

The bag was heavy, awkward. We hid the duffle behind the green dumpster in the park. Eventually Paisley found us. Or we found her. Paisley was around more and more. It was summer, it was a holiday, and the downtown streets were congested with people, mostly Californians. On the Fourth the mad ruled the streets. Police watched from horses, patrolled on foot, from cars. It was a ten-block party with beer booths and T-shirt stands and the annual transvestite unicyclists, all emphasized by casino lights. Police used cordons to contain the crazy.

We visited St. Mark's. On the Astroturf steps, I prayed the prayer to the Holy Ghost, hoping heaven would point me toward the right confirmation name. I was hoping for some divine sign. Paisley watched, and she tried to pray too, but it didn't seem right, she said, praying on Astroturf. I told her it was what we had, and Jesus had had much less.

Father Bowling had chained and padlocked the doors. So we were locked out. He had his reasons. Father Bowling, in fact, once surprised a party that had relocated from the motel next door to inside the church—people screwing in the pews and chasing each other with the processional cross. Billy watered Father Bowling's tomatoes and noted that the lights in the rectory were out, and where could a man of the cloth go, he wondered aloud, at ten o'clock at night on the Fourth of July?

When it was dark enough, Billy heaved the duffle onto his deck and rolled the bag through the park, dumping everything on the crabgrass. Inside was a war chest. During summers, the trees were like tinder, with calls in outlying areas for zero burn. Desert summers were dry, and fireworks were illegal, but Billy had ordered these through the mail, and these, he told us, were necessary. I watched him eagerly plant the grass with rockets and starbursts and pinwheels. A determined look entered his eyes. I helped him. So did Paisley. My father watched from a bench, stuffing his face into a brown paper sack and tipping it back.

At last Billy raised a platinum candelabrum into the air. Lit, the flame leaned in the partial breeze. Then, one after the other, he ignited this field of fireworks. Lunar shadows disappeared as the park transformed into a blaze of green-blue light and sulfur and sizzle. Rockets ripped past the tree line, exploding in view of his mother's bedroom window, dripping down bright tentacles of light. Technicolor mushrooms bloomed. The sky sparkled, as though hung with tinsel. It was easy to see the love Billy was trying to show. Layers of smoke hung low near the grass, obscuring our feet. A bit possessed, Billy cursed himself when several wicks wouldn't light. But then, finally, they sparked and went. And we looked up at his devoted work, this magic trick created for his sick mother on the hill.

+ + +

None of our previous miseries compared with living with the

Christian. After showering, after blow-drying, Gary would materialize from the bathroom looking like that evangelist on TV with the wind tunnel hair. Also, Gary had no problem moving in. He marked territory by shedding pamphlets quoting Mary Baker Eddy in every nook. He left cracker crumbs in cushions, socks on the counter. When he wasn't working behind the blackjack tables, he was spreading his special brand of Christianity around the ground floor of our duplex, his pop music the soundtrack. Mom retreated to the basement, studying hospital procedural manuals. I hid upstairs in the slanted-ceiling room, sweating.

One morning, Mom summoned me downstairs. I was in bed, lubing my bearings. They were sitting at the kitchen table and leaning over empty cereal bowls. We only had two bowls anymore, since Gary had claimed the third for his penny collection.

"Come, sit," Mom said, patting a chair. This looked like a setup, an interrogation. Gary smiled and folded his buttery hands. I remained standing.

"Gary and I have been talking," Mom said, "and we think you should start spending more time together." She paused. She looked at Gary in a nauseating, admiring way. "I think he'd be a good figure for you," she said. What she didn't say was *father figure,* but that was the term that popped into my ears. I stared at Gary, his lumpy cheeks like mashed potatoes. And then I ran out the door.

Gary's presence, more than his music, drove me away. From that morning on, I'd leave early and come home late. At night I'd wait in the alleyway across the street until the last light in the duplex went out. Then I'd barge inside and run upstairs to my room. Gary was no father to me.

Meanwhile Billy was spending more time around St. Mark's. He was seeking asylum from all that was happening outside its doors. He began watering Father Bowling's tomato plants more often. He became generally available, reading comics in the confessionals, cleaning the sacristy with a slug of dip in his lip. He swept pews. He genuflected each time he passed the figure of Christ. It was summer, and I didn't want to spend every day inside the church. And home certainly wasn't a place for me. So I skated.

In our dry desert city there was a neighborhood with streets named for rivers. Paisley lived on Ganges Avenue. I remembered she hadn't returned *The Incredible Book of Saints.* Her house was a square, red brick number with painted white brick shelves beneath the front windows. I knocked on her door, wiping my shoes on a plastic mat. An older boy answered. His face was smooth but his neck was spotted with acne. Paisley shoved him aside, but the kid remained behind her, his two eyes hovering, touching his hand to her back. Paisley's nose was a deeper brown than before, the freckles more screwed into her face. Inside, her parents sat on separate recliners, watching TV, four socked feet in the air, their blunted eyes spellbound by diaphanous blue light.

Her brother continued pushing Paisley from behind.

"Jacob, stop it," she told him. She stepped outside and shut the door. "My brother," she explained.

It was a warm evening, and we sat on her steps, in her quiet neighborhood, paging through *The Incredible Book of Saints,* trying to invent interesting things to say. She lived in a lower-middle-class neighborhood, not far from my duplex. Downtown neighborhoods during that time changed income levels by simply crossing a street. It wasn't like now, with condominiums and urban revitalization.

Paisley closed the book and pressed it between her palms. The unfamiliar smell of clay floated off her. She looked at me, started to speak, and stopped. She rubbed her chin along the book, watching a sprinkler, in the shape of a fountain, water a neighbor's lawn.

"Go to the movies with me?" Paisley finally said.

"I don't go to the movies."

"Why not?"

"Movies cost," I said.

She stood, fisted the neck of my shirt, and tugged me up. "Then I'll pay," she said.

The theater downtown had a busted marquee. Several plastic letters had been abandoned on the sign's unlit background. Only two movies were showing. Paisley chose. Inside, the cool air was welcome, and few seats were claimed. As soon as the previews ended, as soon as we were thrown into coal black darkness, Paisley leaned over and pushed her cold fingers down the front of my shorts, grabbing me. I sat completely upright. For the first twenty minutes, I pretended that nothing had changed, or was happening. Eventually I wrestled my hand inside her shorts too. Paisley was furry, and I petted her, like the top of a puppy's head. Little taps. I reluctantly turned to her, hoping that she'd handle me with care, hoping that she'd sense that I was fragile, afraid.

Instead, Paisley began moving her hand like a single cylinder piston. Soon I had to forcibly remove her hand and bowleg my way to the restroom, where I stood dumbly over an ice-filled urinal, trying to piss. Pressure wanted release. Back in the theater, Paisley resumed her industriousness, and off I went again to stare at myself above the urinal.

Over the next few weeks we went to the movies a lot. I wasn't stupid, wasn't naïve. I knew things. And I was after those things. Eventually Paisley hit the target she was aiming for. And she began to dress up, too. But we never kissed. Our lips never touched. It was as though kissing was an afterthought, a cliché. Our bond was through our fingers. And we never spoke about our intimate connection after the credits rolled. We were simple, blind scavengers foraging for meaning, for sustenance.

On another evening—Billy was still busy at church—I skated over to Paisley's. She crumpled to the porch steps and leaned against me. Her hands went to her cheeks. When she asked me for dip, I was surprised, but I handed her my tin anyway. She smelled it, her nose twitching. Then she put a smidgen beneath her lip, considering its effects while looking at the stars.

"My parents say Billy's mom once attended mass," she said to me.

I had nothing. So I said nothing.

"She stopped attending after Billy was born," she said, and turned. "Do you know his father?"

"He's away on business."

"He's been away on business most of Billy's life."

What Paisley was saying disturbed me. Billy and I never spoke about such dangerous things. Next Paisley would lean on me about my father. My mind raced as I quickly organized a lie. He lived across town? He worked in Spain? He built ships in Alaska?

"Billy will have to live with him," Paisley said, adding, "when."

And I knew it was true. Paisley carefully spit into her mother's potted agave plant and placed a warm hand on my knee. Her head was starting to feel like deep space, she told me. Then the sad tender look on her face changed. "I like your confirmation name. St. Joseph. The carpenter. I like it."

"Patron Saint of fathers," I said.

Paisley excavated the dip and scraped her finger on the porch's railing. A car slowly drove past. Paisley rose and yanked the neck of my shirt. When I stood she twisted our hands into a tight knot. Her house smelled like foreign territory, an invisible padding of indescribable meats and cooking oils, of different detergents and soaps, the accumulation of another family's bodily flecks tamped into the dull, gray carpet. Her parents, always on recliners, turned their heads mechanically and nodded at us. I nodded back. Bags of potato chips, large as horse feed, sat on their laps.

Paisley's bedroom was a well-tended unit with a periodic table poster and intricate, lidded Native American baskets. She shut her door without locking it and rapidly pulled her T-shirt over her head. Next off were her shorts, and then white cotton underwear. She kept her bra on, and socks. Paisley Michaels then lay on her bed, waiting for me. A speck of dip was on her chin. Her body was a lively, hard thing.

+ + +

Through the confessional's screen I saw Father Bowling jam his fingers into his ears, pinning them deep, as though trying to touch his brain. I continued, telling my priest what occurred in those movie theater seats, about the urinal, being unable to piss, finally the thing that happened inside Paisley's unlocked bedroom. Father Bowling said he didn't want to hear one word more. "One Act of Contrition, for fuck's sake, and wash your hands before services," he said, making the sign of the cross in the air.

Billy and I worked the afternoon mass that Wednesday, but afterward Billy didn't feel like skating. I'd been practicing ollies and railstands without him in the park. But Billy just trailed Father Bowling around the sacristy, out among the pews, helping arrange prayer books in seat slots, eventually cornering the priest by the vigil candles. I watched them talk for a while, until Father Bowling seized Billy's arm and dragged him over and said, "Take this kid outside. He needs sun."

Engines were combusting inside Billy. He was speeding up. He didn't like leaving St. Mark's, and on the occasions that he did, he didn't watch for cars anymore, ignoring the fat red flashing hand signals at street corners. He dipped more and whatever he needed, he stole. We were fast on our boards whenever chased.

I was in the second kitchen with Billy one day, watching him open and shut the cupboards. All that remained inside was baking powder, vinegar, salt. I watched him separate spice bottles like he was parting jungle ferns, peering through, trying to locate some unnamable treasure.

"What are you doing?" I asked.

"I heard about this thing," Billy was saying. "I heard it works."

Searching, searching, he was unable to locate what he was after, and when he violently jerked his forearm the spices rained onto the tile. The paprika cracked open. He spotted a small bottle of white peppercorns by my shoe. He snatched it. "Found them," he said eagerly. Then he dumped the round pellets across the chrome counter.

With the side of a butcher's knife, he crushed the peppercorns until he'd made a fine powder. Then he cut a thick milkshake straw in half, held the ends between dust and nostril, bent over the mess, and inhaled. He inhaled out of need. His eyes were buggy with it. He inhaled like he wanted to be taken off the planet. He inhaled, and water appeared his eyes. "Try it, try it," he said, pinching the bridge of his nose. "Oh, oh, oh," he said. "You need to try this."

White peppercorn dust was like a shotgun blast to my nasal cavity, and I couldn't stop sneezing. Then came the pressure behind my eyes, and I held my head in my hands, rocking back and forth.

"Isn't this great?" Billy asked. "Don't you *feel* it? Can't you *feel* it?"

I saw a blurry version of him through tears. "I can't feel anything," I said. "Except hurt."

"What do you mean?"

"Nothing," I said angrily. "I feel nothing."

Tears seeped down Billy's face. He was offended. Snot ran from his nose, and we stared at each other, tears sleeting down our cheeks. We were unable to stop them. I couldn't tell if the tears were from the pepper, or from me.

"I hate this," I said. "What about the wine?" I reached for a box labeled *Friday*.

"No," Billy said.

I removed the box's lid.

"That's for my mother," he said. I reached inside and fingered the top of a bottle, testing him.

With tears in his eyes, my friend considered me with something approaching hatred. Then my good friend bent to a knee, assumed a face of fierce focus, and uppercut my balls so faithfully that I can taste it in my throat to this day.

+ + +

Father Bowling closed the door to Ms. Sorrentino's room, tightening his belt by a notch. I was at the house looking for Billy, who I'd last seen at services, when I surprised our priest.

Father Bowling's bible was in his armpit, fingers at his big Texas belt buckle. I'd startled him. He looked like a man newly burdened.

"She called," he whispered to me. "I'm here for the anointing." He put a hand on my shoulder. "Billy doesn't know about this visit, understand?"

I nodded, and between us passed a silent agreement. I would say nothing. He would say nothing. As I watched him walk toward the stairwell, he touched the wall tenderly.

I heard the front door close. I slowly opened Ms. Sorrentino's door, where she lay melted to her mattress, like the ice under my bed sheets, her head sideways on a pillow. In a tangle on the floor was her silk bathrobe. She was unclothed beneath a white sheet, which summarized every gracious part of her. Her hair was a shining nest. And the newly familiar adult smell lingered like an invisible cloud inside the sunlit room. That afternoon, while looking at her, I began to understand the meaning of beauty. I recognized it. It was the beauty of a woman anointed. Greasy strands of hair fell like a veil over her sated eyes. Ms. Sorrentino was beauty incarnate. I felt her sad loveliness reach out and touch me with each shallow breath. What special blessings had Father Bowling bestowed to make her consider me with such a bold smile? So far down on the donor list, the remainder of her life simply a matter of the clock, and yet she smiled.

And I needed Billy. I needed my good friend. Circumstances at home were no longer acceptable. I found him in the church's small yard, yanking weeds. A black plastic bag, half-full, was by his feet. I said nothing about seeing his mother, about Father Bowling.

"I need to get rid of the Christian," I told him.

He fisted a clump of weeds into the bag. "Yeah, so?"

"I need your help."

He pulled a weed nicely, engineering out the root.

We chose the following night, when Gary would be dealing cards at his casino job. It was a fast operation. We cleared the bedroom's floor and leaned the bed on its side and kicked Gary's Jesus sandals into the closet. Billy held the tape measure straight while I outlined with chalk, over which we stretched black industrial duct tape, creating an inverted pentagram. Billy also left dip in Gary's penny bowl.

What terrible Christians Catholics can be!

Afterward, we took to our boards and skated to the park. A warm breeze brushed our cheeks as we occupied our bench. Not long after arriving, sirens opened up the night. The sirens grew louder, more annoying, and three police cars raced by, their lights touching the leaves in the trees. Then more police units followed. Red and blue light brushed the upper floors of the buildings.

We hopped off our bench to investigate. When we rounded the next block, we saw police cars parked in a wide arc, opening enough pavement space for the man on the roof of the Purple Coyote casino, should he decide to leap, should he decide to dive off the twenty-two-story building.

An eager crowd was already gathering, as ants did around crumbs. Everyone was looking up, amazed and frightened. Police radios squawked. Onlookers held plastic beer cups and casino chips and each other's trembling hands. One officer walked from group to group, hand on gun, informing us that if we yelled *jump,* if we even muttered the word *jump,* we would be arrested.

That lonesome figure, twenty-two stories in the sky, I recognized him. How could I not? He was faceless and outlined against a blue-black night. At one point my father walked along the roof's edge with his arms out, like a tightrope man. He pivoted and faced the crowd below, arms winged, replicating the image on my necklace. Then the man's legs lifted and everyone gasped and he dropped into a sitting position on the ledge.

Among the expectant, tipsy crowd, Billy was the only one to set to his knees, to hold a crucifix, to pray. His necklace draped through his fingers like a rosary.

I watched Billy close his eyes, his head tipped forward, hands rising, his lips whispery and silent. I watched with envy and with awe.

A police officer recognized the importance of Billy's gesture. Soon the policeman was holding his baton with two fists, pushing people back, including me, until Billy was fully encircled, until it was just Billy with his prayers, Billy and his deck, its wheels still spinning. The officer waved his colleagues over. Everyone watched.

Again I looked up at my father on the roof. Wind blew his hair to the side like currents pushing snow off a drift. The slightest wiggle or movement and he would drop. Billy's left toe tapped the ground as he prayed, and how. How my good friend prayed for my father!

And that's the best memory I keep of my friend. I rarely saw Billy after that night. Several weeks later his mother was gone. Father Bowling asked me to work the service, and I did, alone. Gone that morning were Billy's tattered skate shoes. Gone too was any sense of familiarity behind my friend's expressionless eyes. It was on that altar, during his mother's funeral, when I said my last prayer—that prayer, and one other, when later I asked God to melt the ice cubes on my mattress. After that night, I was afraid to look up for several years. Even though the man on the roof was saved, it was terrifying to watch a life suspended in space and time like that. And as Paisley had foretold, Billy eventually left town to live with his father, a Californian.

St. Mark's is no longer St. Mark's. It was shuttered and later became an Italian restaurant. When that failed it opened into a bank. And it still is a bank. Billy Sorrentino keeps some money there. That's the rumor, anyway. Father Bowling eventually left the order to marry. The parish built a new church across the city, in a desert subdivision, now presided over by an Eastern Indian from the Delhi Province. The church is broken and is losing its men.

And my mother, she's dead, but that's another story.

These days I work my job. I husband. My wife is Jewish, and we're raising our son under the banner of that great faith. Even so, when I place my son, Joseph, into his miniature bed at night, I sometimes whisper small Catholic things to him, small pleas to keep him forever safe, but I don't speak one word of it to anyone. Prayers, I discovered long ago, work best in silence.

ESPAÑOLA

Weights help with the tension. Otherwise he's in knots, wound as tight as a baseball. Only two months returned, still adjusting to his studio apartment, green mountains, and cooler temps, to not having nineteen men in his ear, Lucero often considers reenlistment. Instead he grips kettlebells to keep from stumbling backward, from coming apart.

That afternoon he follows Friday's routine—jackknives, pulldowns, and hammer curls—and is nearly, breathlessly done. The gym smells glandular, of ammonia and flesh-salt and men, and his engorged arms feel righteous and good. Lucero computes reps with a knee crushed to the flat bench, single-arming a thirty-five-pound dumbbell, working his delts and traps. He enjoys the burn of concentric contraction. As he goes, a distant foreign Iraqi roadway comes to mind. He remembers a streetscape full of believers. Lucero's body strain loosens. He also remembers that snug feeling of wanting to follow along.

Then cousin HamJo stumbles through the gym's front door. The shifting pressure-suck curls the pages of a *Muscle and Fitness* magazine on the floor. HamJo pads across the gym and interrupts Lucero's meditation by delivering the news: BB has traded Cristina to someone for chiva.

Lucero's masseter jumps, sweat dews on a knuckle. Torn from his workout flow, he's momentarily high on rage. Lucero breathes deeply and opens his jaw to release pressure, then fastens his eyes. When he blinks there's cousin HamJo again, fat and worried and nervously waggling a brown front tooth with his tongue, back and forth, like some switch. HamJo is the only family member without a blown fuse.

"What do you mean she's been *traded?*" Lucero asks.

"For heroin," HamJo whispers, looking guardedly at the other bodybuilders in House of Pain. "Maybe your dad didn't exactly, you know, trade her. Loaned her, I mean. *Loaned.* Like last time."

Lucero drops the dumbbell and it clangs on the rubber flooring. A trainer behind the desk stands, glances over. Cristina is Lucero's baby sister. She's seventeen, not a young kid, but still, his baby sister. "How do you know all this?" Lucero asks.

"Uncle Goner told me," HamJo says.

"But it's Good Friday."

HamJo's eyes settle, almost too sadly, on a power rack. "I know, I know."

Lucero punches his damp sweat rag into a gym bag and mines out keys. He looks at his cousin and says, "That son of a bitch does this during holy week?"

HamJo just stands there and dabs his splotched cheeks with a wad of toilet paper.

Nothing equals the load of Lucero's family. Almost more day-to-day chaos happens in the tiny hamlet of Española, New Mexico, than what he witnessed in all of Diyala Province. Outside, Lucero's large flatbed, a retired tow truck, claims two spaces in the sun-bleached lot. It's a huge number, ridiculous and unnecessary, but it keeps him feeling safe. Often he feels otherwise. He's driven thousands of miles in an unfamiliar land, trawling dirt streets, his 16 aimed at cloud cover, fending off stomach cramps while waiting for that one final death knock that never arrived.

Another driver honks when Lucero accidentally cuts her off. He's preoccupied and, anyway, he always has trouble with blind spots. He puts a hand out the window as an apology and stays within the lines.

Wherever he drives, he patrols, isolating landmarks along roadways. He scans horizons for subtle anomalies, shifts in landscape, locating potential targets in the middle distance, compressing optical data (cell tower, building top, doorway) and determining range (miles, yards, inches) in split seconds. He captures the full panorama. The buildings around town—squat, one and two stories, dirt-colored, with flat roofs—are uncanny reminders of Baqubah. The resemblance is reliably eerie. Somewhere in his olfactory memory he still stores the burnt, shitty stench of raw city sewage.

Lucero's family is big, which means numerous stops. At his father's apartment Lucero lets the brass knocker hit the door loudly. Then knocks again. There's no response, so he sets an ear against the splintery wood and listens. Next he bangs his shoe on the aluminum screen at Aunt Dubie's. Nothing from her, either.

Uncle Goner's old Plymouth is at his barbequed trailer. Lucero realigns old steer horns mounted with chicken wire to the front grill of his uncle's aqua coupe. Uncle Goner doesn't come to the trailer's door anymore because Uncle Goner smokes, because Uncle Goner now lives in a large green tent behind the trailer, because Uncle Goner's junked-up when Lucero pulls back the vinyl flap.

"Sissy, it's you," Uncle Goner says merrily, rocking on a plush recliner. His hands burrow into the padded armrests like fingers into fatty flesh.

"I said never call me that," Lucero instructs his uncle. "Where is she?"

"Where's who?" Uncle Goner responds. "Who, who, who," he goes on. "Who." Now playing an owl. The man's dilated eyes appear freakshowish inside his spherical head. His loose, fifty-eight-year-old cheeks droop down his face.

"Cristina. My sister. That's who," Lucero says. "Seen her around?"

Uncle Goner chuckles. His pale tongue slots several gaps in his smile. A hand goes to his eyes and ears and mouth as he continues his wasteoid game. Goner chases the dragon by tapping brown flakes into hand-rolled cigarettes. Everything about the narcotic hobby disgusts Lucero. After the trailer fire, Uncle Goner rescued the only item left, a prehistoric singed rug, filthy with cereal dust, from when Lucero was a child. Four sloppily hammered boards form a wobbly new end table, now littered with milk cartons, which perfume the yurt with a pungent, past-expiration-date aroma.

From the border, the interstate shoots up the middle of New Mexico like a spine. It's a convenient route for Mexican traffickers. A little farther up, on 285, past mesas more beautiful than any good dream, turn right, make another right, and there's Uncle Goner's tent, minus seventeen steps to the flap. Lucero knows the whole region is infested: highest user rates per capita in the nation. "EPIDEMIC" screams the Sunday paper: grandkids scoring for grandmas, sisters sharing needles, etc. It's part of the community's fabric now, discussed in the same offhanded way people once talked about pies at the county fair.

When Lucero looks again, Uncle Goner has fallen into a druggy sleep, head to the side, beaded snot on his upper lip. Lucero breathes in the stench of flesh going to seed. He knows he's a powerful man. He studies mixed martial arts, bikes, is learning to swim, and attends weekly Mass—the church the only sanctuary left. He drinks powdered vitamin milkshakes every morning, eats bananas before bedtime for potassium. Twice a day he showers, applies lotion for sun protection, flosses, has quit dipping, and generally looks after his health. He could easily disassemble Uncle Goner. A large part of him now wants to pinch Uncle Goner's nose, plug the man's breathing forever. Instead, the righteous part comes around. Lucero checks his uncle's pulse. He senses warm, sour breath on his palm. He looks down at his uncle. Goner taught him to drive stick. Goner took him ice-skating when no one else would. Goner is family.

Lucero pulls a striped blanket from a rusted army footlocker and drapes it across his uncle's undernourished legs. He ties back the flap to let in sunlight. A breeze escorts hints of sagebrush. Lucero sets a brochure from the clinic on the uneven table, announcements for the needle exchange and counseling programs. He hopes Goner will wake up someday and phone.

Lucero drives. He learns nothing from the empty streets, but he drives anyway, hunting down his father. Neither Aunt Elena nor

Jill-Jill knows anything about the recent development, about Cristina going missing.

As the sun drops, waves of orange light daub the sky. The mountains ease from green to purple to black. Eventually Lucero returns to his studio apartment, where one wall is mirrored panels, another wall entirely cork. Lucero dislikes the previous tenant's additions. He pours himself a bowl of fiber-rich cereal, and before long the symptoms hit: eye pain, dizziness, neck strain, jaw ache and click, dry throat—a comprehensive résumé of his myofascial issues. Lucero hates the pain, refuses to accept the condition as a personal weakness. These involuntary jaw contractions began in the Middle East. The pressure sometimes migrates into his back, which tightens into cables.

In the kitchen Lucero opens his kit and spreads everything on the counter. He applies gelatinous conductive solution to small square electrodes. Standing at the mirrored wall, the electrodes taped below his sideburns, he jukes the battery-operated electrostim unit. The gadget pulses every other second, sending electrical currents into the electrodes, rhythmically contracting his muscles.

For a while Lucero watches himself in the mirrors, his mouth in full ugly spasm, recognizing the numerous facial similarities between him and his father, until finally out go the lights. He's unable to watch that twitching madman any longer.

+ + +

Sergeant Lucero Luna made E5 in three years, an accomplished leap through the ranks by any standard. After eight weeks of basic in Georgia, he was transferred to Fort Bliss in Texas and later ordered to conduct urban warfare exercises in a fake desert town built for that purpose. Next he flew to Ramstein, Germany, where he was elevated to team leader in a platoon. One sweltering afternoon the lieutenant colonel gathered the battalion inside a hangar bigger than Delaware. The collective body odor of the colossal huddle formed invisible stink clouds in the rafters. Lucero was near the front of the scrum, elbows raking his side, with a clean view of the colonel's sharp, clean jaw line. Lucero watched him pull paperwork from a manila envelope and read the letter from brigade headquarters: deployment would be fifteen months. Every soldier was humming with fear and anticipation.

As a member of Bravo Company, First Battalion, Sixth Regiment, Lucero was dispatched to the southeastern Operations Center in Baqubah, forty-five minutes north of Baghdad, and a former Ba'athist stronghold. It was a tightly compact city of 200,000, an equal mix of Shi'a and Sunni neighborhoods, where many high-level members from Saddam's regime had retirement homes. And it was hot, both in weather and in action.

Lucero's attention to detail was innate, a gift. He had been a neat, introspective child. No one in his family had ever traveled to California, much less Iraq, so this was a novelty. This was different, exciting. As soon as his jungle boots hit tarmac he felt enlarged, part of him deepening. Lucero opened himself to receiving whatever information the country could lend. At night, as mortar rounds hit miles away, Lucero would place an ear against his thin pillow, feeling the syncopation of his nerves thrumming along with his new, temporary home.

Baqubah's lowland flats were a truer form of desert than any other he'd ever seen. Flat and drab, with two seasons—hot and not hot. The Diyala River cut through the city like a swollen muddy slug, around which sprung lush palm groves. Irrigation canals snaked from the river to nourish orange orchards. Whenever his platoon drew close to the river, sniffing for buried weapons caches, that purple gauzy shade under the trees felt better than any cold bath. Locals stretched thin ropes across the river, ferrying themselves across via homemade rafts.

Baqubah was not pretty, with few public utilities and much less infrastructure than the capital. Baghdad was a city stilled in some weird 1970s time warp, but Baqubah was the developing world, premodern and almost primeval. Along roadways Lucero often spotted donkeys hauling carts loaded with gasoline canisters.

Lucero's twenty-man platoon patrolled northern sectors, providing security, maintaining presence, maneuvering up and down dirt roads in a convoy of four Humvees, coughing along at ten miles per hour, fifty feet apart, in three-hour shifts. Backcountry roads carried strange calving smells. The work was mind numbing and meditative and always vaguely terrifying. From the rear seat, directly behind the platoon's lieutenant, Lucero scanned roadsides for IEDs, for anything suspicious—errant boxes, raised dirt berms. To fight boredom the soldiers shit-talked and dipped, disgorging molasses-colored globs of spit into Gatorade bottles squeezed between thighs. Each of the seven neighborhoods had its own onion-domed mosque, and from speakers strung outside minarets the muezzins chanted the call to prayer five times a day, which was the signal, in Lucero's Humvee at least, for each soldier to excavate sucked, wet dip and reload with a fresh pouch.

Baqubah was also a sharp lesson in asceticism. Its citizens didn't own much. Lucero was all too familiar with have-nots. Española suffered from similar poverty, but unlike Española, Baqubah was, he had to admit, strikingly ugly. Neighborhoods had zero curb appeal. Tan and concrete walls hid inner sanctums. And if a family had any money, the money was thrown into the family's gate. Because Iraqis loved gates. Each home was connected to the next by high walls. The roadways were blocked by walls—so many walls, like mazes. Second-story rooftops were for sleeping and socializing and sometimes made good sniper perches. Plus, sewage was a major problem. Pipes simply ran from homes into shallow trenches in the streets. And the poorer the neighborhood, the more slipshod the wiring. Down many streets wires simply hung overhead like messy spider webs.

The city had so many defects—unwelcoming, and scorching, and treacherous—but during his fifteen-month tour Lucero witnessed several small miracles.

Once, at a routine stop, Specialist Tims called Lucero over to a swung-open gate. The platoon was mid-route, the four vehicles were idling, and Tims was hopping heel to heel, his wide forehead shining like a wet wall in the sun, giddily pointing inside the opened gate, like a child summoning friends.

Lucero eventually ambled over and saw why Tims was carrying on: there, inside, was a spectacular five-by-five-foot square patch of the greenest grass he'd seen in months. The grass was carefully tended, probably watered daily, and bordered by level cement, the green just glaring, nearly burning his retinas. Lucero stood in quiet appreciation until the home's matriarch quietly emerged from a doorway. The woman smiled, her teeth like wind-picked tombstones, and invited the men inside. That afternoon, the entire platoon lowered their barrels to the ground, communing with the loveliest Iraqi family, everyone standing over the square block of fresh grass. Each soldier was calmed by the sight of it. And each, in turn, took to a knee and breathed deeply, including Lieutenant Romero.

Mostly the work was sustainment. At cluttered, open-air markets the platoon would jump ship and mill, like it was social hour, chatting up the people—lots of back-and-forth nodding. The smell of barbequing goat meat and vegetables and flatbreads from the stalls rubbed their skin like salve. As team leader, Lucero kept an eye on his two team members, White and Dyer, a sort of playground-monitor assignment, while Lieutenant Romero spoke to market elders. An interpreter acted as Romero's go-between. How is the water? How is electricity? Any problems? Sewage? Are there too many people out of work? What do you need? Tell us. Tell us.

Middle-aged men wearing ankle-sweeping dishdashas would eyeball the soldiers from the sidelines while squeezing their knuckles and sipping chai. Lucero understood the sharp looks he fielded. He'd envision foreign troops rumbling through his Española neighborhood, and the fury his family would feel, the natural suspicion aroused by men with guns outside the front door.

Lucero's Humvee absorbed two sniper tags, presumably fired by al-Qaeda in Iraq. Both shots spider-webbed the bulletproof glass next to Lucero, and both incidents sent electrical surges through his legs, but he maintained, he repeated his silent prayers, and he waited to reach headquarters, where both times he emptied his stomach in the can.

One afternoon midway through his tour Lucero was flipping through a book in his self-built hooch, which he'd constructed from filched lumber, when he was summoned from the bay by the platoon's lieutenant. He was trying his best to ignore Specialist Scahill, a loudmouth from Philadelphia. Scahill was strutting around the bay's halls, jabberjawing, showing off vibrating cock rings that he'd ordered online. The dumbass was regaling everyone with past conquests and future plans.

Lieutenant Romero, an academy grad, two years younger, was smart and wiry and was waiting for Lucero in his office. The bald dome of the lieutenant's skull shone through thin black strands. Lucero knocked on the door.

"We need another interviewer," Romero told him. The lieutenant rubbed his knuckles against the desk. The platoon was sussing out new terps, he was told. Their most recent interpreter, a plump nervous physician from Baghdad who sweated rings into his red ski mask, had disappeared earlier that morning. Ugly things happened.

"Just jot down your general impressions," the lieutenant said. "See if this new guy grasps English. Today's interview day. Each sergeant gets one." Then Romero handed him a clipboard.

Hollow shipping containers had been transformed into makeshift, Spartan office units, nothing more than ad hoc sweathouses with two chairs and a desk. Inside Box D, a young Iraqi man was waiting for him. He had skin tone like Lucero's, and he sat fidgeting on a chair. Lucero shut the door and the heat closed in. Heat made the cargo unit smell elemental, of a foundry, of melting iron. The young Iraqi had curious, deeply set eyes, under which lay the familiar worry bags Lucero associated with war. The young stranger smiled, revealing a front tooth hoisted over its counterpart. Lucero took a seat.

"So okay, according to this sheet, your Americanized name is Benny," Lucero said, glancing at the clipboard.

"Yes," the young Iraqi said. He nodded. "Benny."

Also per the info sheet, "Benny" had been a petty criminal. Said on the sheet he enjoyed taking things from markets and not paying. So he'd spent time in prison. Now he wanted to help coalition forces. Lucero squared papers with a tap, and said, "So you know English." It was a statement and a question, a trick. Lucero gave away nothing. "Benny" could be snooping for al-Qaeda.

The young man folded his hands. "You got it, dude," he said. "I know English. So cool."

Lucero squinted. Dude? "Uh, why do you want this job, Benny?" he asked.

"Stay out of prison," Benny said.

"And how long have you been out?"

"Two weeks."

"And where'dja learn English?" Lucero asked, leaning forward.

"Movie tapes," Benny said. "My family watch much movie tapes. Action adventure. I read the subtitle. I improve this way." He nervously licked his crooked tooth.

"Translating is tough work," Lucero said, adding, "dangerous for you, if certain people find out you're working with us."

Lucero was struck by certain dark thoughts—that after patrols, back on base, entombed in his air-conditioned hooch, he always could slide on earphones, turn on his TV or laptop, and shut out all reminders of war, while Iraqi citizens like Benny remained on the streets, exposed.

"Yes, but I want to help," Benny said. "I good with people, dude. I do help."

There it was again, that word. "So you want to help," Lucero said. A statement and a question. "Any other reasons?"

"One," Benny responded, and he said funnily, "Yippee ki-yay."

Something about the young man's aslant tooth was endearing. That tooth reminded Lucero of his favorite cousin back home in Española. Plus, the man didn't have a breathlessly thick accent. Plus, he was kind of humorous. Plus, he spoke English well, if oddly. Lucero handed the lieutenant a positive recommendation.

+ + +

The next morning Lucero attends 7:00 A.M. Mass with the faithful, mostly older women praying to end the scourge. Someone's nephew was popped in the ankle with a Glock. Another prays for her thirteen-year-old to keep away from the brown.

Lucero knows the tragedies. He knows his community.

Mass is part of his regimented life. The church of St. Francis is over three centuries old, built by Spanish missionaries, and at this early hour it emanates a kind of hollow loveliness. Lucero sings along when prompted, bows his head when it's time. Lately Father Paz has had a rough run of things. He's said too many prayers over the fallen.

When Lucero kneels, he doesn't kneel out of fear, like others. He doesn't pray to notions of heaven or hell or winged seraphs. He prays to meditate on what's been lost, on finding placement amid chaos, as a private way to pause, for brief moments, during the indefatigable rush of things. God to him represents a passage-way into himself, a way of deciphering small meaning from life's larger commotions.

When he was in Iraq, weekly Mass happened wherever, any-where there was space—on dirt airfields, inside mess halls—and the rituals were performed by military chaplains schooled in the basics of every denomination. His unit, he remembers, had five Catholics, and Lucero had asked the chaplain to teach him to dis-tribute the Eucharist on the battlefield, should a hairy situation arise. The daily turmoil he saw beyond the walls and the concer-tina wire and the piled sandbags served to brace his faith.

At the kneeler, Lucero senses tension around his orbital sock-ets, symptomatic of bruxism, of teeth-grinding. He feels strain in his neck as he tips his head, then the after-click in his jaw's hinge as he receives the Eucharist. Lucero bears the pain, but it's both-ersome. He tries secreting it daily on the weight bench. He's seen two internists, one specialist. That specialist fingered a diagno-sis. To alleviate the discomfort he's tried muscle relaxant pills, acu-puncture, night guard, talk therapy, hypnosis, and biofeedback, each with negligible results. Now he's fooling around with trans-cutaneous electrical stimulation. He bought the unit at a discount. He even printed a MEDLINE map from the Internet, tacked it to his corkboard wall, a detailed chart of the nerves, muscles, and ten-dons in the human head. He keeps informed of his condition.

Outside is cool and bright. Lucero hops in the rig, wondering how much chiva, how much debt, what exact amount makes you trade your own daughter? He feels the radial nerves in his forearms tighten, and they tighten more when he imagines closing his grip around his father's sternocleidomastoideus.

Lucero tracks down his brother Rick at the bookstore. Lucero soldier-steps through the door and sees Rick on a stool behind the counter, squinting over a dog-eared copy of the *Oxford Book of English Poetry*. The old stacks emit the faint aroma of cat piss. Rick's mashed hair looks recently lifted from a pillow, and his drowsy eyes are a side effect of the buprenorphine opiate therapy administered at the clinic.

"So listen, if I took enough courses at the JC," Rick says, starting at the exact spot where their last conversation ended, "I could transfer to state in two semesters. I can do it this time, Sissy. I can. And you should too. Take advantage of that program for vets." His brother squints, examining Lucero's face and the pink squares left by the electrodes. "What's that funny look?" Rick asks him.

"Dad loaned out Cristina," Lucero says.

Rick stands. "What? Again?"

"I was hoping you might know more," Lucero says. "Gave her up for chiva." Just mentioning the word creates a gnawing vagueness in his brother's eyes.

Rick says, "That bastard."

"And don't call me Sissy," Lucero says.

Lucero gives his younger brother orders. They split tasks. Lucero calls his mother's brother, her sister, and four cousins on that branch, while Rick takes his father's brothers and sisters, leaving twelve messages for the cousins and their girlfriends.

Lucero overhears Rick's conversation with HamJo, who's already on the prowl. Rick hangs up and says, "Jesus Christ."

"Don't say that, either," Lucero tells him.

Earlier, Lucero had donned his army-issue jungle boots, not knowing where he'd find himself, under or behind what rough desert hill. His father is a man perfectly designed to burrow inside holes. Half the family is useless, undependable, either heavy users or recreational weekenders—but at least, he thinks, there are more eyes out there now. Rick takes his car in a different direction.

Late March in Española is nippy but the sunlight pacifies the crisp breeze. Lucero drives with windows cracked, scanning parking lots. The cool air caresses his tight sideburns. At St. Francis, several parishioners stand around the parking lot holding coffee mugs, ovals of steam rising into the thin desert air. Lucero hears the sharp tock of hammers working wood. Men are assembling wooden crosses on the pavement for the following morning.

First he tries the bowling alley, next Saints and Sinners—his father's favorite bar. He feels his masseter twitching again. Several cousins, patrolling the streets, drive past him. Lucero waves down Maya, who's freshly rehabbed, and she stops mid-block and rolls down her window.

"Oh, Sissy, I heard," Maya says. "I'm out here like everyone else."

Lucero flinches at the nickname. Eighteen years old, his last night before basic, that guy's ass, Lucero's hand . . . people in the bar noticed, but so what?

"I just checked the laundry mat," Maya informs him. "Nada. No sign of BB."

"Dad doesn't do laundry as far as I know," Lucero says. "But call me when you hear something. And please, nix the Sissy shit."

"Will I see you at Mass tomorrow?"

"If we find my sister," he says.

Lucero loves his father, doesn't know why, was raised under the cold shadow of addiction, but Lucero considers finally hurting him, teaching him through pain. To watch his father willfully destroy himself is one thing. Putting his baby sister at risk is quite another.

Lucero's father heats salt heroin in beer bottle caps. Then he injects a twenty-eight-gauge needle into the femoral vein in his groin. Lucero knows the details because his father explained them. Some fathers talk fishing, his talks chiva. BB also said that his feet were shot long ago, same with the veins in his hands, and he won't consider neck injection. The man is losing places to put it. His father's forearms are so collapsed they may as well be made of quicksand.

Lucero torques the wheel and heads back to St. Francis, waving at the parishioners in the lot before heading indoors, where he lights a votive and recites several Our Fathers. Later, after punishing his muscles at House of Pain, he kicks in his father's apartment door.

Taped to the bedroom window are black garbage bags. There's a mattress, dresser, and three pairs of accordion-shaped blue jeans on the floor, as though his old man had dropped trou and leaped out. The place is an anti-spiritual tomb. Lucero peels back the tape affixed to the bags and sunlight washes the walls. In the small living room, crescent fingernail clippings contrast brightly against brown carpet. His sister's bedroom is neat: an early model computer on a desk, piled socks, hair clips—a perfectly acceptable young woman's room. Lucero takes note. She doesn't own much. Regardless, she'll be living with him from now on. On his father's bathroom counter are packaged needles from the clinic, plus his father's phone and wallet. The man's keys are gone, same with his Dodge truck.

Lucero steps outside and waits in his rig. He watches the ruined apartment door from a distance, rubbing the meaty web of his hand at the LI4 acupressure point, a technique taught to him by a ninety-dollar-per-hour specialist.

+ + +

Children were the best part of Iraq. Lucero didn't want to admit it but finally did. Ever since Fort Bliss, he had been waiting to brush aside the clichés piled on him by returning soldiers, especially what he was told by Captain MacLeod, a father of triplets, who explained through bloodshot eyes that Iraqi children were wondrous.

It was hard to deny. Even with a war going, the children were unusually happy, their smiles like searchlights as they jumped sewage trenches to run alongside the vehicles. Seemingly parentless Iraqi kids appeared from out of nowhere. Several emerging little capitalists tried selling pirated DVDs to the men. Others posed questions in shockingly Kentish English accents: Do you have a wife? Are you rich? Can I live with you? Give me a ride?

Of course, the streets had more than children on them. The men in his unit drank in the lovely faces of women, the women glancing without glancing, smiling without smiling, their eyes like burnished jewels edged by silky headscarves. Private First Class White, the Humvee's gunner, was a chronic masturbator and often described his discharge after rubbing one out. During patrols, White also had the annoying habit of hollering down from the gunner portal the phrase "I would" whenever he spotted a particularly attractive lady. "I would!" Leering at another: "Her too, I would! Most definitely I would!"

Lucero often felt guilty when looking for too long. All around were young women and children scurrying into dangerous roads from hidden recesses, and he and the men had their fingers against triggers—this was open war—but civilians were just *out there,* minding their days. There was a cold, clear segregation between military and populace. The brigade commander thought goodwill should be spread via the peekaboo approach: roll loudly and heavily armed into open-air markets, say hello, and roll back home. Yet all they ever did was block traffic, get in the way.

"Act like friends"—words from the brigade commander— "Remember, we're here for sustainment. Smile. Be friendly."

Lucero was averagely built and strong, and wearing full battle rattle added significant bulk and only emphasized unfriendliness: camouflage pants bloused into tan jungle boots, upper blouse, flak jacket with 16-pound ceramic plates, Kevlar helmet, six thirty-round vest-strapped mags, night-vision goggles, a CamelBak for hydration, zip strips, knife, tin of chew, mag light, sunglasses, tags around neck, crucifix around neck, and his 16. He was an Americanized machine. How was that friendly?

In the down hours, to distract themselves, the soldiers placed orders on Amazon. Men's magazines were scattered around the halls, as were CDs, movies, video games, acoustic guitars. Lucero read a lot. His books were shipped to the Army Post Office in New York, later routed to his air-conditioned bay, enjoyed first by him, then passed along to others, and finally handed to children along patrol routes.

What continually surprised Lucero was the ease of communication between the war zone and his small New Mexico town. Following patrols, he would log in and receive e-mails about what was happening in Española. Another family member was hooked, stealing, in jail. So he logged off, wandered around the bay, hoping to find someone to distract him until the next patrol.

+ + +

The platoon's newest terp refused to wear a ski mask. Wearing a mask was the smart choice, the safe choice, but Benny refused. Still, the men soon found that Benny was an asset during tense home searches. Licking his crooked tooth, he put families at ease by acting casual, by joking around, by pretending this was just an annoying game.

Benny was a sort of clumsy and oafish young gentleman, but he always thanked the women when they offered chai or Coca-Cola. And women always offered. Lucero's task during home searches was to stand by the door, half in sunlight, turkey-peeking around walls, side-glancing rooms, and looking for approaching shadows. There was a Koran in every home, always on top of a pillow. And often there were pictures of prophets, but otherwise not much— especially in comparison with the unlimited bounty available to soldiers inside the base walls, that false paradise.

One afternoon, as the platoon rolled rowdily back toward the Operations Center, Lucero listened to the men's nervous laughter increase in volume as they drew closer to base—they were safe once more. At the checkpoint, the vehicles stopped beside twin sandbag citadels. For security purposes, returning platoons were required to turn over ammunition before continuing.

Lucero hopped out to check on White and Dyer.

"Christ, I need a piss," Lieutenant Romero said, throwing fists up and stretching.

They had done a sluggish tour of the northeast. No surprises. Men in the markets, women gathering water and perpetually busting their asses waiting on the men. Kids chasing kids. Lucero kept a close eye on Pfc. White, the unit's bona fide geardo, who stood around polishing his matte-black, polarized Oakley sunglasses. At one point Lucero saw White staring admiringly at his own reflection in the Humvee's window, modeling his specially ordered buck knife with an antler handle, which hung awkward and ridiculous from his belt.

One by one the soldiers approached a fifty-gallon drum impregnated with sandbags. They ejected magazines from 16s, cleared chambers, and caught the rounds. Then each man fired into the barrel, each weapon answering with that reliably soft click. When Specialist Castillo stepped forward, his weapon discharged, and a high sharp snap cracked the air and currents coursed through Lucero's legs. Lieutenant Romero jumped. The MPs palmed their guns. Sergeant Castillo looked around, embarrassed. It was an act of carelessness. Everyone knew there would be an investigation.

"Embrace the suck," Lieutenant Romero said, taking Castillo's weapon.

Sergeant Castillo was relieved of patrol duty. From that day forward the unit's new terp occupied Castillo's old seat, in the back, beside Lucero.

Benny had a kind of nervy energy. He was ceaselessly shifting in his seat while amusing the men with his movie-styled English. As the weeks passed, Lucero began liking him more, especially when Benny would mime biting the standing gunner's kneecaps.

One calm morning, Benny said, "Yo, this be slow." He was watching tawny neighborhoods pass by at ten miles per hour. He was obviously bored. "You think we can score some chronic out here?" he said later.

Benny's mishmash way of speaking was punctuated with *dude* and *fuck* and *dope*. Whenever the unit finished searching suspected insurgent bivouacs, the men would quickly prepare to leave, but Benny always mounted up last. He would remain on the street, like some cowboy, hands on hips, scanning rooftops. When every man was loaded in, he'd yell, "Let's roll up out of this bitch!"

Guy talk bounced around the Humvee like a loosened rubber ball—sex, tits, baseball, tits, sex—but that line of talk paled in comparison with the richly weird slang Benny taught the men. Conversation was nearly impossible whenever moving over twenty-five—the Humvees growled—but during slower trawls Benny would start the lessons again.

Lucero's unit was accustomed to thoughtful, taciturn interpreters: businessmen, men of the academy, men who wanted Iraq to calm down so they could get on with their lives. Benny was different—Shi'ite by birth, father he didn't know, raised under a succession of aunts and uncles, and a first-rate smartass.

"That mean, you are a donkey," Lucero would hear Benny explaining to the lieutenant. Romero would nod thoughtfully and repeat the Arabic phrase.

"Good. Now try 'You are son of donkey.'"

So many donkey put-downs!

Later, Benny tutored the men on nastier morsels. Lucero would watch Lieutenant Romero eagerly scribble into his notebook. First the phonetic pronunciations, then the translations: *fucking your mom, your grandma, your mom's tits on a pole*. Pfc. White laughed so hard at *my dick in your conscience* that he nearly swallowed his dip, pounding his chest while wet flakes rained down onto Lucero's shoulder.

Around Benny the men refrained from referring to enemy combatants—AQI, al-Qaeda in Iraq—as skinnies, as Hajji, as Ali Baba or Johnny Jihad. The men liked him and didn't want to offend.

"You sure you won't wear a ski mask?" Lucero asked Benny on another three-hour patrol.

"I don't need that shit," Benny responded, batting his hand in the air.

"At least think about wearing a skid lid," Lucero said. "You're from these neighborhoods. Somebody might recognize you. Take a shot. Report you."

White, peering down from his standing position with his fists on the fifty cal, bumped Benny's shoulder with his boot. "Listen to him, goddamn. Shitheads hammering folks out here."

From the front seat Lieutenant Romero peered back, as if to say, *"Lay off."*

But Lucero continued staring at Benny. Lucero wanted to show the younger man his concern. But Benny just balled a fist and, as sort of a thank-you, lightly tapped Lucero on the shoulder. Then the young Iraqi grew unusually still and quiet, as though Lucero's worries were an uncomfortable trigger. Benny put his head against the window, falling off someplace, his cheek vibrating at each road rut.

Later that day, as they were returning to base, safe once more, the lieutenant said to the driver, "Specialist Dyer, do you see that abnormality, up ahead, in the road?"

"I do, sir."

The lieutenant was pointing at several trenches that met and formed a large black puddle. It was deep with sewage.

"Gun the vehicle, Specialist Dyer," the lieutenant said.

Specialist Dyer smiled and drove his heel into the accelerator, aiming headlong toward the puddle. The resulting wake rolled over the vehicle's hood and broke inside the gunner's portal, dousing Pfc. White, and his Oakley's, and his moronic buck knife.

+ + +

So what if Lucero kisses guys? That doesn't cancel out how he waxed one in the thigh and another in the clavicle after his unit was ordered to move to contact. It was extremely hot that night in Baqubah, but Lucero doesn't enjoy remembering the vivid, almost mechanical way the deeply green figures crumpled inside his night-vision eyewear. These days he's slowly exorcising traumas that loop like old film footage behind his eyelids.

He's working out, maintaining. He doesn't like thinking too much about it. Thinking leads to remembering, and remembering only brings on more jaw pain.

And he hates that his father gave him the nickname. So all Lucero needs is one more person to call him Sissy, and when Paul Baca gives it to him, Lucero forearms the impish bartender farther into the vinyl booth. Several customers in the pool hall walk over to inspect the ruckus. But Paul waves the gawkers away.

"I'll ask you one more time," Lucero says to Paul, feeling strain bloom around his frontalis, the signal for an approaching tension headache.

Paul lets out a scared fart and says, "The Cruz. Okay? I've seen your father at The Cruz. Come on, Lucero, let go of me."

What's happened to Lucero's high desert town? It now resembles the last sick tailings from an ancient empire. There was a moment, when Lucero was young, when families gathered at the park on Sundays after church, kicking soccer balls against barbeque grills pumping out sausage smoke. Picnic blankets once lay like oases across wide lawns. Now the roads are scattered with newsprint and plastic bottles. What is going on?

At home, Lucero waits for night to fall with gelled electrodes wrenching his facial muscles. This self-treatment supposedly boosts endorphins, blocking nerve signals and battling the pain. When the sun sets, he swipes his keys off the plastic countertop made to resemble wood.

The Cruz is a weedy drive-in with three old screens. Cars listen in via radio. In his youth The Cruz featured short cartoons before the main presentations. As business slid, the fields turned into swap-meet grounds, but the drive-in eventually reopened. The new owners decided to feature only porno. Men of Española like the place. Lucero pays and parks beside the cinderblock concession stand, which sells condoms, soda, butt plugs, French fries. His truck idles under the shadow of an eave. Dust twinkles in the projector's misty beam, bringing to mind space and stars and galaxies, a thin section of universe where Lucero now sits. For a moment he isolates a distant star, wondering what's happening between there and here.

And he waits, bored by the on-screen hetero-gymnastics, until finally, at 12:23 A.M., his father's truck arrives.

There are twenty or so other vehicles in the field. Each is parked a good, safe, wankable distance from the next. Seeing his father's brake lights illuminate and darken, Lucero grabs the keys and creeps through the field, partially lit by the reflection of an actress's ten-foot tooth. On the screen are a man, a woman, and another woman, each barely dressed, playing lawyers in a courtroom.

Lucero yanks open the passenger-side door and his father's hand jumps to his heart. "Ah, *Dios mío,* Sissy," his father says, "You scared me."

Lucero piles in and grabs his old man's damp, chicken-skin neck, nearly lifting his father off the bucket seat. He shakes his father's dusty head, holds him, and shakes him tighter. Eventually his father touches him, gently petting his bicep. The man's touch is so foreign that it almost burns. Lucero opens his mouth, dizzied by his own strength, realizing how long it's been since he's delivered this kind of hard hug.

"Damn it, Dad, you fucking disappoint." Lucero lets his father's head go, and BB adjusts back into his ass-worn seat.

"Sorry to," BB says. His father is thin—a dead, skeletal bird.

Lucero swipes tears from his eyes and listens to the sound of his father's shallow breathing. "Did you already hit?" he asks his old man.

His father nods, even though Lucero already knows the answer. He can tell by his father's low lids and sedated eyeballs. The man just sits there, deflated and pathetic, his cracked hands gripping the bottom of the steering wheel.

"Hiding out now, too," Lucero says.

"From you," his father says. "Thought I'd be safer here. Not your kind of movies."

Twin erections larger than the historic obelisk in downtown Santa Fe appear outside the windshield. Bits of the theater's screen have gone auburn, from sun damage, yellowing one woman's naked thigh as her body wanders into that quadrant.

"Haven't seen you at Mass," Lucero says.

His father laughs. "Haven't seen me at Mass, son, in twenty-odd years. You know better than to say that."

"Is it true?" Lucero asks. "Did you loan out my sister?"

His father's sun-wrinkled mouth bunches, like a beanbag. "I owed money."

"I should destroy you, Dad. And during holy week, for fuck's sake."

"How'm I to know?"

"Where's Cristina?"

His father doesn't put up a fight. There's nothing left in the sad man but air and bone anyway. With a pencil's nub, Lucero writes the name and address on an old receipt. Her location is more than an hour's drive. Lucero looks at the time on the dashboard. It's late. He thinks about leaving immediately, but he reassesses: if he left now he'd arrive in the middle of the night, during the darkest hours, a time when people sleep beside loaded guns. His masseter spasms as he imagines the possible horrors already exacted on his baby sister, by some cretin named Angel. Each scenario makes his lungs feel tight. Last time this happened, Cristina was fine. He tells himself that she's okay, she's okay like last time, she's definitely okay.

"And who is this punk?" Lucero asks. "Should I be worried?"

"If there's one thing in this world I wouldn't do," his father says, "it's give my baby daughter to the devil. Angel's a cream puff."

"Uh huh," Lucero says and toes the truck's door, opening it wider. It creaks and the yellowy cab light turns on. Lucero says, "Okay, now that necklace. Give it over."

"What?" his father says. His eyelids lower.

"That necklace," Lucero says, "give it. You don't deserve to wear it."

The old man's faith is faith to junk, nothing more, and buried in a bush of white chest hair hangs a thick silver cross, one of the only jewelry pieces his father hasn't hocked at Dynamite Pawn.

"My momma gave this to me," his father tells him. But there isn't much fight in those flabby words either. Eventually the old man sets the necklace on the pleather bench seat.

Lucero tries rubbing out the tarnish with his thumb, feels its weight, and then, reconsidering, sets the necklace on the dash. Shadows cut across the old man's forehead. "Never mind," Lucero says, "keep it. You need it more."

+ + +

"Benny," the lieutenant said, "You ever watch those movies they screen at the base?"

"Shit no, dude," Benny responded.

"But they're free."

"Too much comedy. I like action. Like I say."

The Americans laughed. The corner of Benny's mouth lifted whenever he saw his new friends laughing, even if they laughed at his movie-got English.

The convoy was moving along a cool March morning, listening to unusually loud chanting coming from the minarets. The unit would rendezvous with three Romanian engineers, hotshots who'd problem-solved issues with the power grids in Kirkuk. The team would provide security alongside Iraqi security forces.

At thirty-five miles per hour, Lieutenant Romero was skirting protocol, but that was his order: maintain at thirty-five. Neighborhoods blinked by faster than usual. Lucero had eastern streetscapes memorized. He knew when umber walls would yield to orange groves, knew when to expect certain dirt colors again. He searched horizons and zeroed in on kids playing soccer in the streets. Beside him, Benny was scanning west, spooling and unspooling thread around his thumb. Since joining their crew, Benny's constant shifting had become more frequent, the boredom in his eyes more evident. Army work hadn't turned out like it was in the movies.

"Watch that box at two o'clock," Lucero called out.

Specialist Dyer steered wide, giving a cardboard box a wide berth. Up front, Dyer was yapping again, though it was hard to hear anything at thirty-five. Lucero knew he was probably talking about his family in Boise—Dyer was a Mormon man, and there was always lots of talk from him about family. Lucero hadn't heard much from his, other than sporadic notes from HamJo, who sometimes sent books, canned olives, cheap logs of dip bought from Native American stores. HamJo also scrawled notes of scuttlebutt: his sister Cristina's confirmation, Uncle Goner's trailer fire from leaving a busted toaster plugged in.

Lucero was thinking about his father, who hammered roofs to pay rent and sustain his habit, when the lead vehicle's taillights lit up. All trailing vehicles stopped.

"What's going on?" Specialist Dyer said.

Via radio, the lieutenant instructed the lead vehicle to continue around and past a traffic circle bearing a statue of an orange. Sweat beaded on Lucero's chest. He was itchy. It was growing warm inside the Humvee. No one looked forward to summer months, and not one man in his unit liked discussing it. Lucero could still feel that massive heat from a particularly cruel summer day in the Buhriz neighborhood, heat so large and complicated that it nearly drove the men insane. While they were positioned outside a mosque, securing its perimeter wall from rumored threats, the temperature on that shitty day peaked at 140 degrees inside the Humvees. Frozen water bottles eventually arrived from resupply, half-melted by the time they reached lips. Pfc. White had folded from his standing position and had to be rehydrated by IV saline.

Soon Lucero's patrol began stopping, moving, and stopping again. They started encountering more and more people. Along the roads were groups of men and women, wearing black, some crying. At each successive crossroads more people poured out into the main flow. The vehicles slowed to ten, then to five miles per hour. Gripping his radio, Lieutenant Romero kept asking, as though talking to himself, "What is this? *What is this?*" They were four American armored units creeping through a predominantly Shi'a neighborhood rapidly filling with people moving in the same direction.

The lieutenant's eyes nictitated with darkening worry. He hooked a finger and dug tobacco from his lip, flinging the wad. "Come on, come on, come on," he said to the windshield. "We need to meet the guys from Bucharest. What are these people doing?"

The small convoy managed to cleave through the crowded streets for several more blocks, but at the next intersection they stopped completely. Hundreds of people created an impassable artery. To continue without bumping into anyone would be like driving through a cornfield and not treading over a cob.

"Fucking gridlocked," the lieutenant said.

People flowed around the Humvees like river water around boulders, clutching one another and releasing low, guttural cries. Lucero told the lieutenant that it was a funeral, probably some kind of funeral, and it would pass. He touched the lieutenant's shoulder.

But the horde didn't recede. And the slow-going march of sorrow didn't look like any funeral. Soon fingertips began appearing on the windows, followed by curious eyes as people peered in at the soldiers. One old man spotted Benny, an unmasked Iraqi, wearing a NASCAR T-shirt, sitting inside an American vehicle, and the old man sternly wagged his finger at him.

"Ashura," Benny said to the men. "I forget. It is Ashura today."

The lieutenant glanced back. "Fucking HQ doesn't tell me about this?" He grew more fidgety. "Four fucking armored lily pads in a pond of people," he said, adding, "We're surrounded."

"Ashura what?" Specialist Dyer tapped the wheel. "What the fuck is Ashura?"

"We mourn Imam Hussein," Benny said.

"Yeah, and, who? What?"

"People walking to Karbala," Benny said. "Pilgrims."

The soldiers in the other Humvees asked the lieutenant for permission to turn around. Each vehicle was stopped, blocked, exposed. What should they do?

"Shit-all," the lieutenant bristled over the radio, "We can do shit-all but sit and wait. Fuck."

Then a column of men came down the street. Blood was running down their faces in brilliant red lines. Blood dripped from chins onto long white dishdashas. The spectacle looked fake, somehow staged. But clearly it wasn't. Lucero and the others were astonished when they saw the men bashing sabers into their foreheads. More men did the same.

"Holy great shit," Specialist Dyer said. "That's a joke. Did you see that? That is a joke."

Lucero quietly watched. All of them watched. Behind mirrored sunglasses, the gunner above him swung the fifty-caliber east-west and west-east, his right leg starting to tremble. Lucero was unafraid. He gazed out the window, rapt by the ritualistic display and by the dedication, and astounded by the numbers. Here were people clawing meaning from this wasteland. War was on, yet people were flooding the streets, mourning some mythic figure enlarged through the centuries into tribal adhesive.

Lucero felt his fingertips buzz, felt his jaw strangely pop, felt the door open and air rush inward. Benny carefully stepped out, walked into the crowded street, and turned. He smiled at the men with his arms raised.

"Get back inside the vehicle, Benny," Lieutenant Romero yelled. To Lucero he said, "Firm that door until his donkey ass returns."

The numbers, nothing compared with the numbers—each one a believer. Lucero felt spiritually aligned with the searching eyes. War bred such enormous absence in the soul, yet these people were coming together to form a presence. The women, the men, and the children, each of them beautiful under blue sky tinted with silver clouds. The air was warmed by manufactured suffering. Despite proof, despite odds, these people were clutching at ideas of greater designs—opposable-thumbed, warring, cruel, yet lured by the hope of salvation and renewal. Lucero believed he saw Benny's crooked tooth shining as he twitched his head to the side, as if to say, *Come with.* The door wasn't closed. And for a moment Lucero considered hopping out, setting down his 16 forever, and joining the human tide. *Come with. Come with.*

The soldiers watched Benny shape his hand into a pistol. Their interpreter then pointed his hand, dropped his thumb like a trigger, and winked. "See you, dudes," he said. His arm fell heavily at his side as the soldiers watched their terp step behind a woman, and then he turned, and his baggy NASCAR T-shirt disappeared.

Lieutenant Romero sighed.

"What was that?" Specialist Dyer asked. "What was that about?"

"Something bigger than us, obviously," Lieutenant Romero said. He lifted his finger off the radio.

There were attacks and explosions that day in Karbala and in Baghdad, nearly two hundred dead from mortar rounds, roaming gun squads, and suicide bombs. Shi'a Muslim pilgrims were targeted, but Lucero and the men of his platoon didn't hear about it until after they returned to base. Instead, they were safely surrounded, unable to back up, encased in a moving womb of mourning, of Iraqi citizens searching for a higher source.

One young girl tapped on Specialist Dyer's window. She smiled up at him, showing off her pink tongue. Dyer nodded at her. Then he looked away as he spit into his Gatorade bottle.

+ + +

Lucero throws back the polyester sheets before dawn, wraps his hands, and works the heavy bag in his dimly lit apartment.

The ceiling bolts moan as he attacks an imaginary solar plexus, his mind listening for the pop of bone fracture. When his upstairs neighbor, Ms. Ybarra, taps her floor with a cane, Lucero showers and shaves. He blouses blue jeans into tan jungle boots and carefully attaches fresh electrodes to his smooth jaw, just below the temporomandibular joints. He inserts new batteries into the digital unit and flips the contraption to "on." Behind the wheel of his rig, he positions the rearview mirror upward to avoid seeing his contracting face.

All night his dreams dug deep holes and applied pain. Now he drives south, wound like a diamondback.

Albuquerque is a decent place to meet men, several okay clubs with beat music and dance floors lit like minor galaxies, but this trip heats a different sort of anticipation. Lucero likes the sprawling city. But it's a place, apparently, where a man named Angel lives, a man who accepted his seventeen-year-old sister as payment for chiva.

In a blue sky with zero wind, the stilled pillowy clouds look like meringue ladled onto flat plates. Lucero can still remember the serious feel of his 16. The weapon wasn't hard to give up, but part of him now wants it back. It had three positions—safe, single fire, three round bursts; and was magazine-fed, .556 caliber rounds. He sublimates flickering memories of how those rounds interact with walls, how they act against a shoulder, a leg—little harnessed lightning strikes, like powerful extensions of his finger, very hard and bloody pokes.

The address is in a middle-class neighborhood, faux-adobe tracts in a planned subdivision, the streets named after native pueblos. A blue door, heavy curtains, small satellite dish over the garage. Lucero parks across the street. At last he peels off the electrodes. The pink squares on his face feel hot and tender. With the chance of a struggle, he removes his crucifix necklace and places it in the glove compartment.

Inside the open garage is a blue F-150 truck with a polished chrome bumper. The garage smells of dripped oil and long-ago woodwork. Lucero silently pokes around. He searches on a tool bench for evidence of weapons—gun oil, bore brushes—but sees nothing. Finally he tries the door to the house and it opens. The washroom reeks of pine disinfectant. There's a wash going, and he hears the sound of a television coming from another room.

After four years in the United States Army, Lucero returned to New Mexico and kept up a steady workout routine. Lately this has been complemented by a diet of books, to keep his mind tight, and of fiber in the morning and echinacea and acidophilus at night. His musculature response is as triggered-up as a cat's.

He hears a drawer opening in the kitchen: the shiver of utensils. Then the low sound of a man's laughter.

Lucero walks into the living room open-palmed. A thin middle-aged man, belly like a bowling ball, lounges on a blue L-shaped couch. He's watching TV with a glass of milk in his hand. The man has black parted hair, a T-shirt too small, and purple house slippers. He sits up.

"Don't," Lucero says to him, thinking the man's watery lips look like ejaculate.

Through a doorway Lucero spots his baby sister in the kitchen. Black hair and fine skin and long limbs and eyes the color of his. She's beautiful. She's holding a dish plate. And she has yellow washing gloves on her hands. She's surprised to see him. He watches her slowly arrive at the realization that he's here, that he's come for her, as she wraps her arms around her shoulders and releases a single, animalistic sob.

"And who are you?" the man asks Lucero.

"I'm Sissy," he says. "Now, please drop to your knees," he adds, and the man's eyes widen.

"Lucero," Cristina says, her eyes glistening.

"Turn your back, Cristina."

"I thought your name was Sissy," the man says.

There's nothing significant to remember other than the pleasurable sensation of his boot toe razing into spongy, floating ribs. It's a powerful kick. Lucero has done, and seen, much worse.

Then he touches all of her, raising Cristina's shirt to inspect the small of her back, searching for bruises, proof of trespassing, any reason to inflict bonus pain on the man moaning and curled into a question mark on the recently vacuumed carpet. Lucero prays for her. Sometimes she's the only reason he attends Mass, to pray for his sister's well-being, and to pray the addiction out of his father's veins. Cristina grabs Lucero's forearms when he reaches for the buttons on her jeans. "Stop it," she says angrily. Her tears have already gone dry, and then he thinks he sees his mother's face ghost across hers.

Cristina hooks her fingers inside the yawning lips of the dish gloves, turning them inside out, and drops the wet limp things beside the man on the floor. She stands over him, inhaling two large breaths, her skinny shadow dropping across his back.

"Hurt him again," Cristina says to Lucero.

His mother, father, brother, his collapsing family, and now his sister—he must put an end to it.

"Hurt him more," Cristina says, even louder.

"That's enough," Lucero says. "It's enough."

"I know you," the man says when he rallies sufficient breath. He hoists himself up, wincing. He leans against the couch and tenderly pokes a finger around his rib cage. "I know you. Oh, I know your family. Tell your father I'll be seeing him."

In the rig, Lucero's face spasms. He presses his palms into his temples, closes his eyes, and breathes evenly to unstitch the pressure. When he blinks he sees Cristina, his baby sister—safe once more.

She fastens her seat belt. "If Mom was with us she wouldn't have let this happen."

"Mom," he says, "allowed far too much to happen. You must know that."

Lucero drives north. Along the way they begin spotting cars parked on the highway's shoulder. Earlier, heading south, there were none, but now Lucero remembers. It's the day: Jesus reborn. Cristina remains silent, a newly released captive, reorienting herself, her glazed eyes drifting off absentmindedly toward the hills. Lucero touches her arm but she doesn't react. Already he can see the clock moving and her mind hardening, her features rusting. He sees a fragile seed hindered by coldness, the next generation repeating the mistakes of the past. He doesn't want to see that happen. He will not watch it happen.

The highway slides into a yellow valley dusted with juniper, then ascends the back of another lonely hill painted with a wide strip of pavement. Lucero counts the cars beside the road, considering the magnetic, almost necessary friendship between humans and belief. He feels a muscle in his neck shoot, followed by a moment of disequilibrium. He opens his mouth and the sensation fades.

Farther north are more cars alongside the road, and soon the pilgrims begin appearing, mostly small family clusters, many wearing fanny packs. It's an ant-line walking in the same direction, on the same side of the highway, aimed for the mountains, the Sangre de Cristo. Several men bear the weight of homemade wooden crosses on their backs.

"I forgot about today," Cristina says. "They're heading to Chimayó. The shrine."

"Easter Sunday," Lucero says.

Cristina yawns, and he thinks: where did she sleep these two nights? Under what strange bedsheets? He prays for chronic, daily pain in Angel's ribs.

A green highway sign tells him how far to Española, to Taos. Lucero glances at the dashboard clock. Mass has already ended.

As he removes his foot from the accelerator, steering the rig to the side of the road, Cristina says, "Sissy, what are you doing? I'm hungry. I'm tired."

"Eleven miles," Lucero says. "We can walk that."

"What? I don't want to walk that."

"Only eleven miles," he says.

"But I'm tired."

"Me too."

He parks, hops out, and feels his boots on the dirt, feels how the ground still has him on it.

So many families are out today, water bottles in hand, walking toward that dim chance. Under a white, magnesium-colored sky, Lucero gambles weekly, pressing knees to kneelers, because there's not much left. But he has his sister, and she has him, and they have each other, and they have this: a long walk, the sweet and woodsy smell of juniper, and an expectant spring morning.

*Thanks to Caleb Cage for helping me understand
the soldier's experience in Iraq.*

LA LUZ DE JESÚS

LAX to ABQ, only one hour twenty minutes, tarmac to tarmac.

James realized the short flight, a puddle jump, really, took less time than driving to Vegas in his MINI. But whatever: he was busy eyeballing the old guy from the seat behind. The man's face was gritted as brick, and the fuselage smelled footy, and James's quad majorly itched, and he wanted *off* the plane already. The old guy was outmaneuvering James, setting a frayed paisley carry-on in the aisle first during the processional de-plane.

"In a *hurry*, Ace?" James asked the man, drawing numerous stares.

Other passengers were ornery and waiting, bent under luggage compartments. Another man sneered at him, but whatever, James was secure with himself, stamped golden with the knowledge that he was from Los Angeles, city of angels.

So's to perfect his New Mexico role, James wore cowboy boots. Made from sealskin and purchased from a Russian in La Brea with an orange rub-on tan, the boots were illegal of course—and therefore supremely hot. He would be in the state for three months, and James figured he needed to look the part. Everyone in his friend circle, in Los Feliz, in Echo Park, in Silver Lake, looked the part.

It was a seventy-eight to thirty-five degree slide, but even so, James shivered gladly. Outside, the New Mexican air was bracing. And that massive northern mountain range was super Jon Blazin'. Under the biggest carport of blue sky he'd ever seen, bluer than the Beverly's swimming pool, the cold made James's testicles harden to walnuts and rise. And his voice notched up several octaves when he said to the kid behind the counter at the off-site car rental place, "That piece-a-shit? No *way*. I simply refuse."

"I'm afraid that's all we've got," the kid said politely. A single car sat in the fenced, asphalt lot.

Buck-a-Trunk rented beat-ups and clunkers for long-term use. To James they leased the last available, a jaundice-yellow El Camino, dull chrome along the sides and faded mauve interior. "It'll have to do," James said at last, sliding the keys off the counter.

He would need to acclimate to the elevation and February temps, the southwestern dead-of-winteriness, but it was a bright day, the sky was purring, and he had nothing but free time ahead of him. James had his bags. In his bags were paper and pens and a laptop, everything he needed. Finally, at last, he was here to finish his screenplay, which in its early draft was superior in every way, he was certain, to *Thunderbird,* technical shots of which had been filmed at the new studios next to Albuquerque's airport. Several massive hangars could accommodate five helicopters flying in-doors simultaneously. Or so the rumors went.

For years James had been hearing whispers about the New Mexico scene. Everyone in the business had. Suits from the state's capital wanted to lure industry away from California, wanted to siphon from the billions, and so they offered fifty-cent returns on every dollar spent. The state built professional sets. The state bought an old prison, transformed it for film use. The state prom-ised well-trained talent and invested in infrastructure and adver-tised location spots and reliable vendors.

The incentives were smart. The studios came. Cue Tamale-wood.

James cruised north. It was all distances beyond the bubbled window. His rental car was comfy, tatty bucket seats but not half bad, considering how the tires hummed along the interstate. His gonads descended as vents blew hot against his lap.

According to a slim guidebook James had destroyed during the flight, and left inside the seat back, this landscape was high desert shrub-steppe. He pushed into higher desert, headlong toward the

Sangre de Cristo range—the Blood of Christ Mountains, also via the guidebook, *if you can believe that.* The Blood of Christ Mountains. Too perfect, he thought.

Too too, he thought.

James thumped the steering wheel with his palm, and in the rearview watched how his long, tinted bangs draped agreeably into his eyes. Boot heel depressing the accelerator, he flung a gum wrapper out the window, where it fluttered in the dry, subthermal desert air, coming to rest somewhere out there, he didn't know where, just somewhere amid all this weird reddish dirt.

+ + +

James Miles loved movies. James *adored* film—or "Cinema Arts," as his $128,000 undergraduate degree stated, in black Winthorpe font.

Whatever you wanted to call the business of capturing images and sequencing them in blocks of celluloid moving at twenty-four frames per second and blasting them via bright light onto screens worldwide, James worshipped it. From the age of twenty-two, he'd worked on film sets as a production assistant, driver, location scout, extras wrangler, wardrobe assistant, fly on the wall, absorbing.

James remembered often and fondly the film that marked his early conversion; how *Apocalypse Now* flooded his impressionable seven-year-old synapses to the point of near-epilepsy; how on that fated afternoon he softly genuflected in the sticky movie theater aisle, freshly sneaked-in from *The Muppet Movie,* his mother unaware; and how on reddening knees he crossed himself again and again, enraptured and awestruck by syncopating light and sound, as though the whole cosmos was convulsing.

Nothing was the same afterward.

Nearly every afternoon during high school, James would rent VHS cassettes and lock himself in his westward-facing room, which sopped up West Covina heat, sweating under a hot television screen in his airless, stultifying teenage stronghold, watching movies, learning from them.

He started with Action and systematically moved down the

shelves by title, A-Z. Next he ingested Drama, Comedy, Foreign, Documentary. He *suffered* for movies. In the near-tropical heat of his bedroom he watched fade-ins and camera angles and tracking shots and outtakes, his mother always yelling at him from downstairs, her wedding ring tapping against the wrought iron banister. "Come down and act like a human being, or so help the Gospel of Mark!"

He analyzed shorts, indies, feature lengths, prequels and sequels, and the extra cookies that rolled during credits. He studied cuts that worked, edits that didn't, when to overlay montage with soundtrack, and how many gratuitous buttocks to shove inside a trailer to lure crowds to the box.

Also, he developed special gifts. He could tell whether young starlets would make a bigger payday someday if they blew his synods at least three times during simulated coitus scenes. Rewind, play. Rewind, play. Rewind, play. Actresses of that caliber became legends. If they delivered lines without too much wood in their throats, if they were Bathsheba-beautiful, if they had been blessed with the right coloring and genes, they *endured*. Virginia Madsen, *Creator*. Angelina Jolie, *Gia*. Bo Derek, *Tarzan, the Ape Man*. For example.

His Cinema Arts degree was a rerun of those high school afternoons of willful solitude, but with terminology. There he met Ricardo Morales, who ended up directing *The Get Go*—with a huge opening weekend. There he also met Joy Paz, actress, later his girlfriend, or live-in lover, as she had called him. After Joy's liposuction surgery, she began pulling down large coin for early motherhood leads. Joy's first role, forgotten by everyone but him, was in James's opinion the greatest, saintliest work ever put on celluloid.

But these days, it seemed, everyone was fast-forwarding but James.

+ + +

He secured his SAG card after a humiliating series of background performances, cinched finally by saying, to a well-known dopehead, "Excuse me, is this your fork?"

[Handing over the fork.]

[*Aaaaand . . .* cut.]

That particular film nearly got canned before it was ever finished. The production was a three-week, straight-to-video throwaway, a bomb made as a wedding present from the director and producer Gil Soto to his latest nineteen-year-old wife, Mims. Mims was a high-pitched, screechy person, and she reminded James of a hummingbird, only ramped up more via methamphetamines. Mims wanted to "carry" her own project, but after the first day of shooting everyone knew Mims' acting was such a colossal farce that Gil Soto simply refused to leave his StarTrailer, an Airstream outfitted with chrome dials and a pro range kitchen.

On the set, rumors swept through the impatient crew. Mims was nowhere to be found. And the producer wouldn't come out of the Airstream. People wondered, was the job over?

That afternoon, James leaned against the producer's trailer and heard babbling coming from inside. The TV? Or perhaps, James realized, he was just hearing the sad, dying sounds of a has-been. Years of working in the business had toughened him to the affliction. Still, James *yearned* for his big chance at catching it. He'd been lounging around sets for years, communing at night with up-and-comers on his television set, and at twenty-eight he was *nowhere.* He rented a twelve-by-twelve room in Los Feliz, drank at Skybar, dated an earlobe model, but he wanted real entrée.

At last James knocked on the Airstream's door.

Gil Soto's eyes were bright with self-loathing. The man had a disarmingly familiar TV-commercial face, was sixty or so years old, and he usually carried himself like a trophy, but not on that day. Standing before him, James reached deep and pulled from his pocket a tiny round and blue Xanax, holding it to the light ceremoniously, in offering.

Gil Soto cricked back his neck, which James interpreted as an invitation, and when he stepped inside, Gil Soto fell into a leather Eames recliner, motioning for James to approach with a curling finger. James stumbled, dropped the tablet on the tight-woven carpet, and fell to his knees. He did not give up. He soldiered on.

He reached and parted Gil's great and full lips, gently placing the pill on the man's gray tongue.

Gil closed his swollen eyes and swallowed, without asking, *What chemicals?*

Then the man's eyes opened. Unexpectedly, he raised his feet and propped them on James's shoulder, slowly forcing James onto all fours. He positioned his sockless, fuzzy, naked feet on James's back, using him as a footrest, leaving his feet this way until night fell, as the writer and director of *Paddycakes,* the biggest money-maker of the Reagan era, watched cartoons on a flat-screen television and short-monologued.

That afternoon, Gil Soto hired James Miles.

For five years James worked alongside Gil, quote-unquote learning the *ins of the biz.* Perpetually locked to the man's side, James gave pep talks when called upon, championing Gil Soto's comeback at every opportunity, raising him like Lazarus; which of course happened, as everyone knows, the classic Hollywood fairy tale, now an award-winning documentary.

Oh that Gil Soto, James now thought, gnawing on sugar-sucked gum and driving into the road's shadows, farther into the mountains. Soto's last film, featuring monsters, pulled in eighty mil in four weeks. Oh that Gil Soto, the *fuckin' asshole!*

North of Rio Arriba, James passed a patrolman dozing on the side of the highway. He accelerated. James would do just fine out here, away from Gil Soto, that *fuckin' asshole!*, and away from that flittering wife of his, out here among the aired-out, sunburned hicks.

+ + +

Piñon Hill, as it was known, was owned by Gil Soto. Or rather, Piñon Hill was owned by Gil Soto, but operated by the Gil Soto Trust. Tax reasons. Gil Soto was the kind of *fuckin' asshole!* who owned stuff—like a western film set.

It was tucked in a low valley between foothills, at the base of the Sangre de Cristo. Piñon Hill was leased by premium cable networks and, lately, Western movie projects—they did okay at the box—and was miles from the interstate, through a padlocked gate, down a narrow gravel road, a perfect replica of an old-timey town, complete with raised wooden walkways and splintery buildings approximating those from late nineteenth-century Western America.

James had seen many films shot here, but he could hardly believe the place when he arrived. Semi out of it from travel, he blinked. His Tag Heuer had the wrong hour. "Dude," he said, staring sag-eyed out the window.

He parked next to the corner building with wood shingles. In *The Sandbaggers,* the building was central to the bar fight. It served as the brothel in *Queen Flea and Her Highwaymen.* (Only one viewing of Sara Black, he now recalled, but nothing became of her, proving his system was valid.)

James opened the car door, knee popping, and surveyed. Hairs inside his nostrils stiffened in the brisk air.

Two rows of wooden, near-dilapidated buildings faced each other on a block-long stretch of eerie filmscape. Business names in peeling white paint were etched above each structure: Saddlery, Jail, Mercantile. James laughed to himself. It was just too much. A wide dirt lane ran up the middle, horse posts over troughs and, at the end, through cold pale air illuminated by the El Camino's headlights, James saw the shadow of a single-room church with a bright white cross on top.

Already thin layers of dust had settled on his black sealskin boots. He wiped them clean, shivers coursing up his ribs.

The door creaked as it opened, spreading cold light over wood flooring. It was a prototypical westerny bar, mirrors behind it. Piano, stage, bar stools. The wood tables were half-ass props, unsteady and wobbly. The film in his head unfurled with each careful step. Every detail would matter. Every detail would be right. His film would be a stunning achievement. He'd suffered years of emotional abuse at the claws of Gil Soto, and he would not waste this opportunity to prove himself.

Upstairs, next to the whore rooms, or the lodger's quarters in *Lucien's Revenge,* was a fully equipped studio apartment, as promised.

The room was wintry, musty but adequate, occupied by directors during longer shoots.

James spent the evening unpacking, arranging his clothes, computer equipment, and seven body hygiene kits. He set up his small library of DVDs next to the television and stereo combo system. Thankfully, also as promised, the unit had surround sound. Four remotes, TV centered, chair situated beneath the arrangement, it was an altar of sorts. And that night, he worshipped the glowing node, the single room on the second floor of the corner building shining like a bright star amid the surrounding darkness, and visible for miles.

Before bed, James put in Joy Paz's earliest movie: *Fresh Mangoes,* a boner-comedy set in Fort Lauderdale. He skipped forward to the 40:12 mark. God bless modern tech, he thought, remembering the wasted hours in his boyhood bedroom, fast-forwarding and rewinding to land on the exact half-second.

Toggling the super-slow-mo button with one hand, he unzipped with the other. He unfurled one sock and set it neat and flat on the light-blonde wood floor. At 43:53 he sighed "Hallelujah," inhaled deeply, and reached for the sock.

"Time to hit the hay," he said to the room, repeating a phrase from the Old West phrasebook he'd brought along, for research purposes.

He was tired, worn plum down, and he felt good. He felt western and good and clean.

+ + +

Backdropping the set were foothills pocked with juniper and piñon and rising to high snowcapped mountains. The next morning James stood at the window, captivated by the scenery. The trees on the mountains looked like fancy ornaments from Neiman's. It was ridiculously serene, even inspiring. Quiet, with nobody to coax him into going to The House of Blues. No distractions. And the absolute isolation and *feel* of the place was Jon Blazin'.

He flipped open the computer shell and wrote, without coffee, for three hours, sunlight filtering through lace drapes and warming his knuckles.

Later he walked the set in his new parka. The coat was massive, so warm that he only needed a T-shirt beneath it. It was like wearing a gutted polar bear. He said the names of things during his slow meander. *Outhouse, chuck wagon, prospecting pick.* He loved the Western film genre. Windows in several buildings displayed their wares, horse tack and glass bottles now dressed in spider webs. He walked around the buildings and, not surprised, discovered they were mere shells. Four walls, unsteady roofs, the insides gutted and fake.

The church at the end of the lane was something different. Its adobe walls were shellacked cocaine white, with heavy pews inside, and a huge dark wood cross at the front, which sat propped on a ledge. The church appeared real, or real enough. Someone had done a remarkably believable construction job.

Behind the church, James came across a tamped-down trail, something made by time, from coyotes, or mountain goats, or trespassing health nut hikers from Rio Arriba. He followed the trail around a bend, figuring on some exercise. Away from L.A., his tri-weekly yoga sessions were on hold. His abs could use a workout after that bag of peanuts on the plane.

Ascending hills, down ravines, James soon forded a creek half-frozen by winter. The amniotic smell of dew and earthy shoots and mud was pleasurable. Farther up, through a copse of aspen, was an opening that led to a leveled outcropping, where he saw a great valley to the west. And shaded by a tree's branch was an oblong, adobe structure with a corrugated steel roof, now rusty. Several earthquake-like cracks decorated the building's exterior walls. The strange building was about the same square footage as Joy Paz's well-furnished casita on Ambrose Avenue. It looked like it had seen better days. James wondered if it was somehow part of the film set. He did the calculations, figuring the building sat on Gil Soto's land. One thousand acres was a lot, right?

James was startled when he heard scruffy, shoe-like sounds coming from inside the building. He stopped, his fist involuntarily clenching. He thought he was alone.

Late February in the foothills north of Rio Arriba was certainly far from Los Angeles, but what he saw next could have come straight from Hollywood Boulevard. A half-naked, white-haired man emerged from the building's doorway, his skin as umber as heroin, a synthesis of Spanish and American Indian, jeans sitting ridiculously high on his waist, with a shirt bunched in his fist. The man was perspiring, little beads collected on his neck. The man looked at James as though seeing a ghost. Perhaps seventy years old, the man's left sideburn was as white as goose feathers.

No phone reception in the hills. This James knew.

Without a word, the man turned and began walking away from him. James saw that the man's back was scabbed-up like mange, red scratches along his vertebral column, as though a sharp comb had been run up and down it. Worse, there was blood trickling down into the hollow, the upper portion of his tighty-whities gone pink.

"Um, hey," James finally said, politely trailing the guy. But the man quickened his walk into a geezerly semi-jog. "Dude, wait! Hey!" James yelled after him. He followed the man as far as the high ridge, where a trail switchbacked down the other side and faded into trees. "Do you know who owns this land?" James called out.

The man took to the trail and soon disappeared. Branches covered any trace of him.

"Ever seen *Paddycakes?*" James yelled down the trail, his voice echoing around the panoramic valley. "Do you know the name *Gil Soto?*"

Even saying the name roused pangs of indigestion. James knew the name all too well, and James wanted to forget the name. He knew far too much about that *fuckin' asshole!* Gil's reemergence had kicked off with a big budget, teen-teeth vampire movie.

James looked down into the pretty tree canopy. But the man was gone.

+ + +

Later that day, when the sun dropped, a chill ran through James's calves: the hike, the elevation.

Self-pity wrecked him whenever he sat too long in a room, bubbled in from the outside world, forced to recall those long afternoons in his childhood bedroom, watching and studying movies. *And for what?*

Here he was, still struggling, still completely unknown. Where was his film? Where was his Maserati? Where was his villa on Lake Como's shores?

He'd passed several businesses five miles west, past the chained gate and the cattle crossing, just off the interstate.

James fired up the El Camino.

Every building had been closed at one time, then reimagined for different purposes. The no-name town, if it even qualified as a town, was a loose collection of slipshod roofs and converted businesses. The bar, called Filling Station, was once an old auto shop. El Cheapo, the grocery, had once been a barbershop. And so on.

James approached the grocery store, but there was a Post-It note stuck to the glass window that read, in chicken-scratch handwriting, GESLOTEN. The door was locked, the lights out. James thought, closed? And what *language* was that?

Filling Station was a soft bar, unfortunately. No hard liquor, which was what James was after. Watching a half-naked stranger haul noodles off a high ridge was a fine reason for a shot of Jameson.

"Really? No whiskey?" James said to the bartender, a woman.

She returned the same look as the saleswoman at Maxene's when he'd asked if she carried belt buckles with rubies—he'd seen one once.

The bartender had nothing on tap either: bottles only. So he ordered a 12-ouncer from the rough-and-tumble lady with the nasal bump. She wore a long tan Carhartt jacket and had eyes as green as street signs. Her curls jumped off her head and hung like wisteria.

"Well, then, any food in this place?" he asked the woman next.

"Frito pie, is all," she said.

"What's that?"

"Open one bag of Fritos and drop chili and sour cream on top," she told him. "And serve with a spoon."

James felt as though she'd punched him. "Do you know how many *calories* that is?"

The hops bounced up his sinuses. Several nights later he ordered the same beer, managing to wheedle out the bartender's name: Linda. And James was Linda's only customer. He sussed out that Linda was some kind of artist, as evidenced by brown and gray paintings of mud puddles hanging lopsided on the cinderblock walls. She lived cheaply too, off the grid, nomad-like, and was the caretaker of two horses, she told him. But after this brief exchange, Linda didn't give up much. Every woman he knew in L.A., especially the earlobe model, talked nonstop.

Small red tags beside the paintings stated prices. Linda sold them for fifty dollars apiece. On the concrete floor was yellow and black caution paint, daubed out by oil stains. And duct-taped to the wall behind the bar was a list, printed from the state's website, outlining the penalties for DWI infractions. James was shocked to see the list run to ten. Ten DWIs? In California, after four, he was pretty sure authorities sailed you into the Pacific.

Wind blew, rattling the shop's aluminum garage doors.

Beer helped, but his thoughts were still triggered by what he'd seen in the hills. James couldn't put the matter to rest. What he'd witnessed was eerie, Anthony Perkins eerie.

So he placed an elbow on the bar top, a household door propped horizontal by twin saw horses, and said, taking a casual sip, "The other day, I saw a man without his shirt. He had a bloody back. Up in the hills. For some reason he ran away." Then he held in a breath.

Linda listened, gathering a moment before responding. "Just give those guys space."

"Those guys? There's more than one? You know about this?" he asked. "There's a building up there, too. Old building. Bad roof."

"It's called a *morada*," Linda said, her tongue doing yoga to squeeze out the word with a Spanish inflection.

"What?"

"Mor-a-da." Said as though he wore a helmet.

"Look, I no speak-a the Spanish. I know, I'm from L.A. It's a problem. I get it. But I'm not an idiot."

"Okay, listen," she said. "Just give the *penitentes* room for their silly holy rites." Again with the irritating inflection. "Leave them alone, and they leave you alone. That's the deal around here. Get it?"

"But that's Gil Soto's land," James said. "Ever heard of him? *Paddycakes?* The blockbuster?"

"I'm telling you. They've been around a hundred years. Maybe more."

James swigged. His beer was tepid. "Whatever, dude. I *own* in Los Feliz," he said, adding to that lie another, "on the *hill,* walking distance from the *observatory.* I don't let just anyone walk around on my property. You know? That's like, not American."

For whatever reason, Linda was unimpressed. Informing certain ladies in L.A. that you owned property in Los Feliz could get you invited into their rectories. Instead, Linda stared at him coolly, and they sat like that for some time, eyeball to eyeball.

Linda looked like she would be comfortable hunched over on rangeland, nibbling alfalfa. And she smelled of burnt tires. Her dog, Cockroach, a mother telling by the teats that hung like icicles, followed Linda everywhere.

Linda intimidated James somewhat, but he liked her hair, how it was curly and long and dusty and honest. James decided he'd do the same: start wearing his hair longer, sprout a beard, and embrace being here. As long as he was in New Mexico, why not? And he had to admit that he liked the way Linda handled beer bottles, firm and purposeful, like Alice Wells at the 55:01 mark in *Cosmica,* especially Alice Wells on wide-screen, and *especially* with Kiehl's Crème de Corps lotion.

He left Linda a three-dollar tip.

+ + +

Another night, soon after, James returned to Filling Station. During the drive he remembered with a primal shudder the number of blind-alley jobs he'd held without significant advancement. Best boy, 2nd AC, lighting tech. For years he was a gopher for Universal, primarily a paper jockey gig. Things were different now, and much, much worse. Now he was Gil Soto's grunt, the man's foot soldier, the assistant to the power player, Mr. Brentwood, *Mr. Fuckin' Asshole!* Vikings made cash rain down after Gil had produced a one-off, at James's suggestion, like always.

After hooking himself to Gil Soto, James had been certain his luck would change. He thought opportunities would open, meetings would be set, people would call and ask his opinion, the Holy Grail within his grasp. Instead, working for Gil was a major backslide, with increasingly costly therapy bills.

Everything had been smooth sailing until that night James prophesized the next big three.

"Emily B., Cody L., and Moni G.," James whispered into Gil's flesh-colored hearing aid, without letting the man know about his divine skill set. A year later, his prediction proved correct: Emily and Cody and Moni soon had swarms of paparazzi bothering them. And after that, Gil Soto downgraded James to busboy duties, as if, because of his gift, James was angling to usurp the throne.

James went from thumbing through film treatments to picking up Gil's dry cleaning.

Then he was tasked with scrubbing Gil's five outdoor barbeque grills. This transitioned into painting Mims' toenails sepia as she slurped vodka from a straw while they waited for Gil at the Marmont. There was much smoking of Gil's neatly rolled joints— "I want someone around here to be high, just not me"—and months of putting Gil to bed, raising thousand-count Egyptian cotton sheets to his chin, and quietly reading to him Dr. Seuss's *Oh, the Places You'll Go!* And of course, responding in the affirmative when Gil, drifting off one evening, asked him, "Pound out Mims tonight for me, will you? My sciatica."

Every subsequent disgrace was endured in the hope that the golden door would eventually open—that James would eat enough shit to earn his own project. What had come of his suffering, however, was this: three months on a writer's fellowship, of sorts. In

New Mexico, in the late winter, alone. James had demanded it. Or, he'd told Gil, he'd walk. Or, he'd threatened Gil, he'd tell *Variety* about those weekly meetings with Men's Ministry, a Christian life network.

"Please, oh no, please don't ever," Gil said.

The following week, James's feet were solidly on New Mexico hardpan, his man-purse full of nonsequential hundred-dollar bills.

+ + +

James developed routines. Mornings, he ate on the dusty downstairs bar, two yogurt cups and an apple, his breakfast ritual watched over by the black bowling ball eyes of a severed buffalo head. Ten to three, he wrote, edited, and swore. Afternoons, he wandered around the deserted town, expecting to see tumbleweeds rolling across the lonely road. His hair grew, his beard thickened. He underlined favorite sayings in the Old West phrasebook.

One morning, he broke. He'd had it with words, space breaks, with dialogue, and he decided to stir his blood. He marched down the lane to the church and began deadlifting the boulder-heavy pews, nearly popping out twin hernias. Decades of dirt berms lay beneath the seats. He returned to the church with a broom and swept soggy leaves and dirt out the door. James had a knack for interior design. When the set designer on *Stardust* fell ill with flu, James saved the day by arranging the drapes and tables and flowers . . . just, perfectly, so.

Nights, he frequented Filling Station, where he engaged Linda in hours-long staring contests. Big, hulking Linda started looking better and better as the weeks rolled by. Midnight, he'd sit and face the stereo-TV ensemble and watch movies, ending the night around 2:00 A.M., watching Joy Paz in that singularly stunning gamic performance: unzip jeans, remove sock, the business, and then cry.

One afternoon he sped to the no-name town earlier than usual. He wanted to reach El Cheapo before the proprietor put the damn Post-It note in the window. Two men were arguing over a stack of lumber when he cruised into the dirt lot. About fifteen feet in length, the wood boards stuck out from one man's truck. James bought a tissue box at El Cheapo—the crying. And when he came out the men had managed to settle their argument and had already relocated the lumber from one truck to the other.

When one of the men slammed his truck door, James saw a pure white sideburn behind the window's glass. James recognized him: he was the character from the hills, from weeks earlier. It was the same man who'd run, his back slashed and bleeding. The man's truck coughed exhaust and James's eyes burned. The man drove off.

James approached the proprietor of wood as he was securing his tailgate. "How much are 2x4s going for these days?" James asked him. He wanted his snooping to appear casually inquisitive, friendly like, as though he was just another local yokel.

"Two bucks per twelve-foot board," the man told him. "Why? Need some?"

"Oh well, thinkin' on it," James said, overemphasizing his drawl. "Might do some framing work soon." He stroked his beard thoughtfully. "Say, that guy, who just drove away, what's he building?"

James watched the man's chest jump as he chuckled. "Stairs to heaven, son," he said, and smiled.

There was a Cadillac in the middle of Filling Station, taking up half the bar. And the garage door was open. Tables were moved, chairs stacked, clearing space for the vehicle. Linda was on her back and fiddling around underneath the carriage, her bent knees the size of grapefruits. She wheeled out on a rolling contraption, swiped her hands with a rag, and said to yet another stranger, who was sitting on James's stool, "Oil's changed."

The guy was the only other customer James had ever seen in the establishment. Three empty forty-ounce bottles were on the bar top. James watched Linda help the man into the driver's seat. Then he watched her actually start the Caddie for him. She said, before the man backed out, "Remember, keep one eye closed. Set the steering wheel on top of the yellow road lines. At the yield sign, make a right, and coast on home down the hill. Easy, like last time, okay?" The man through half-shut lids nodded happily.

"How on earth do you stay in business?" James asked Linda, after the drunkard drove away.

"We're busy the rest of the year," she told him. "Right now it's Lent. This area's big on Lent. And folks drink less during Lent."

"That's not what I mean," he said. He thought more about it. "Anyway, if it's Lent, what about that guy?"

"Frank Rodriguez? Frank doesn't follow Lent," Linda said. "He and his family are what people around here call crypto-Jews."

There Linda went again, talking nonsense, but she did look at him differently. She even complimented James on his luxuriant beard, saying it was a better look for a man with such soft hands.

+ + +

It snowed. Great parachutes of crystallized water dissolved like cotton candy on his tongue. That night, the night of early spring snow, James walked the set. When the clouds parted, the moon shone like klieg lights over the buildings.

Inside the church, James perched his boots on the pews, surveying his cleanup job. More and more it resembled a truer church. A proper church. The place was the only genuine-looking article in town. After a while he began aligning the pews into neat rows. He swept snow from the entrance. He wiped down the pulpit and shined its brass base.

Around his middle—he noticed; oh, he noticed—weight in his body had dropped, leaving him with a slight paunch. All those mornings of yogurt without following up with yoga. He wondered what Joy Paz, or the earlobe model, would think, seeing James Miles like this, all mountained-up. For once he did not care. He felt oddly safe here, sheriff over his own forsaken town, examples of his sweat and hard work all around him. The big dark wood cross on the ledge was the final item that needed cleaning. When he tried taking it down, the thing wouldn't budge. It was heavy. So he shimmied its base, and suddenly it faltered, and the arm of the cross bore down. He quickly pivoted and caught it on his shoulder, which ached under the weight. "Oh, Christ," James said.

The wood was so old and dry that it was almost held together by splinters. It definitely needed oil.

Hitched on his shoulder, James dragged the cross outside, snow flurries jumping around his face, and walked the full lane, leaving a long, crooked trail in his wake. Then he proudly set the cross, with a thump, on the barroom floor under the buffalo head. What a shoulder workout!

The creaking stairwell was like an old woman's complaints. James returned from upstairs with a bottle of lavender massage oil. He'd brought the stuff along in the event he met someone special, but so far the only woman around these parts was Linda. The stuff smelled calming, and when he fully unscrewed the cap he was reminded again of that aromatic young nymph from The Standard Hotel on Sunset, her sole job to lay in a nightie, behind the reception desk, encased in glass like a buxom hamster, scribbling into an oversized journal, a pink feather dancing at the end of her pen. Los Angeles seemed to him now, looking down at the distressed wood cross, a distant solar system. Months of mountain air had woken up his synapses in new, unexpected ways, and his task for the night was to burnish wood.

Lent, Linda had said. That time of year. Oh, how he'd forgotten. Yet James remembered how hard he'd tried throughout his life to forget, suppressing what he was once taught, and how long it had taken him to clean his mind of sacraments and absolutions and replace them with things of greater importance.

On his knees he picked away the splinters with eyebrow tweezers. He used a white Atomic Rock T-shirt as a rag. It had armpit stains and had to go anyway. He doused the fabric with oil and rubbed the prop. It was, though, a prop, wasn't it? Hadn't it been the same cross from *The Old Pueblo?* Regardless, the wood drank in the oil. James was surprised when he reached the upper portion. There, under layers of caked paint, was a hand-hewn engraving. He picked at the paint with his fingernail. The flakes fell away and revealed the image of Mary. The mother of Jesus. Mary in her shawl, Mary with rosary beads hanging from her arm. Mary inset in the cross. It was the first time he'd ever seen that done.

He restored Mary to her previous condition, rubbing in more massage oil than was necessary, even shining her forehead.

Parallel drag marks lay in the snow after he was finished. As he walked back to the studio apartment, swiping dust from his hands, he thought he saw a shadow drop on the snow in the shape of a person.

The shadow came from near the saddlery building. He also thought he heard the crunch of boots on snow. When he looked again, the shadow—or whatever it was—had vanished. Anyway, he was tired, the tissue behind his eyes was frayed. He was seeing things.

James fell into bed without watching Joy Paz that night, and in the morning the sun was high and the snow was gone, the lane turned into mud.

+ + +

It was a bright morning, several days later, when James decided to take a hike. His lungs needed air, and he wanted to wear down his muscles, shed the paunch. How could he face his Pilates class in his current flabby condition? And how could one person gain this much weight by eating only egg whites for dinner? His bones were moaning under his skin. As an added insult, he'd just run out of face-mask cream.

Six weeks in, he had fifty-nine pages of his new wave Western completed. It electrified him to imagine the film premiering at The Vista, his favorite theater, with a friends-only guest list. Then onward to festival circuits, a distribution deal, a National Society of Film Critics Award. From that point forward everything rolled out for him, doors opening, the remainder of his career wondrously Jon Blazin'.

Still, after forty-three days in the desert, hair past his ears, beard fuller, he needed an ending, a title. He lathered his face with SPF 100, hypoallergenic lotion, and admitted to himself that he was stuck. He'd hit the wall.

A hike might loosen things.

Up the hill, the creek ran harder from the melt. The yellow

eye of the sun never seemed to recede. It was so unlike L.A., where smog created a comfortable, blurry shield. The creek was really working, would be hard to hop, and for the first time in his adult life James manned up. He dragged a branch toward the creek and created a natural bridge. He was proud of his ingenuity. The cold, high air dried his eyes, but the hike was good, his heart was going. Perhaps thirty more pages to the end, he told himself.

His cast of characters spoke a distinct language. L.A. slang crossbred with oldfangled, western maxims. It was revolutionary dialogue. At least James thought so. Mamet-like, only not. Perhaps Jarmuschian. Of the books he'd brought along, one, published by UCLA, documented the latest linguistic street slang. The other, the leather number, which was falling apart from age, was written by a reverend and linguist from the Nevada Territory, noting the hee-hawisms circa 1876.

To bed down a man was to kill him.

James liked that. He liked other sayings too.

Full as a tick, i.e., drunk.

Soiled doves, i.e., prostitutes.

His untitled screenplay was based on *Paradise Lost,* its style influenced by Fassbinder, to be shot like *Days of Heaven,* with a surprise alien at the end, and it was going to be huge.

He borrowed the first five pages from his undergraduate thesis.

When he reached the flat ridge, his heart pounding in his neck, there were twelve horses standing around untied, necks down, feasting on the permafrosty meadow. James wheezed. Two freshly assembled wooden crosses lay on the ground outside the long adobe structure. Mor-a-da, it was called, per Linda.

He heard faint slapping noises coming from inside the building. He remembered the older guy with the bloody back. He thought about quickly turning around. But he knew this was Gil Soto's land. And he was curious. James touched the cool dry wall, tiptoeing around for a closer look. What he saw was unfilmable in some southern states. Twelve men, shirts off and near nude, were whipping themselves. Among them was the man with the white hair and distinctive, pearly sideburn. The simple movement was like tossing salt over a shoulder, to ward off bad luck, only these men had the motion memorized, whips connecting with the skin on their backs.

One man glanced up, spotting James's wet forehead, his eyes peeking into the darkness. The man raised a finger toward him.

James's adrenal glands emptied, a flight response so intense that the tip of his penis tingled. James ran, but he was never a track star, and the sound of galloping feet caught up with the speed of an avalanche. Someone grabbed his arm, flung him around.

Long shadows fell around him, as though dropping from sky-scrapers. James was breathing hard. He was encircled. Not one man was younger than him, but they were certainly faster. The men's left shoulders were red, their backs spotted with blood. Everyone was huffing, including James. Clearly displeased, the men looked him up and down, considering his hair, his beard, but he was not the mountain man they were seeing, not just some random in-truder, even though he did resemble Bum #1 from that bit part in *Beverly Hills Beckett*. This was a *look,* he wanted to say, a *character study.* This wasn't him. He was James Miles, from l.a., basically an okay guy who liked the coffee at the Casbah. And besides, this was Gil Soto's land.

The man with the monochrome sideburn said, "You again? Seriously? Can't you just leave us alone? We're having a private ceremony."

"I've already told you. You're on Gil Soto's property," James re-sponded. He was indignant. He wasn't looking for a *dustup,* but he knew *what was what.*

The stranger shook his head. "Listen, *pardner.* We have an ease-ment, okay? It's on file at the county recorder's office. Go check at the courthouse in Taos."

"Whatever, dude," James said. "I think *Gil Soto* would have warned me about this kind of weird business. You do know the name *Gil Soto,* don't you?"

Each man wore jeans and big silver belt buckles.

Another man spoke up. "Hilario," he said, jutting his chin at James. "Do you think—he sort of resembles—"

"Sure, sure," Hilario said, touching his white sideburn, squinting harder. Then he added, pointing to the trail James had followed, "Just leave."

"And if I don't?"

That night they came on horseback, with torches.

First James turned on the electric teapot, to make green tea, to keep alert. He was out of adrenaline. Yet it was all so ridiculously familiar that he almost laughed, unable to pinpoint the mishmash of films the scenario resembled. A blend of many: the distant clack and thunder of hooves, followed by the appearance in town of sepulchral figures on horses—with lit torches. But this was real life, his. Cue the drop in the gut. Cue porcelain-staining diarrhea.

Sarsaparilla: that was one nice-sounding word from the dead reverend's phrasebook.

When he returned from the bathroom, he lit a vanilla candle to cover the stench. Then shut off the lights. From the second floor he watched through a slit in the drapes. Torches raised, the men on horseback were assembling around town. He listened to the clacking hooves.

Epic fail was one term from the UCLA slang book. He'd used it fifteen times in his screenplay.

Fear pulled inside his intestines. The magnetic draw of the toilet was fierce. James wished he had the fire poker from downstairs. The fireplace was fake, so was the poker, but it looked the part. James watched the group, surprised when most of them disappeared, one by one, finally leaving a single man behind. The flame of his torch eventually burned out. But the man remained beside the church for hours, watching James, on the second floor, watch him.

By morning's first light, the man was gone.

+ + +

These men, making James wrestle with concepts he hadn't wrestled with in some time. Church doctrine, he knew, would always be with him, hooked in like intestinal amoeba, but for as long as he could remember James told everyone he did not know. How could he know? How could anyone know? He bought the truth as it mattered in the material world: darkness bursting open, like the Big Bang, into white light. Born wet.

That was that, and that was everything he understood or cared to understand.

His mother, his father, his older sister, and James once lived as a family in a tract home surrounded by a square patch of grass, each house on the block a facsimile of the next, each its own mini-castle, and everyone inside his home believed. Everyone but James. His mother balled her fists and prayed for him, two red knots thumping together, but he never got it, and he never believed. The whole brouhaha, after all, was a lot to swallow without choking. One dude, *really*, the Son of God, *really?*

Each subsequent night he watched the men arrive on horse-back, torches lit, always leaving one man behind, who disappeared by morning. James worried and wondered what they were after, what they wanted, and what their plans were. They were trying to intimidate him, clearly. And keeping tabs.

Their presence in the town, though, roused him into action. He grew obsessed with finishing what he began, locking himself inside his studio apartment. And he rarely, if ever, thought about his patron, his benefactor, his boss, the *fuckin' asshole!*

Serpentinia, Gil Soto's first foray into CGI animation, was about to be released.

Over the next week the clouds unzipped. Rain fell, and snow liquefied on the mountain, sending sheets of water down arroyos and creeks, creating marshes and temporary bogs in the under-land, a glacial kind of melt, everything around the set soaked, as though the mountain was crying.

"What is it *with* those *guys?*" James asked Linda one night. He sipped from his beer bottle. His eyebrows were wet, from drizzle. He turned the door handle on the bar, back and forth, back and forth, preoccupied.

Behind the bar Linda was repairing an eighteen-wheeler's

flat tire. She held it down in a metal tub with her thick, muscular pinkie. "Those guys," she said to him, "like to flagellate. They probably didn't like you seeing them. I warned you."

"Flagellate?" James said, momentarily confused. "They *touch* each other?"

"No, dumbass," Linda said. "To prove their faith and pay penance they whip themselves, among other things."

"Among other things?"

A half-lit cigarillo drooped from Linda's dry lips. Her eyes blinked from the smoke as she told him about the whips, the hymns, this New Mexico brotherhood of atoning men. "They're the penitent ones, all right," she said. "Believers all."

James narrowed his eyes, disbelieving. The feeling was similar to when he watched *Naked Lunch* for the first time, dark confusion overcoming him, as though something was offering itself to be understood but in the end proved impossible. He took a bigger swig of beer. Neither could he understand, for that matter, Gil Soto's fleeting fascination with similar fetishistic territory.

"Oh, and we won't be open on Friday," Linda said.

"But it's *Friday.* I always go out on *Fridays,*" James said. "Where will I drink my beer?"

She shrugged. "Other bars down in Rio Arriba. They keep them open for tourists."

"That's sixty miles."

"Sorry, it's Good Friday," she said, and winked.

James wondered what she was trying to pull. And after that wink she wouldn't look at him. He missed their eye game. He only had two more weeks left, and his screenplay was unfinished. He was desperate for an ending. He needed inspiration. A title. He needed to be shaken. For the first time in a long time, he needed to believe.

James set his palms convincingly on the bar top and said, "Linda, look at me." And after a while she eventually did. "Linda, I want you to show me."

"Show you what?"

"How hard those men believe."

"I don't think so," she said.

James set his jaw. He bent an elbow and gulped his beer. He tapped his knuckles together, thinking. Finally, he pointed to a vaguely gross painting of a nut-brown mud puddle on the wall, its cloudy water surrounded by rounded pebbles. "I will give you five hundred dollars for that gorgeous masterpiece," he said to her. "But first you need to show me."

"Well," Linda said, suddenly nervous and scratching her throat. "I do know some things."

James sped to the set in the El Camino, nothing but static on the radio, and played Joy Paz's celestial, underexposed, payoff shot seventeen times, using two socks, the ceremony lasting two hours and forty-seven minutes. Afterward, he held his breath and waited for the flash of insight. But there was still nothing.

One detail, however, was certain: he no longer thought an alien invasion was appropriate for his film.

+ + +

He was raised in it. So he knew it. Still, he didn't understand any of it. And he'd forgotten much of it.

Baptism. First Communion. Confirmation. The whole nine. He attended catechism classes and survived the eighth grade altar-boy post without being groped. He held on at each ceremony, endearing the full ride, as large checks arrived in the mailbox from distant relatives, which he spent on video equipment, on clothing, on looking good.

But he never got it. Mostly, he did not know how to know, or how to know what to know.

To prove their faith, again per Linda.

At least he could partially understand that line of reasoning. Living in L.A. for as long as he had, working in the business, he knew what it meant to prove one's devotion.

Over the next few nights he dreamed of humping mounds of wires and frames and nets across hot studio warehouses, of delivering C-stands and grips and Jimmy Jibs to back lots, of driving dollies through soundstages, of sitting on beach chairs under weeks of sun, of waiting, of watching, of wondering what it all meant beneath the big white letters on top of Mount Lee.

Perhaps he would never understand that, either.

+ + +

On Friday morning, the answer arrived. He heard a scream.

"Milagro!"

James awoke early from a dream about the dog park in Silver Lake, beside the reservoir, watching coeds pick up green poodle shit with purple velvet bags, and in the gauzy background someone was hollering.

"Milagro! A miracle! A miracle!"

There, again, that shouting. His eyeball twitched. He threw back the sheets and scanned the road from the window. One of the elder horsemen had dismounted his beast. The man hadn't left during the night, which was highly unusual. He was pacing outside the church with a cell phone to his ear. James's phone didn't work. Maybe he had the wrong provider. Soon another man joined him, also on horseback.

James sighed. These old dudes. Why these guys couldn't just leave him in peace he didn't know. Resignation settled in his throat like an irritating nasal drip. If these men were not going to leave, fine. He would still face the morning. He would face whatever Linda would show him.

Downstairs, at the bar, he ate breakfast, listening to horses clop-clopping about the town. He washed up, preparing himself. Linda would be arriving shortly.

He put on his sealskin boots without socks—fresh out. He changed into his red flannel, hundred-fifty-bones Martin Gordon shirt, his kangaroo belt, his handmade Gomorrah jeans. He moisturized with Kiehl's Restorative Argan Body Lotion and clipped his fingernails to the quick. The beard, and his hair, he kept messy. It was his look now, and he wanted to claim it, to be at the forefront of the trend, on appearing like he hadn't tried.

"I am a screenwriter," he said to the cold room. He unlocked the downstairs door, letting it swing back. A block of golden light enlarged around him.

Morning shadows held at angles along the boardwalks.

James stepped into the middle of the dirt lane, thumb tucked purposefully in his belt. There were now three horses by the church. The man with the funny sideburn, Hilario, dropped down from his saddle. The two others were taking turns coming and going from the church, whispering. What James needed was inside. The muddy lane had dried and hardened. He walked it, his wallet chain clanging against his thigh, the distant sound of spurs in his ears.

And the men, standing mutely, watched him come. The friendly expressions on their faces surprised him. One man had a mustache so thick and full and unreal it looked like it was almost impersonating a mustache. The man walked over and touched James's hair. James flinched and batted the guy's hand away. The man withdrew, but his eyes were already organized into awe.

Hilario stepped forward. "Did you do this?" he asked James.

James slit his eyes. "Do what?"

Hilario gazed into the church. One man was sitting on a washed pew, mesmerized by the restored lady on the wooden cross. Mary. James had only cleaned away gunk, as a hobby, as something to do, nothing more. Even so, James nodded, *yes.* Yes, he did that.

"It's Good Friday," Hilario said to him, "and you've given us the Virgin."

James had never heard such strong words coming out of anyone's mouth who wasn't at least an assistant producer.

"Please step aside," James said. "I have important work to do."

Inside, James looked up at the cross, and then glanced down at himself, growing uneasy and nauseously ashamed. Tight black shirt sucked to his torso like skin, his form-fitting soft flannel, the careful hem of fade-wash jeans draped perfectly over shiny pyramidal-toed boots, and he realized with a stab of pain behind his eyes that, outside of an urban metropolitan area, he looked like a *fuckin' asshole!*

He wrapped his clean hands around the base of the cross, and pulled.

"A miracle," one man said to James. "You know. A milagro," he said louder, watching him lug the burdensome cross out the door. James was unfamiliar with the word, but he liked the sound of it, like the name of that hip coffee spot on Hillhurst. Outside, the sun warmed the rims of his ears.

"What are you going to do with her?" Hilario asked him, setting a finger on the cross, near Mary's buffed forehead.

"The question is, what is she going to do to me?" James responded. At the far end of the lane, his dear bartender was standing beside her horse, Black Widow. Linda's truck was parked nearby, a trailer hitched to it. She was holding Black Widow by the horse's bridle.

Everything Linda did to him that morning, everything Linda showed him, happened with care and love and patience. Later he had a hard time remembering the steps and everything that came to pass under the blue New Mexico mega-canopy above them. It went down a hawk's dive from the Rio Grande—per his phrasebook—as the local men looked on, wondering and whispering.

James remembered visiting the Stations of the Cross prior to Confirmation, the preparations, the renewal of the baptism promise, the laying on of the Bishop's hands. The worst part was watching the Bishop's face during Confession change from bewilderment to horror as James, just fifteen, admitted the number of times he'd played and rewound and played and rewound and played and rewound the crowning slow-mo scene in *Fast Times at Ridgemont High*, the one featuring Phoebe Cates, Monad of Monads. The number of tube socks alone.

That humiliation was nothing, however, when compared to what L.A. could deliver to a soft, unprepared soul.

Linda began by respectfully petting James's beard and calling him *Jesús*. Pausing for a half-breath, James did as she requested, shivering out of his ridiculous clothes, until only his ninety-dollar boxer shorts remained. "Show me," he said.

"Okay," Linda said, nervously eyeing the older men. "I've heard enough to know how this goes." She slugged his shoulder. "I hope."

His skin pimpled up from the chill.

James was made to wash and dry Linda's feet, boot lint and callouses and all. She sat on the boardwalk, him beneath her, his knees crushed into the dirt. At one point, as he was leaning over a bunion, she sliced into his shoulder blade with a sharpened rock. James winced. Then another cut, and another. After a while she unloosed rope from her saddle, and she gently, and reverently, started whipping him.

Like the mountain had done, James began to cry from her tender abuse. He whimpered for all that time lost nurturing to Gil Soto, *fuckin' asshole!*, and he mourned the friendship Joy Paz had given him before she tightened her tourniquet and let him fall away. He wept with the same soft force of New Mexico rain against loose windowpanes.

As he'd done on the night of snow, he was made to hump the full weight of the cross the distance of the dirt lane, as Linda called him names, as she called him names with a dim smile. She helped him up whenever he stumbled. Onward, he marched, toward a freshly dug hole. James struggled with the cross, bent and bearing it.

One man's cell phone rang out behind him, its song of bells.

To prove their faith, Linda had told him.

The three men clutched each other when Linda pressed James down on the well-oiled cross, binding his forearms, one, the other, and then his feet. She drove office thumbtacks into his palms, into the bony tops of his feet, the pain like great scorpion stings. Blood opened on him. Over these months James had been lonely for human contact, and he thanked her profusely, his giving bartender.

His breath sucked away as Linda smacked Black Widow's haunches, as the rope affixed to the saddle tightened, as the base of the cross nudged into the hole, as the single cross, with him on it, rose into the day's sparkling light.

Mounted high, James had views over the town, the miner's exchange, the saloon, the church, and the men beside it. Wagon wheels were propped against raised boardwalks. He saw the ghosts of actors and actresses appearing and dissolving on acetate, famous faces captured for brief moments of glory.

The stench of horse manure was rampant and deep, and good too, and memorable. Finally James looked the part, and what he saw was totally Jon Blazin', including the vision of Linda below him and the men across the lane, silent and overwhelmed and wide-eyed, crossing themselves in that way he had once done and didn't know why.

Hilario touched his sideburn and staggered forward until his knee seemed to buckle, and he kneeled. James was *up a tree,* he knew, but he was no longer a *yellow belly.* He was James Miles. And he was from Los Angeles.

James mentally lined out every stupid word of his screenplay he could remember. Sweat dribbled into his eyes, powering retinal stings, creating optical effects in the troposphere, so that everything was golden, wondrous. He previsualized ending, lighting, even cast, his very own cosmogony crystallizing as the storyboard now took position below him, like some holy map. He had his title, his ending. Sun on his shoulders, the incisions burning, he had his story too, as though delivered down from the few bright clouds in the sky.

DEBORAH

*What is sweeter than honey,
and what is bolder than a lion?*

—BOOK OF JUDGES 14:18

Men always asked about her bandages, the tender attention she paid her hand, and she always said a burn, her stove, glowing electric coils, some careless accident at home that would likely leave a scar. This particular man had earned his scar, a buttery slash above his lip, from a boyhood accident. So they had things in common—"me and you," he kept saying, punctuating with a wink. He moved in closer, giving the bartender two fingers to indicate another round.

For months she'd been keeping a close eye on the man's trailer, a yellow doublewide on Route 89. On his roof was a satellite dish trained at the sky, like an ear to the universe, but mostly she looked for the rangy black border collie outside, in the dirt, chained to a rail spike and without a water bowl. There were nights she drove past the trailer and was shocked to see, in the halo of her headlights, the mongrel lying on the ground in darkness.

She followed the man's pickup up Route 89.

She knew the way, and she already knew how his callused hands would feel on her naked ribs, and the way, afterward, he'd drape the bedsheet over his lower half, as though ashamed of what he'd shown her. Of course the man fell asleep. Of course he didn't expect her to remain throughout the night. She was just a figure passing through his inebriated consciousness, and in the morning the man would barely remember the smell of her neck.

Poor thing was still outside when she opened the aluminum door, its eight-foot-long chain gripped by the spike. The animal had scratched a concave nest in the ground, where it now lay. She lowered her good hand and the animal brushed its whiskers against her fingers.

"It's okay. It's okay," she whispered to the animal. "You're safe now."

The dog was female and painted in dust and brilliant. She set down an old Mexican blanket and the animal eagerly hopped into her pickup, newly attentive, her ears perked, free at last from bondage.

On her ranch outside town lived two horses, a mule, an alpaca, a cat named Moo, and seven—now eight—rescued dogs. All shared twenty-three acres of desert juniper and piñon trees and desert broom in a valley boxed by low hills.

Along with national chain stores and strip malls and a renovated downtown plaza, her high desert Arizona town, pop. 46,673, was home to Safari Fun Zoo, a spiritless twenty-acre park comprised of fake rock habitats and low fences that allowed visitors near-close encounters with flamingoes. Safari Fun actually lacked African Animalia, save for one tired elephant, Bertha, which was acquired from a Nevada casino and appeared, judging by the pain in her red wet eyes, like she fully understood that her life was just shifting versions of the same Hell.

Safari Fun was too much concrete and didn't provide enough shade for its captives. Her season pass brought her there on most Sundays, just before closing, when caretakers were busy cleaning the javelina enclosure. She had their schedules memorized. Her gaze was on the most secretive, seductive of the bunch, a sleek male cougar that usually sat—unloved, alone—inside a shallow cave or upon a fake rocky ledge.

Months previous she'd discovered how to access him: hop a low fence, bend under three baby palms, shuffle beneath a desert willow, and sidle against the steel perimeter fence, where there was enough room to fit her hand through the barbed mesh.

On her first attempt she made sucking sounds, fluttering her fingers to gain his attention. But the cat remained on his hot ledge, staring. After several more failed visits, she discovered that raw hamburger meat could draw the animal's notice.

During that first communion, as he neared, his muscles moved like liquid beneath his hide. And when he turned away and turned back and pounced she understood, shaking, they were becoming one. His incisors held the kind of strength she could only comprehend whenever walking under moonlight, contemplating the power of a star. All the Sundays ahead she tried giving herself to the animal, feeding herself to him, which was the closest she'd ever gotten to saintliness, she providing gifts, her pain blossoming into pleasure, feeling his teeth against bone, his saliva writing scripture on her skin.

On that Sunday afternoon she felt the after-sting of too much alcohol in her throat, and she wished she hadn't lent herself to the man. But it was necessary. To secure the collie, it needed to be done. At the ticket booth the teenage girl nodded at her, as she usually nodded. She proceeded through the park with the laminated pass around her neck. She knew the way, the number of footsteps. The big animals, those that lured crowds—striped hyenas, elephants, cougars—were housed in the park's outer fringes. Before hopping the fence, she waited for two new parents to leave the area. A father slowly pushed a stroller. There was a minimum-wage guard on site, who wore all white, who sometimes patrolled, but she'd seen him near the entrance, at the concession stand, flirting with the popcorn girl, tapping his pepper spray whenever the girl laughed.

Carefully she unwrapped the bandages. Beneath the top layer was more gauze, with faint brown amoebic stains around her wounds. She swallowed pills during the week to discourage the pain, but never on Sundays. Sundays were reserved for worship. With her working hand she peeled away more gauze, revealing three ugly nubs torn at the knuckles. She pulled a ball of wrapped hamburger from her bag and spread it across her hand like salve.

Two grand leaps and the cougar was upon her, its Asiatic eyes near and bright and determined. She was closer to one of God's great beasts than she'd ever gotten. His breath was warm and bacterial, his head larger than hers.

His nose sprung to the left, sniffing, and he looked unsure, always mistrustful, but all at once her ideas and thoughts and breath left her. She left herself, the source of things upon her, which drove her inward, feeling pain so true as to convince her of meaning. She shuddered as the animal tore and jerked his head until at last the pretty creature padded away, part of her now with him, and he with her, as one.

In those moments when she was not wordlessly inside herself she was upon the land. Despite fences, despite boundaries, the land was everyone's land, the universe's vast yet finite gift, and she was its guardian, often crying at the thought of the annual harvest.

If you did not have a hunt permit, you hired an outfitter, and the outfitter had a hunt permit, and he or she also had guns, and maps, and access to private ranches. The hunters were after deer, elk, antelope, oryx, ram, javelina, which she would see at the Mini-Mart near her house, their dead necks draped over hoods, corpses shoved inside truck beds, eyes open, tongues like lifeless hanging hands. Each sighting published specific goals in her mind. Each sighting would make her think of her name, its origins, sweet and honey-giving, but as a collective could be a horrendous swarm.

She drove her pickup one night to the gravel parking lot outside Pine Cone Ranch, a gorgeous 100,000-acre watershed rich with wildlife. Three vehicles were in the lot, dark, empty. Men set out from here during open season, women sometimes, and children too, where they hiked to shacks higher up in the hills.

The only advantage her animals at Safari Fun had over their brethren was imprisonment—safety in imprisonment, yes, free from man's continuous hunt.

Her stainless steel blade entered the van's tire with a push. The front, the back, multiple entries. She went vehicle to vehicle, until each sagged closer to the gravel.

Another car drove along the dirt road, eventually passing. She crouched amid brush weed, out of sight, as she had been doing for some time.

The tower had come down and with it her husband, her lover, her best friend of thirteen years, one giant mess of metal and glass and particulate that threw plumes so poisonous over her life that for a year everything was darkness. She relocated to a place with sun, a place where no towers stood, where no towers threatened to fall, where at no time of day could a building's shadow cross her face and serve as reminder.

The land and light gave much. Both existed, and gave, and that was enough. She would acquire more land when the moment was right. One hundred and twenty acres hugged her land, and the parcel would soon jump on the market. A real estate agent had given her inside information. And she would acquire it and expand her loving domain.

The following day she heard the dogs barking near her small ranch house. The newest, the border collie, had alpha instincts. The dog was still working out the pecking order with the German shepherd.

She walked her land, in cowboy boots. It was that hour in the late day when snakes appeared to put sun in their blood. One night, not seven months previous, she was returning to the house from a walk when she came upon a pretty scaled creature. She had walked toward it, watchful and curious, as its bony triangular head distinguished itself from the muscular coil. She twisted her heel in the dirt until fangs flew, embedding in the side of her boot.

A rickety wood fence lined her land. She hated the fences. She hated the lines. With her heel she kicked at a rotted post. The earth gave and it toppled. The land beyond the fence would soon be hers and hers to care for. Every cent she had with her husband was liquefied and spread across this wondrous desertscape, where the sky went on and on and was only stopped by mountains forty miles away. She loved the state, and what the air did to her lungs, and even the humdrum town with its pastel-colored barrio.

She discovered a messy spider web hiding in a pile of wood. Its erratic design, full and confused, looked like a frozen puff of smoke. The plump shiny spider was in there, dangling inverse. She imagined plucking its web, playing a kind of hollow music for the creature.

Back at the house, on her five-by-five porch, the dogs came and gathered as though around a schoolteacher. After she'd been washed, deloused, the border collie had eased into the troop without many problems. And she looked happy now. As were the horses and mule and alpaca. Her cat Moo owned the house's interior, with her strategic perches on furniture and pillows.

She gingerly unwrapped the bandages, peeling gauze from the bloody stumps. There were now four. One digit remained on her left hand. She flexed the nubs and felt dull deep throbs that caused nausea. On the backside of her hand was a scratch, gotten from an overeager incisor. She held up her hand to the day's failing light, looking at what approximated, in her mind, a paw.

Some nights she bawled so violently she believed her ribs might separate. Often she could not catch her breath, as tears streamed into her shepherd's soft fur, holding him to her as a buoy—and he was. They all were, each gentle, loving one, all of them crowding around whenever she sobbed. Her husband's energy went somewhere in this universe, along with thousands of others. The vacuum their collective absence created would become the center of gravity around which the world's concerns now orbited.

So she'd reduced her life, streamlined it. All she needed to live was a simple ranch house with enough room for her friends and a walking trail that disappeared in the distance.

Around this region she knew, from the local daily, about the fights. It was hillbilly activity, mostly, with money involved. Animal Control would encounter wandering strays from time to time. The dogs would have a patchwork of suspicious lacerations, from bouts. She'd put in volunteer time at the local shelter, and she knew about this kind of thing, and she asked questions about the blood sport, curious and listening, and she later compiled information into a spreadsheet at home.

To end the ugly business she needed to stop the breeders. A single breeder could raise fifty, eighty dogs at a time, on rural ranches, on rural roads, putting the smell of blood in their mouths as puppies. To stop the breeders she purchased a break-action double-barrel shotgun, used.

She asked around, at the supermarket, at pet stores.

Who around here bought food in bulk?

Slight, petit, she was small as a bee, and people asked about her bandages because she looked injured, but she was well, she told everyone, she was well and as motivated as she'd ever been.

One man's name piqued her interest. His name kept appearing in her conversations around town.

The man was older, a former sheep rancher, a lumbering presence who wore camouflage ball caps. His truck, she noticed, as she followed him, was missing its left mud flap. She trailed his truck to his ranch several nights in a row, watching his headlights turn at the gated entrance. Beneath her seat was the double-barrel, as ready in that moment as it would be the next day. She wanted to be certain. And now she felt like the hunter, and he her prey.

The rancher liked the bar. It was a common place for common men with common thirsts, and dark.

One night she put her elbows on the bar, her rear end in the seat beside his, legs open, her flesh the bait and the key to his attention. The old rancher, of course, noticed. Another man walked in and called him by name—Frederick—and slapped him friendly on the back. These men, this bar, the mileage on their sun-lined faces. She thought of the holding and exhibit areas at Safari Fun, what the animals would think if they peered in on her species, lolling in plush recliners, feet up and pointed at TVs, a general lazy comfort protecting everyone from ever having to form a question.

The man did not have a ring. There were no signs, in fact, of any female presence in his life. Most men with women had a particular aura, some sense of togetherness and confidence around them.

He smiled at her weakly. She gained traction on his interest when she ordered the same drink as his. He sipped, and his dry red Adam's apple, as he swallowed, repulsed her. She would give herself to him if he asked, if he would lead her past the locked gate and closer to the source of his madness. Dogs and dirty kennels, she imagined, each bullied into winning. She wanted to throw a mountain at him. A television behind the bar showed golf.

After some time, he tried his best with words.

"Pretty boots," he said to her.

"You like them?" she responded. She played coy.

Their conversation caught the bartender's eye. Without any local friends, no job, no familial connections, she was anonymous as a breeze sweeping under doorways, unnoticed except for those who noticed.

This old rancher probably did not engage many women in conversation. He took his words slow, as though discovering every letter for the first time. He asked about the bandages. He commented on the weather. He talked of seasons.

She imagined his house as wooden, burnable. She imagined herself gathering the swarm inside her, a thousand tiny angels brought together for a purpose, capable.

A hand touched her shoulder from behind. She turned. It was the man from the other bar, the scar visible above his lip. He smiled, showing yellowy teeth, and he was glad, truly glad, to see her. "See, things in common," he said, "me and you."

She felt herself falling through air, the floor beneath her going, the ceiling above coming, the collision and instantaneousness of mass blooming into energy and opening to the universe. A silent howling swept between her and the rancher, and the older man turned away, his interest lost by the interruption of a younger, stronger kind. Her plan failed and she pushed back her stool and left, and over the following days she reconsidered her designs while walking the land. Beyond her twenty-three acres was a mountain-fed stream, its water as clear as glass. She walked alone for miles, protected by her companions. They followed dutifully.

The trees and mountains were as high as she ever wanted to find herself. She was done with cities, their systems of interconnected reliance. A can of soup had to pass through hundreds of hands to finally end up in her cupboard.

She came across an animal's skull. Rabbit, perhaps. She crouched, peering closer. An explosion of fur lay around it, mixed with the mud. This dead thing was still providing mineral and sustenance to the land, as it had provided for whatever had taken it, such direct contact with its hunter, a chase, a swoop, an intimate transferal of energy. Every being, she thought, sitting beneath a piñon, was just stars and dust.

The dogs put their noses in the dirt and read the land. The border collie's ears perked as she listened to sounds lost on her human's ears. With their paws, her friends mingled with the source of life. So she removed her boots, her socks, placing her good hand to the ground, her bare heels in the dirt, her breath fusing with the wind.

That Sunday she arrived late at Safari Fun. She went directly to the cougar enclosure. As she hurried she unraveled the bandages. She moved against the flow of departing visitors, confident now in her task. Over the fence, beneath the desert willow, she crawled upon the animal's enclosure, safely out of sight. Hamburger meat went greasy and cold onto her thumb.

He was beautiful, he was always beautiful, and he was slow with his approach, his great solid paws spreading with each step.

She touched the animal's dry nose with his last feast. "For you," she said to the animal. She silently urged him to take her, remove this last offering. From her to him, he was free to unleash his animal heart and steal away. Her species had taken everything from him, this wild beauty, this God. He looked at her impassively, without recognition or love, but in his eyes, behind his eyes, she knew, glimmered the look of penance.

The pain hit more than with the others. She clamped her mouth with her other hand as his jaw worked, and she saw stars and white light, a plane approaching, a momentous explosion, all-consuming fire, and then nothing.

She awoke. There was blood. A lot of blood. She pulled her paw to her hazy eyes, amazed. The flow was too heavy to staunch. She put gauze to it, noticing a figure on the far side of the enclosure. A man, the caretaker, with a radio to his face, watching her. Soon the desert willow's branch lifted, exposing her to the security guard, a young man clad in white. She'd lost the power of speech.

She ran at him, knocking him off balance, and scrambled on hands and feet over the fence, going, going into the day.

+ + +

He followed the blood trail. On the brick were imprints here and there of a bloody hand. Never in his twenty-six years had he witnessed something so odd, such bold madness, a woman feeding her hand to a caged mountain lion. It shook him. His stomach was not right because of it. He came across a cowboy boot, and then another. With him he carried pepper spray, his industrial flashlight. The blood led him to her. The caretaker met him near the toilet pavilion. They exchanged a look that signaled alarm and confusion. Between the building's wall and some bushes was a small woman, in hiding, cowering like some kind of hurt animal. Her hands were in front of her, protectively, creature-like, one of them bleeding heavily.

The caretaker was speaking with the office on his handheld radio.

The guard fisted his flashlight and shined it on her. "Ma'am?"

The woman did not have a human look in her eyes, which frightened him. "Ma'am?" He stepped forward, running into her loud hiss. He took another step, and he encountered her howl.

TWO KINDS OF TEMPLES

for Amy Hempel

I.

Their toes met under arsenic water. The man pulled his foot away first. It was a spirits-seeking place, clothing optional, open-air hot springs backed by high desert mesa cliffs. The man knew all of her before her red toes entered the oblong, smooth-rock pool. A brochure said arsenic waters helped treat ulcers, arthritis, skin conditions.

There were two other bathers in the pool, twin white mounds of Texan flesh. The Texans spoke quietly about mileage on a new car.

The woman's toe, sliding around polished crevices, found the man's again. This time he did not withdraw.

"At this rate," said one Texan, "we'll reach one hundred thou in no time. Sedona next, love?"

+ + +

Later, a communal dinner featured kale and lentil patties and quinoa. Eating family style, the woman claimed the empty chair beside the man. They listened to adventures narrated by hikers, river rafters, and birdwatchers. A national forest cuddled the resort.

"Massages here too," one Nevadan said, holding the green stem of a strawberry. "Warm oils and hot rocks. Never before in my life." A seed stuck between his teeth.

Management suggested clients wait forty-five minutes after meals before bathing.

The dark lithia pool was unpopulated, except for the man. Stars sent down somber vigilant light. The water was still. The woman found him there and broke the sheeted plane with her red toe. The water swallowed her worked-out legs, her stomach, as she sat, quiet and stalking. The man was here an escapee from a two-story home, a three-car garage. She was a huntress in search of prey. Her toe quickly went to his in the shadowy waters. She wore no ring.

"I'm married," she said later, halting their kiss. She stood wet and shivery in the red-tiled entrance of her assigned cottage.

"Good," the man said. "Married. Marriage. Two people. Me too."

Their hands writhed like tentacles around each other. His skin was the skin of a cleansed man, his pubic hair dewed and soft from days of soaking. She was fine sand hills and grassy valleys. Her wet hair drooped down the sides of her face, angled like a pine tree.

"I could tell you I'm married and you wouldn't know," the woman said. "I could tell you I wasn't married and you wouldn't know." She traced circles around his hardening nipple.

There was no visiting the bed, with its four pillows, soft cotton sheets, and pleasing design. The cold tiled floor was hard, the right place for this. A wicker chair scratched an autograph into her thigh as she assembled on top of him. He fed himself to her. She moistened his mouth with hers.

Later, after midnight, they sat like nourished prisoners on the floor, backs against walls, staring at each other across the moon-lit room, an empty bottle of red wine between them. She talked, and he listened, and to her it was a fine thing to be heard again. Along the hillside were other cottages. Agreeable chatter rose from a shared board game at the lodge. The man thought he recognized the Texan. He felt sore. The woman had worked him like a tractor.

"This," the woman said. "Every woman should have exactly this. More of this."

"We've had it," the man said. He played with his fingers like worry beads.

"I could have lied to you about being on the pill and I'm here to get pregnant and I don't know your name and we'll never see each other again," the woman said. "Maybe that's how the story goes."

"Yes," the man said. He stood and pulled on his white resort robe. "Maybe."

He walked toward the door and she reached and held onto his leg, finally kissing the tender fold behind his knee. "I want more listening," she said.

+ + +

The next morning the woman wore a black two-piece at the iron pool. There were many who felt uneasy about showing themselves to such brisk air. She did not seem the type to own such a barely suit. Alongside three burly Arizona men, who swapped baseball stats, who sat at a comfortable distance from each other, who did not make eye contact, the man watched her dip that red toe. The iron spring was fed by water gliding down discolored copper chutes. From all corners came pleasing sounds: fountains, dripping water, water grooving rock, the slap of wet feet on flagstone. Few spoke during mornings. Mornings meant awakening, calm.

Iron water aided blood, the immune system, so said the brochure.

The woman dropped into the pool to her neck. Small waves lapped the man's chest. The other men's nude bodies were magnified and distorted through the water. She glanced at each man. One of them, by the water's trickery, appeared as large as her forearm.

Across from the man, she dropped her plum lips beneath the waterline. She touched his toe again with hers. Her breath rippled the water while birds talked in the trees on cliffs. The sun dried each man's chin.

The woman did something remarkable then. She unclipped the top portion of her two-piece and flung it like a wet napkin to the flagstone. She did the same with the bottom. Undressing, before the men, seemed to the man a declarative, almost grotesque statement. Removing a towel, entering unclothed, was the better way.

Lunch was Mediterranean salad. Dinner was tofu burritos with couscous.

She found him later walking along the raised wooden board-walks. The resort was a small country of wooden walkways. To prevent erosion, the brochure said, to live harmoniously with the land.

Each cottage had its own tree, its own wooden bridge, and its own silence.

"Thought we lost you," the woman said.

"I'm here," the man said.

"Are you?" she asked. She looked at a squirrel's shadow relocating along a branch. "We should try the waters," she said.

Each other's bodies were toys to be gazed upon with childlike wonder. Sheets of muscle moved inside his back. Her nipples, when the breeze touched, were pink supple miracles. The steamy soda pool was hotter than the night's air. Other bathers visited it like brief vacations, in and then out. The two remained, toes touching underwater, bearing the heat. They did not speak. Around others, they treated each other like passengers on a train.

Inside cottages, on top of oak cabinets, sat sage bundles, the ends carefully singed. The man and woman swayed outside her cottage on hand-carved rocking chairs, robes opened loosely, overlooking the bridge, which connected to the resort's boardwalk system. This late, few people wandered. Moonlight fell on their supple skin. A loosened board creaked from the rockers. A nail rose from the end.

A friendly group sipping wine was visible through a scrim of tree branches.

"This is one of those magazine stories," the woman said. Warm night air held them to the chairs.

"A men's magazine," the man said.

"Or a women's magazine," she said.

The woman adjusted herself when the man carefully slid his hand inside the mouth of her robe. Her skin was hot, her pubic hair spiny as cholla needles.

"Or maybe a porn magazine," the woman said softly.

"You are married," he said.

"I am," she said.

"Yes, you are."

The loosened board creaked often and louder.

"I am, I am," the woman said. "I am."

That night they did not share the same cotton sheets. His cottage lay in a different district of trees.

+ + +

Pools had varying temperatures. Visitors entered watchfully, as people do shrines. They beheld the waters like holy sites. People stood under showers, heads bowed. People walked slowly, robed like monks. Each person's hair was tinged wet or dried into sculpture. People carried small water cups with them, gazing at the pools with tender gratitude.

She found him waiting outside the deep mud baths. The man was peering at the tubs with clenched fists. "I like the idea of arsenic water better," the man said.

She shrugged her shoulders, her robe bunching at her ankles. "Give, and let's paint each other," the woman said. She stepped on another man in the tub, hidden as he was, like a frog in a marsh. The other man rose up, a brown stucco creature, and lay on a wooden platform in the sun. His mud tracks were prehistoric.

"Give," the woman said to the man again. She held out her hand.

Knee-deep, the man stood still, as the woman arranged warmed mud on his chest. She built cities on his shoulders, a house on his nose. Her breasts swayed.

"I'm here for myself," the woman said.

"I'm here for my wife," the man said.

She layered mud into his hair. "Does she know you look like a monster?"

Mud dribbled down his body like wax down a candle.

"I leave tomorrow night," the man said.

The woman smiled, parted his mouth, and inserted a handful.

+ + +

People checked in at a front desk hewn from a granite boulder. A gift shop sold oils, lotions, teas, and incense sticks. The uninitiated

133

arrived through doors clothed, wide-eyed, as though entering a foreign country. Its citizens milled in white robes, in tan plastic flip-flops, holding tiny recyclable cups. Their skin was pink, scrubbed, exfoliated, renewed. People picked tall desert grasses and put them in their mouths like country boys.

The woman walked up the steps, down the steps, along boardwalks, under trees, past cottages, to an upper platform that opened on the crown of the mesa. There was a natural path, and she followed it. Beyond the trees and a blue spring, deep with snowmelt, she saw high desert hills in the distance and gorgeous mountains under a pale sky.

He looked in every pool but could not find her.

Dinner was roots, purees, more roughage. The man tasted soil with each bite. She was late, but finally located him, his table already full of Californians. The Californians were new and nervous colonists, their cotton belts pulled tight around bellies. She watched him fill water glasses. Her red toe remained cold.

At another table she ate slowly, like an ox. With each bite she felt flowers rising in her stomach. She felt the earth part, the shoot rise. Travelers exchanged maps at her table. Travelers discussed distances in miles, in kilometers. Several harbored distant accents that brought to mind old pictures in a box, at home, a place far from where she sat.

An employee, at forty-five minutes, blew a horn made from birch, its song low and mournful. Many descended into the soda pool, for digestion. The man and woman passed each other on deliberate marches from hot to cold, from steam to sauna. Her skin puckered in the icy splash, his boiled in soup.

They met again under arsenic water, her toe finding his.

"My cottage?" the woman said as they walked barefoot along the walkway.

"Your cottage," the man said.

They passed over the bridge as if it were a threshold. Inside, she positioned him against the cottage's wall, ordered him to stay, and sat, studying his silhouette. The man was awkward art, wondery and apprehensive. She asked him to turn right, left, right again.

"Now let's try without the robe," the woman said.

The robe fell, soft as a tissue. His skin had turned shades from the sun.

"Maybe this is a movie," the man said.

"Maybe a sequel," the woman said.

"Maybe it's a bad movie."

"Maybe not," she said. "Put your hand on yourself."

"How?" the man said.

"Like in a movie," she said. "You are the star."

The woman opened her robe as she admired the star's skill. He knew his role well. Her thighs parted, and she joined the film.

Soon the man directed her to the bed. Her cottage had more pillows than his. With one wedged under her stomach, her hair smelled of arsenic.

Moonlight moved across the floor during the night. She curled around him like a vine. In the morning, she put on the robe, the plastic slippers. She studied him, from a chair, waiting for him to wake. When he woke the woman said, "I want to show you."

"You've already shown me plenty," the man said.

"There's more," she said. "I like to surprise."

In robes, in slippers, they walked along the boardwalk, passing Ohioans new to the nation. The woman led him up, through a stand of trees, as warm sunlight dropped to touch her favorite spots of earth. Higher, the world smelled of juniper, of sage, of piñon, until finally the platform ended at the beginning of a tamped trail.

"Go," the woman said, and followed him. She watched him review the deep spring, the hills where trees formed communities under gigantic humped mountains. The trees were larger than any spire.

The woman cinched her robe. His was untied, parted, opened to it.

"Maybe we already know each other," the woman said. "Maybe we're married, and you're married to me."

"And maybe we can work this time," the man said.

"Maybe."

"Where are we?" the man said.

"Maybe we begin again here," the woman said.

II.

On my way through this desert border town, I'd plucked an orange HELP WANTED from the motel's office window. I'd been heading someplace else.

Zephyrs sharp as knives slashed grooves into the endless dirt. The motel's yellow-bulbed arrow had shifted with the wind. It now pointed away from the office entrance toward the hot, lonely flats.

Mondays, I did towels. Tuesdays were carpets. Thursdays and Fridays, I wiped dust from the windows I peered through. Nights, late, I stood in the office, lit up by blue neon, staring at the TV, my sunstruck mind fluttering to a close.

Toothbrushes in the vending machine drooped like fallen soldiers. The belly of the icebox was a dirty trench.

+ + +

The newlyweds arrived in an old Ford. There was a dent in the hood in the shape of a hand. A purplish birthmark dripped below her ear down her neck. Green-red dragons snarled on his arms. She did not wear a diamond. His third finger had a white band, from someone before, from someone not the wife.

At dusk, they cooled down on plastic beach chairs, shaded under the breezeway. They propped their feet on the old Ford, plugging their laughs with beers. I hid behind soiled linens.

"Toss me a full one," he said.

And she said, "But you forgot to say the word *precious*."

A wood-panel door, bolted for privacy, separated their room from mine. At the bottom was a two-inch gap. Their shadows flickered inside an orange glow. Their low discussions were edited, abbreviated by the door.

"Wake up," she said, in the middle of one night.

He said, "But I'm awake."

+ + +

Guests did not leave tips. Guests left toilets clogged. Guests hid loose pennies in the backs of drawers.

I found: bloody towels, lipstick-ringed cigarettes, a child's soft blanket. A handgun on a pillow, loaded. I buried it in the desert, inside a jackrabbit's rust-colored hole.

All the remotes in all the rooms were doweled into the end tables.

+ + +

Afternoons, they went for drives. Her T-shirts clung damply to her ribs.

Nights, he caulked the door's gap with a wet bathroom towel. Wheels squeaked on the queen-sized bed.

+ + +

People pulled in late with garbage bags beneath their eyes. They slipped their keys into the slot before I woke. This had been a place obstructing them from where they wanted to be.

+ + +

Believers sent Bibles as offerings to a lost flock. I placed one inside every chipped end table, not because I believed, but because small tasks helped fill a lonely day. Guests used them to scrawl laments. Children drew in fat crayons. Each night, I placed mine at the foot of my bed. By morning, it always found its way to the floor.

+ + +

Her gleaming toes smoldered on the Ford. Her fingers danced on his belt in the breezeway.

"Say the word *chocolate* to me," she said.

And he said, "Chocolate."

+ + +

That afternoon, when they went on their drive, I doused their bed's wheels with oil. The sheets were coiled like snakes. I bounced on top of them, making sure. The husband's sweat-stained shirts, his jeans, lay scattered. In the tiny closet, on nondetachable hangers, hung the wife's.

When they returned, they reclined, as always, on the plastic beach chairs.

She said, "We should fill that kidney pool with water."

"The heat would only drink it up," he said.

+ + +

Bleach fumes burned deep, giving me a sometimes-cough. Room 15 required four vacuum bags, three sets of heavy-duty gloves. I did not always clean under the rims of toilets. Wastebaskets filled up with postcards addressed to eastern cities.

I entered Room 17 for a quick once-over and found nothing in it, except the remote, doweled into the end table, its batteries gone.

+ + +

Weeks passed, and the couple remained. Underneath their door, I slipped reminders, but they did not pay on time.

+ + +

I poured gallons down the thirsty throat of my swamp cooler, to keep it nourished. Outside, dry arroyos waited for a raindrop. Thorny mesquite trees liked to bite when you walked too close.

+ + +

One morning I walked a mountain of replacement linen to their room. Warm, tucked under my chin, were red pillowcases, their frayed tips worn down to pink.

The door was open, and she lay across the bed. The window framed her as in a picture. Her petite toes were corked with white cotton.

She swung the black soles of her feet onto the carpet, waddled over, like a duck, and put her hand on top of the sheets.

+ + +

That afternoon, the Ford did not leave the lot. After my shift, no towel appeared. Their shadows, under the door, resembled crossing swords.

A sudden cry dug through the drywall.

In bed, I sat up. A door opened. A door slammed. That night was their twenty-sixth. Her sobbing broadened into a song. On TV, reminders of places unlike ours played themselves out.

"The minister didn't have his book with him," he said.

She said, "But it's still valid."

"No witnesses, either," he said.

His tires threw gravel-pings against the Ford's undercarriage.

Her knock was gentle.

In bed, I stacked two pillows on top of my chest. I wanted to feel as light as possible.

Her door clicked shut, and the howl from a zephyr erased her silence.

After some time, her TV mumbled on. The channels snapped until one aligned with mine.

Small lime-green toes appeared beneath our adjoining door, a smaller one crossed over a larger one. She tapped on the wood of the door with her fingernails.

The handle slowly turned.

DAY OF THE DEAD

One man I remembered from my childhood walked the streets without looking. He was top-bald, with salt-and-pepper side hair. This same coloring looped from around the back of his head and swept into his tense beard, like one continuous brush stroke. The man would appear in my neighborhood at dusk looking medicated and burdened. He had terrible posture, and his slumped shoulders seemed to ooze down into his soft belly, which broke an invisible plane as he stepped off curbs and onto busy streets, unyielding. Cars braked to avoid hitting him, raising great, white, burned rubber plumes. Drivers usually checked themselves first, and then their passengers, before their faces rearranged into fury. The man always continued on, indifferent to traffic, to the people screaming high holy, and soon he'd ford another nearby street, steadfast in his march, the sound of screeching tires and horns reliable in his wake, like some brutal chorus.

There was something tragic and off about the man. His eyes were dark caves. You had to peer close to see they were tearless, dry, and unblinking. He stared straight ahead, and his arms never swung, so he looked like a mechanized version of a man, one not properly wired. In his hand he held a white Panama hat, the wind sometimes bending its soft brim. With his other he'd tickle car grilles and hood ornaments as drivers yelled. Their knuckles around those steering wheels were as white as bones beneath skin. People looked at him as though he held some sort of devil magic, as though he were someone who might one day levitate.

My friends and me, we knew the man was around whenever we smelled burnt rubber. Each day he floated through our neighborhood as though wanting to be hit, unfazed, not one concern or worry or human connection binding him to this earth. One day a car absorbed him. I wasn't there. It happened a neighborhood over. I felt a great vacancy in my chest when I heard of our loss. Even then, even at that young, tenderhearted age, I understood that whatever had existed in him also existed in me. My friends and me, we called him Rudolph. I don't know why.

+ + +

Not two months after my oncologist delivered the results—"inoperable," her word—I made the decision to swap one great desert for another: the airplane bumpily approached El Paso by night. During landing, I watched golden lights below the airplane's left wing beckon and wink. Juárez, El Paso's border-sharing city, looked from above like a continuation of the same gauzy radiance, but separating the cities were fences, towers, searchlights, Border Patrol trucks, and different interpretations of the laws of humankind.

I rose the next morning in hard, wide-open West Texas. I was motivated and disturbed and increasingly excited by the itching promise of closure, and I marched frightened and elated across the bowed length of the Bridge of the Americas. Below oozed the brown Rio Grande, channeling along a concrete chute, an ugly demarcation between my new country and the one I was leaving behind.

Across the bridge was an old, bruised turnstile that cost thirty-five cents. Thirty-five cents to enter Mexico: some things could still surprise me. My fellow southbound journeyers looked apprehensive, heads lowered, eyes shifty, fists balled, and mine was the only white face.

It was a clear, dry fall morning with a gentle southeastern breeze, and how! how! how! those jagged brown mountains loomed! Spread across one mountainside were gigantic words arranged from white painted rock. La Biblia es la verdad. Leela. The Bible is the truth, it said. Read it, it said. As a born-and-bred southwesterner, I was familiar with such God advertisements, religious iconography tweaked into background noise, but none of it, whether on murals, tailgates, menus, etc., ever really had much impact on me. To the west, however, stood an unmistakable white cross on top of another grand hill, firm as a rock candle, its outline embossed against the sky. I was bothered by how I found it bothersome.

Already I felt sweat behind my knees. The city was approaching the mid-nineties. It was hot, but bearable, and not nearly as scorched-out as Phoenix. Sunlight dimpled every exposed surface. Avenida Juárez was largely absent of people. A consequence of the cartel wars, obviously. Everyone knew about it. Numerous Norteño bars and mercados and restaurants mentioned in *The Purposeful Pill* guidebook were boarded over. Shutters were sheeted and fastened to locks inset in cement. Another mass grave had been unearthed. Another small town police chief killed. Another birthday party massacre. Another missing journalist. Another drug mule found with his hands lopped off. The violence was increasing. And the city was emptying. Even the mayor of Juárez, even the mayor, made his home in El Paso.

The few brave citizens still on the streets hustled. Everyone considered me with suspicion, as though I was some kind of gringo operator. Still, I carried myself like what I was, a gringo tourist.

One elderly man, his eyebrows like wild crabgrass, stood outside a cookie shop and swept the sidewalk. He was a sweeper, a cleaner, an industrious man. He brushed debris from sidewalk to gutter. Beside him was a garbage can chained to a concrete wall.

The man stepped in front of me and put his hand on my chest. My shoes crunched on shattered glass.

"You must go back," the man said in English. I studied a purple mole on his temple. He smiled faintly, uncurling an arthritic finger, pointing north, toward El Paso, and America, and safety. "Very dangerous here now," he said.

This guy! Oh, I knew all about it, I assured him. Sí, Juárez was treacherous. Watch out! Drug cartels! Azteca street gangs! Highest murder rate in the Western Hemisphere!

I kindly brushed the man's hand away. It was a striking white-blue day with the promising specter of danger hanging like ribbons over the multicolored streets. It was a good day for rushing a turista, taking his wallet, his kidneys, possibly his life. So take it, take it already, I nearly called out. Juárez was unsafe, but who cared when you sort of hoped for a knife?

The commercial district didn't have views of the foul slums I'd seen on TV, the ones I'd read about in newspapers, makeshift shacks piled like lopsided Legos on hillsides, or situated in rocky underlands near multinational factories, somewhere out there, farther into the desert, where plant life threw spikes. Oh that unwashed swarm, oh that poverty, oh those sad, heart-squeezing lives: and just one more goddamn reason. Perhaps, if there was time—and there wasn't much time—I'd pay a visit to the barrios before the Day of the Dead.

Mercifully, there were still some bars open in the Centro, including Western Where, the establishment I needed. Not every business was shuttered. Life, in other words, was trying to carry on amid smells that were quite something, spiced meats underlined by hits of raw sewage, the soup of industrialization. I noticed a staggering number of pink crosses slapped onto black squares on telephone poles. And yellow school busses were everywhere, ferrying people from place to place at high rates of speed. The police were out too, as were Army trucks, which were parked to protect the commercial zone by blocking street access, like logs jamming creeks.

I strolled past one soldier in a black ski mask who clutched a beautiful black semiautomatic. He was surprisingly friendly. He nodded at me as I turned on Avenida 16 de Septiembre. I hunted down my hotel.

At last I found the place, on Noche Triste. The hotel was trying hard to be boutique-y but the fountain in the courtyard held a pool of green, stagnant water. Spartan, far from charming, but it would suffice. A creaky staircase ascended to the third floor in a spiral. Upstairs the door lock was an old-fashioned riddle. I solved it and set my suitcase on the queen-size bed. My corner room had west-facing views and overlooked a plaza. On the far end of the plaza was a large cathedral and, beside it, a smaller white adobe mission.

My decision had enlarged over these final months, just like the unwelcome visitor. And, I won't lie. It comforted me to know an amended version of my Last Will and Testament was safely inside a mauve file folder at R.J. Braunstein Associates, East Indian School Road, adjacent to Mo' Money Pawn, Phoenix, Arizona.

That night, after carnitas and beer, I sat in bed with the lights low and listened to the sound of distant gunfire. The faint popping reminded me of Fourth of July firecrackers. For a while I fussed over my obituary, which I still hadn't finished. I hoped to approach the document with a blend of humor and sincerity. I wanted it brief, to the point, and tightly edited. It would be the final say on a thirty-three-year-old life. There were problems with this sort of endeavor, naturally. The more I wrote, tweaked, and fine-tuned, the more I realized how much in thirty-three years I had not accomplished, the number of places I'd never visited, the women I'd never touched, which was all very irritating, but not as much as a certain, maddeningly bright light that shone from behind the mission across the way.

Some sort of high-intensity halide floodlight pulsed from behind a medium-sized cross, projecting its silhouette directly into my hotel room, an eclipse-like outline that fell squarely across my queen-size bed. I jumped up, my legs tangling in the scratchy sheets. It was incredible: the cross's shadow perfectly overlay my mattress.

I drew the tatty pink drapes, nothing more than frayed lace, but couldn't block the cross's ghosted outline. I looked out at the cross. A blaze of light evenly limned the damn thing. I thought about changing rooms, but eventually found that, if I didn't move, if I remained nearly motionless, I could position myself within the cross's shadow. A well-placed pillow also helped solve the problem.

+ + +

Months ago, I was at my desk, surrounded by student papers, my second cup of decaf on the soiled coaster, waiting for the most important phone call of my life. Something hard, something off, had been found. Scans were ordered, blood drawn. Magazines and waiting rooms and nurses and paper shoes. It was a typical day around campus despite the excruciating wait: e-mails, committee forms, student recommendations, etc.

So I was trying to plod ahead, trying to sublimate fear, trying to remain impassively numb, trying not to ease my hand down my pants, where I had first felt the marble, and then *another,* on the superior pole of my testis. My thoughts pinballed. I couldn't concentrate. I imagined the concerned faces of my friends, my family. I tried not to picture their faces. And after waiting a bit longer—after 127 revolutions of the minute hand on the wall clock—after pacing tight circles on the gray, industrial carpet, I finally surfed to an Internet search engine and typed HOW TO TIE NOOSE into my computer screen.

Up popped 1,590,674 results.

The number of Internet posts discussing the variety of noose-tying methods startled me. I gripped my desk and pulled myself closer. There were videos. There were even step-by-step, downloadable instructions. Then I discovered more. A fascinating world revealed itself. I got up and shut my office door.

Of course, we were too late. The marbles had redeployed to my lung.

Not long after my doctor's prognosis, I began subscribing to listservs. I began perusing Usenet discussion boards. Participation required a handle. I thought it over for several days. I awoke in the middle of the night, sweat-drenched, and settled on a name: "Vikingsholm." The name just came to me. I had distant Scandinavian blood and thought the moniker was appropriate. Anyway, I soon became another faceless member of this largely polite yet desperate message board tribe, which actively swapped fantasies, which offered advice, which consoled. People were engaged in heated, anticipatory discussions on exactly *how to do it.* I never knew acute despair could elicit such passion. Cries for help were often answered with links to support groups. The terminal cases, like me, openly pleaded their cases. My preferred message board—alt.catchthebus.methods—voted weekly on the best procedures, the best places to go about it. Mexico often topped the list. I was terrified of sickness, terrified of each slippery organ succumbing to the spread, and *this, this, this* seemed the preferable option. It seemed the only option.

After a while, I decided to post a message.

Three people responded.

I posted another.

Several more responded.

Someone claiming to be a Swiss doctor e-mailed me information on how to order a copy of *The Purposeful Pill*—the how-to, where-to travel guidebook.

Eventually a small group of us broke ranks with the larger group. We created an invite-only board, for those of us with developing plans. To obscure our purpose we anointed it with a semi-innocuous name: alt.objects.sharp. By day I tried, best I could, to care about my job. By night I scoured the message board.

The Purposeful Pill arrived in my mailbox. Folks were departing for Mexico weekly. Some to Tijuana, some to Nuevo Laredo. Others chose Ciudad Juárez.

I had the literature of help on my bookshelf, of course.

I had the pamphlets of solace.

The doctor had mentioned experimental drug trials, of course.

My family would miss me.

Of course, my decision made, none of that mattered.

+ + +

I awoke to rhythmic beats juiced over from a boom box across the street. I got up and parted the pink drapes.

Several teenage boys were on the bandstand in the plaza. They were practicing Michael Jackson-esque dance routines, the music semi-scratchy, from a fritzed speaker. The leader was an energetic guy, even more handsome than Paul Porte, of the campus a cappella group and my Tuesday night Milton Seminar. I watched the kids spin, and grab their crotches, and slap each other's backs, yuk-king it up.

It was an interesting city, and strange. Odd to think this was where Marilyn Monroe had divorced Arthur Miller, where the margarita was supposedly invented, where Sinatra had crooned. These days it was just a pit of industry and dirt and concrete, a violent moonscape, the prettiest thing about it the sky. Yet here was this spunky crew across the avenue at the start of a sunlit morning.

The streets remained largely empty as I waited out the day. Whatever business had been happening prior to the cartel wars had receded, revealing a city stripped to its tendons. Old Tara-humara Indian women begged on the sidewalks, knees pressed to chests, shaking paper cups with loose coins inside. Their sun-carved faces were pathetic, lovely. You would think, this being the end, I wouldn't have errands. Yet I had to find a Correos de México outlet, where I purchased handfuls of stamps, and wouldn't you know it, the letter stamps were decorated with skeletons wearing formal attire.

That night I made my way to the appointed rendezvous. Western Where was at the center of the axis, close to numerous veteri-nary clinics. I was surprised to find the bar swarming with expats, foreigners and English speakers, mostly men, many wearing color-ful soccer jerseys. The interior was dingy with a slightly schizo-phrenic décor. Silvery Christmas tinsel hung from exposed air ducts. Discarded peanut shells littered the floor. Tom Petty played on the jukebox. Apparently the international set was all too famil-iar with the place. I overheard Australian and British accents. Wait-resses escorted bottles to tables. Customers were here to drink, to celebrate. One man with a sharp funny mustache handed me a card emblazoned with a skull and crossbones. It was cartoonish, but soothing, and when he smiled the lines under his eyes creased like an accordion.

I spotted one of the screen names across the bar, in the last booth. Just where he said he'd be sitting. "The last booth. The most-distant booth. The farthest from the door." The man was sitting with perfect, concentrated neglect, his pallid face seemingly only ever tanned by the glow off a computer monitor.

Father Carlos Luera, aka "FatherCarlos," was the only person on the alt.objects.sharp message board to use his real name, and occupation. Somehow I knew the priest would be wearing, even in this heat, a long-sleeve black shirt and clerical collar. He and I had spent many late nights commenting on each other's posts, making plans, and now it had come to this: face-to-face, in Mexico. His reasons for being here, which included unsavory allegations raised by members of his parish, read like a Russian novel.

Beside him was a young man with a perfect part in his hair, rose color in his cheeks, and vein-laced forearms that poked out from a blue tracksuit.

I set my knuckles on the table. "Well, so, wow, you made it," I said to Father Luera. The old man looked up and nodded limply. "Have you seen the others?" I asked him.

The young guy beside him grabbed my arm and said, "I'm sitting right here."

The kid was sturdy as a brick, clearly worked the weights, and he smiled wide, and invited me to sit, and fingered back liquor without blinking. When he told me he was "H82Live," a handle I knew all too well, I struggled not to laugh.

"Have some tequila," the young guy said, raising a glass. "Really first-rate hooch down here."

I sat, and I looked at him. He was not the same H82Live that I knew from the message board. The H82Live that I had come to know was a moody character. From his posts I'd gleaned he was girlfriendless, unemployed, and five years on the verge. He supposedly lived with his mother in Cincinnati and expressed his depression by angrily posting in ALL CAPS. I tried to divorce old notions of him from the new ones that began to form. The guy was excitable, in high spirits, and when I attempted to locate any sort of death wish in his eyes, I couldn't find it. He looked content, and really fit. He detached his gaze from me and eagerly scanned the bar.

Father Luera, on the other hand, was visibly struggling. The older man's gestures were slow and pained, as though his limbs were encased in concrete. I watched him carefully unzip a fanny pack and withdraw a coin-sized Jesus wafer. Eventually he ate it. In person the priest matched his screen presence: a man of the Catholic order, well into his sixties, and nearly devoid of personality. He had the puffy gums of an eighty-year-old.

"We're missing our fourth," I said, after a bit. We'd decided on meeting as an anonymous foursome and then pairing off.

"Relax, dude," H82Live said. "She'll be here. She's coming. We've e-mailed. She'll make it."

Over mojitos the three of us reviewed our travel itineraries, as though this were a business junket. Father Luera barely spoke while H82Live snickered and laughed and spat out jokes. The kid was jumpy and, I hated to admit it, he was friendlier than a concierge. After another mojito he put The B-52s on the jukebox, and tipped our waitress well, and ordered more beer, and slugged a friendly Aussie on the shoulder, and why not? Death tourists had little to lose. The Australians laughed alongside the Brits and everyone was handling everyone else like fellow players on a team.

Everyone except Father Luera. The priest just sat quietly in our booth and nibbled down another Jesus wafer.

As outlined in *The Purposeful Pill,* exiting should happen with a partner. It was the buddy system. A buddy would help allay fear. A buddy would help if you found yourself babbling and sucking your thumb. A buddy would join you in crossing over. We had decided to catch the bus on the Day of the Dead and, apparently, the other bar patrons had the same slick idea. We could all appreciate how Mexican culture celebrated the dead.

Father Luera finally set down his glass, fighting to give birth to a complete sentence. "So," he said to me. "You're a professor." Speaking seemed to sap him.

"Assistant professor," I said.

"A fine career path. That deserves some respect," he said. "You're an educator."

"Was," I said. Then I looked at him deeply, seriously. "Is it too soon to use the past tense?"

The man's lip cracked as he broke a small smile. Seemingly embarrassed, he tried covering his mouth with his hand.

Our first meeting was going well, as well as it could, until our fourth member arrived around midnight. I nearly spilled my beer across the table.

"You're our number four?" I asked the girl. And she was, indeed, she was a girl. Hovering over our corner table, arms crossed, dressed in tight jeans with fancy embroidered rear pockets and big furry boots, she smelled like mall perfume, and she was adorable.

We stared at her.

"Slam-a-Gamma" was definitely not an overweight divorcee from the Midwest who worked in a bead shop. This girl had clearly lied. A revolving disco ball spangled her light blonde curls. Father Luera was clearly startled by her age. "How did you even get here?" he asked her.

"Flight, taxi, these two feet," she told him, chewing off a loose cuticle. "Duh."

"But why are you here?" Father Luera asked.

Slam-a-Gamma looked momentarily lost, helpless. She glanced at H82Live. They seemed to recognize each other. H82Live leaned back. A sly smile lifted on his face. He inspected her in the same way a butcher did meat.

"I didn't make the squad," she said. Tears welled in her pretty, green eyes. She shouldered her way into the booth. Her Delta Gamma sorority sisters, she told us, were not a mothering bunch. She gave us the whole sordid tale. Apparently their hazing had reached hurricane proportions. "They're just complete assholes!" she screamed.

I could tell Father Luera was speedily computing her age, his responsibilities to her as a priest. He asked why she'd even consider catching the bus with us, down here in this ugly hot dirt.

"Now, now, now," H82Live said. "We don't judge. Everyone has a reason. Look around."

He was right. Western Where was packed with jet-set depressives, nearly every one of them now, weirdly, laughing. H82Live slung an arm around the young coed, and after buying her a drink, he asked, "So, tell us, what will you miss the most?"

"Nothing," the young woman said. Her lower lip produced an illustrious pout. "Absolutely shit nothing at all," she said and knocked back her beer.

On the message board H82Live was a troll, a reliable downer, but in person he charmed. He set his hip against hers, whispering a quiet joke into her cute little ear, and she smiled, but beside her Father Luera was drifting off to his own private land. I watched him launch another Jesus wafer onto his tongue. I looked closer at him. Father Luera wore all the warning signals. His eyes were as red and flat as a STOP sign.

Still, I didn't want us to lose focus. We were here for a purpose. Our foursome was complete. And now we needed liquid.

+ + +

Father Luera had steered a blue 1966 Plymouth Valiant fifteen hundred miles from the suburbs of Chicago to Juárez, and the old car was beat, he told me. He'd also crossed the border without buying temporary Mexican insurance, which was always recommended.

"Not necessary," he said as he unlocked the car's door.

The idea of him sleeping in the backseat, as he'd planned, was too much. So I invited the priest to stay with me for our final nights on the planet. The last thing you wanted was to exit without choosing your method. These streets were dangerous. And lawless: I even carried my half-finished beer with me onto the sidewalk. Nobody noticed or cared!

When H82Live and Slam-a-Gamma bid us farewell for the night, it became apparent that they had decided to pair off. I watched the dimming glow of their shared cigarette bounce away. He bumped her with his hip. She grabbed his shoulder for balance.

Sirens wailed somewhere close, though I hadn't heard gun bursts in a while. The moon was up as the priest and I staggered back to my hotel. It was odd to see the gray outline of the American mountains to the north. Just on the other side of the fence was one of the safest midsized cities in the States, and the only thing separating well-being from danger was a line in the sand.

We arranged for a cot to be put in the corner of the room, near the window. Father Luera flung his small leather bag on it. He hadn't brought much. The annoying light from behind the cross oozed around his unshaven jaw as he unzipped his bag and removed a small vial. The priest had arrived in town early, had already gotten to work. He sat, the cot squeaked, and he held the gleaming vial between his fingers, mesmerizing me. I set my beer on an old dusty Bible on the end table.

"We'll need more for you," he said.

"At least one hundred milliliters."

"Each," he said. The method was supposed to be painless. "We're doing this," he said.

"Are we doing this?"

Father Luera leaned over to remove my beer from the Bible. He was an exceedingly quiet man, and he would be the last person to see me alive, so there was some heaviness, some tenderness in that, and I tried to get comfortable with the idea. A priest, I figured, was a pretty lucky draw.

Father Luera quickly made the cot his home. He produced a thick mystery book, which he would never finish, and propped his head against the wall. I'd seen the book, a page-turning bestseller, at the airport. Every so often he snatched a handful of Jesus wafers from his fanny pack, munching on them like potato chips.

I still had tasks to complete. On my way to Sky Harbor Airport I'd picked up customized invitations. I'd spared no expense on the eighty-pound natural paper stock, on the letter-pressed printing, set in black ink, in Palatino font. I addressed them to friends, to family, putting the skeleton stamps on the envelopes, and stacked them on the old Bible. Not included with the memorial invitations, obviously, were RSVPS.

My new roommate slept well, and deeply, and snored. I expected the beer and mojitos and tequila and travel to wipe me out, but sleep was my enemy. I just lay there in the dark, one eye under the cross's unrelenting flare, which floodlit my brainpan, while inside my head I began to imagine a deep, funeral parlor kind of voice trying to trick me away from my decision.

Late the next morning I awoke to see Father Luera staring at a lower portion of the wall. He'd slept in his clothes, and he was now sitting with his back to me. Sunlight fell through the drapes and onto his shoulders. For some reason he'd nudged his cot away from the wall.

"Morning," I said.

The priest didn't respond. I threw back the thin covers. He was hunched over, forearms on his knees, concentrating on a wall outlet that was missing its protective plastic outlet panel. Two exposed wires were jutting out, seductively, like shiny, brassy fangs. The priest was meditating on them. I held in a breath. A part of me wanted him to reach out. A part of me yearned to reach out. He was tapping a pencil against his knuckles. I watched him wipe spit on the pencil's eraser and touch one wire. A blue spark cracked, and I jumped.

"Padre." I put a hand on his shoulder. "Come on, let's go."

Over these final months I'd learned that the Japanese were skilled at this seppuku business. They were inventive, and often successful. Some used simple household items, igniting bath sulfur and toilet bowl cleaner inside unventilated closets. Others burned charcoal briquettes inside cars. There was also the plastic-bag-over-the-head-and-helium approach. Two spoonfuls of powdered caffeine worked too. Death was easy to buy in the right place, and with the proper information.

One problem with *The Purposeful Pill* guidebook, however, was that it was a popular resource, in part because it named names. It named places. The book provided leads, with glossy photos of businesses, complete with addresses and phone numbers, but when we ran into a friendly group of Kiwis coming out of the first veterinary office on the list, I knew they'd already vacuumed everything up. And sure enough, the vet was fresh out. The thin booklet hadn't been updated in years, and the next three veterinary offices were sold out of pentobarbital, too. We were again denied at the next spot.

Liquid barbiturate was the last medication I'd ever need. Ingested with yogurt, taken with antiemetic pills to control nausea, it was a death dessert of sorts, but the animal tranquilizer was a hot commodity in these parts.

"Those Brits and Australians are screwing everything up," I said to Father Luera. I wanted to tear the expensive booklet in half. "This stupid book. Everyone has a copy."

Worse, for a moment I actually began to pay attention to the whispery, cross-examining voice in my head, which went on and on, throwing out question after question.

Worse than that, the priest was slow moving, which made it difficult to hustle to the next office on the list.

We ventured as far south as División del Norte. But the veterinarian there refused to sell to us. I offered the man money, quite a lot of money, but the guy just smiled and looked at me sadly.

"I no help kill you," he said to me.

Word had spread. People were catching on.

"Please," I said to the man, but he just shook his head.

"Someone at Western Where will have extra," Father Luera assured me. "Life always works out that way."

"Life," I said.

"Trust me."

"But tomorrow is Day of the Dead. Tomorrow is the day."

"Calm down. Everything will be fine."

Nothing was fine! Cells had mutated, spread! There wasn't much time before I became incapacitated, felt pain, grew nauseated. I refused to think about hospitals and nurses, tubes and bedpans and body scans. I refused to think about what was happening *inside* me, whatever it was that was happening.

Another problem with *The Purposeful Pill* method: the buddy system. What about the buddy? Who would look after the buddy once the first had exited?

Father Luera was eager. And thinking on it. I could tell. And of course, he wanted to be first, he told me, as we strolled down the street. In the event, he said. He wanted me to promise him that he would exit first, while I watched, while I made sure it happened. I thought about his suggestion under the burnished, cloudless sky.

"Screw that, I'm going first," I said.

His request irritated me, and my mood was souring, and each step felt like the final paces of a marathon. A yellow school bus raced past us, gushing hot exhaust. A convoy of massive, bulletproof vehicles, rifle barrels poking from cracked windows, followed. In the distance, above the sad messy streets, the top floors of the Wells Fargo building in El Paso stood like a safety beacon, sunlight reflecting off its black glass windows.

On Avenida Juárez we saw H82Live and Slam-a-Gamma holding hands and sucking on sugar skulls. They were now acting like quite the alliance. They broke their grasp when they noticed us. We crossed the street. For them this could have been a visit to Disneyland or something. They looked strange, like happy people, as though the easy act of smiling squeezed the misery from their pores and made their supple skin shine.

"Tell them about your teeth," Slam-a-Gamma said. She stood at H82Live's side, clingy, like a barnacle.

"Oh, you know. I decided to get them cleaned," H82Live told us. "It was only twenty bucks. Such cheap health care down here. It's unbelievable."

"He got them brightened too," Slam-a-Gamma added.

H82Live shrugged. "I want to look my best for tomorrow. You know."

Indeed, his now-florescent teeth shined, and he was in a different colored tracksuit, and he looked downright chipper and American and ready for a visit to the nearest country club. I left Father Luera in charge of the kids and went on the hunt, alone, anxiously in search of liquid.

I'd wanted to see the slums to remind me how life could eviscerate the human spirit, but there wasn't much time. Tomorrow was the day. But I did manage to track down enough anti-nausea medication. The stuff was easy to buy. Farmacias lined the sidewalks. Still, I couldn't find anyone who would sell me pentobarbital. To boost my mood I stopped at a copy shop and paid to rent a computer terminal and typed my obituary from memory. I printed two copies. At the hotel, I addressed the envelope to my lawyer in Phoenix, stacking it on my pile of invitations.

Later, Father Luera was nestled on his cot when I emerged from the bathroom after a hot, nipple-chaffing shower. Steam rose from my shoulders. He was deep inside his mystery book, a finger tracking his progress. I dressed quietly and refused to look at him. After a bit, Father Luera leaped to his feet, parted the pink drapes, and looked out the window toward the plaza, at the Catholic cathedral, at the smaller mission beside it. I watched him place a stiff Jesus wafer on his gray tongue and close his mouth. But he didn't chew it. He just waited for the damn thing to melt or something. He just held it inside. It nearly drove me insane. And that particular way he stood at the window, looking out, searchingly, was perhaps the same way ancient peoples might have looked when scanning ocean horizons, wondering about it all.

+ + +

Late afternoon was eerily quiet around town, and I agreed to accompany the priest on his final spiritual errands.

We went to the smaller of the two churches across the street, the Mission de Guadalupe, apparently the oldest building in Juárez. With thick white adobe walls, wood doors, oval windows, it was similar to other early Spanish missions in the Southwest. At the center was a stone altar. Above it was a portrait of the Virgin in all her asexual glory.

"Under that altar," the priest informed me, "are bodies."

A chill shot up my spine.

Several elderly women occupied the front pews. Father Luera looked more relaxed inside the Mission. His fists unclenched and his posture improved. He moved like a swan as he sat in the back, and kneeled, and pressed his hands together in that way. I thought about how far he'd travelled. And how far he had to go. The hotel, I decided: the hotel would be best. First me, and then Father Luera. Yes. He would need to be convinced of the order. But watching him now, as he applied his faith, left me feeling like I was at his mercy, left me feeling guilty for not participating in his ritual, and hungry for that same kind of outside assurance. As a man of the cloth, I wondered, would his decision defy the order of things?

I sat in an empty pew near the front, tipping my head back and studying the intricate woodwork on the rafters, wondering how many hands that had taken to carve, how many notches, and how many breaths. Surrounding the Virgin was a golden panel. Her son, on the wall beside her, was put on the cross at thirty-three, my age. He was a man, just a man, like me, paper in the wind. With us gone, the planet would continue to orbit. Sun would shine.

When I eventually turned around, Father Luera was gone. In his pew now sat a man and a toddler. The guy was explaining something to the kid in Spanish. Left behind in the pew was a white clerical collar.

Outside, on the step, an elderly Tarahumara lady approached me. She had pitted cheeks. For some reason she grabbed my arm and shoved a rose in my hand. The rose was a deep burgundy color, its petals wilted. I had no idea why she chose me, but it was a nice gesture, an alarming, beautiful gesture. Most remarkable, though, was the woman's smile. I patted her hand and stuffed two hundred dollars inside her thrashed paper cup.

Father Luera was waiting for me on a bench in the plaza.

"These people. Everything around them is ruined," I said. "And yet they smile. Everyone, somehow, still smiles. Have you noticed that?"

"I've heard there's lithium in the water down here," the priest said. "That might explain it." He threw another wafer in his mouth.

"Why do you eat those?"

"Helps me feel weighted down," he said. He looked off in the distance absentmindedly and tapped his chest. "Otherwise, it feels as though I might drift away. Poof. Just a wisp of smoke. But I'm not ready yet. Just yet."

+ + +

"Nice boots," I said to Slam-a-Gamma that evening at Western

Where. Feet propped up in a booth, she was showing off new cowboy boots, tapping the pointy toes together.

"This cute boy bought them for me," Slam-a-Gamma said. She winked at H82Live.

This pair, and their antics, were getting on my nerves. Where was their deep commitment to despair?

"One hundred percent ostrich," H82Live said proudly. "Store owner made them right then and there. Measured her feet with string. He was some sort of magician."

"I want to look my best," Slam-a-Gamma said.

Father Luera and I joined them in the booth. We ordered Gran Centenario Leyenda tequila, but Father Luera opted for a bottle of red wine, which he blessed by making the sign of the cross before drinking straight from the bottle.

It was getting later, and Western Where was beginning to take off. Tomorrow was the day. ABBA was on the jukebox, and drinks flowed, and H82Live was asking again, "What else will you miss?"

"My mom," Slam-a-Gamma was saying over the loud music. "I'll miss my mom."

People danced. People drank. Two men at the urinals in the men's room recounted their greatest disappointments, trafficking in laughter, as though shame and guilt and pain were distant illusions. The disco ball spun counterclockwise, catching our eyes. A bit of fun before the end wasn't a bad thing, I supposed. Each of these isolates had come from faraway places for one final send-off.

At one point two local toughs entered the bar. Both wore gold chains, and oily boots, and cowboy hats, and had bulges in their pant legs, an indication they carried weight. At least the guys thought they were tough until a depressed Brit confronted them. The Brit showed them a look of such destruction, his face so thoroughly blank, that he managed to scare them off.

Still, the Aussies hadn't shown up, which worried me. Midnight came and went, and I hoped they hadn't already hopped aboard the bus. I was waiting, had been waiting, eager and waiting, hoping one of them might have extra liquid to spare. Australians were usually exceedingly nice, easy to talk to, and friendly.

"What about my stuff?" I asked Father Luera. "The Australians haven't shown."

"Well, we've got ours," Slam-a-Gamma said. She looked at H82Live for confirmation.

"Oh, sure." He sipped his fifth or sixth or seventh tequila. "Like I promised," he said. "Everything's taken care of. Hey, let's dance."

I was the only member of our little group without the liquid. I was the only one not carrying. Even the kids had some! I milled, hoping someone else could lend a hand to a patient in need. I bumped into a Frenchman with a forehead the size of a billboard, and he had enough, for a price.

"Five hundred," he said.

"But it's a fifty dollar vial."

"One thousand," he said.

"You said five hundred."

"Eight hundred."

Now it was eight hundred! I would have bargained with him, but this was my life. "Stay here. I'll be back."

I marched through the scary, empty, past-midnight streets. In the hotel room I unfurled a tube sock. Cash spilled out. Things had shifted in the room. The bed was made. And there were fresh towels.

And my pile of stamped envelopes was missing.

I raced down the stairwell, dinging the bell on the front desk.

"Sí," the woman told me. She smiled dutifully. "I send."

Numbness, as I looked at her, as she blinked in response, spread downward through my arms. I walked back to Western Where in shivers. But what, anyway, did it matter? The invitations were out, birds gone to find their nests. They'd arrive within days—or, I didn't know, this being Mexico—weeks? By then, anyway, I wouldn't have any more worries. From somewhere in the city I heard popping again. Against the advice of the funereal chattering, I began my preparations by chewing on four antiemetic pills, which tasted like cleaning solvent.

It was that hour, the dark purple sky turning lavender, and closing in on dawn. In the booth H82Live and Slam-a-Gamma were still acting like a newly minted couple. They disgusted me, even if they were cute together! Even if!

And the others, dampened by drinks and the impending cancellation of their futures, were already beginning to depart, dragging their jolly selves out the door. The Swiss, the Laplanders, the Kiwis, everyone was heading out. After handing over eight hundred to the Frenchman, I finally secured my vial.

I was inspecting the precious liquid under the bar's muted lights when H82Live and Slam-a-Gamma sidled up next to me. I overheard them order more drinks.

Again H82Live was probing. "What else, sweetie, will you miss?" He was tickling her ribs. "Tell, what else?"

I looked over, waiting for her response. But the girl's eyes darkened. A lash fell to her cheek. I watched long enough to see H82Live gently swipe it away with his thumb.

"You," she said to him. "I'll miss you." Her shoulders shook violently, as though she'd just swallowed a full-bodied cry, and she looked around at the men, the older and younger men, at their sad and desperate enthusiasm, at their ill-fitting soccer jerseys, and she said, "Wait."

"What's that?" H82Live asked.

"Wait," she said. She put down her glass, pivoted, and walked quickly toward the door. She grabbed her hair with fists. Over the sound of the music I heard her yell, "Wait!"

H82Live smiled at me. And smacked my back. "I admit it. This isn't the best way to meet women," he said with a shrug. "But it sure works."

Then he followed after her.

Slam-a-Gamma pulled the door and sunlight swept across the floor, wet with our spilled drinks and strewn with peanut shells. The luminant desert light hurt our drinky eyes. Beyond the doors we heard the sound of Norteño trios playing accordion music, a clash of sound so awkward and enticing that it dragged the rest of us outside.

The celebration usually happened at cemeteries, inside homes, as part of planned festivals, a holiday to honor family and friends who'd died, a day that summoned memories so the dead would live again for another, but in Ciudad Juárez, outside Western Where, the celebration took over the streets. I saw mothers and daughters and sons on the gummy sidewalks laying down marigold flowers and candies and bottles of tequila. Grieving relatives set down offerings. And nuns, nuns too, scattered plastic flowers every few yards, where people had dropped, where people had lost their lives, which was everywhere. It was amazing, dreadful. Some had painted their faces to resemble skulls. Others carried skeleton puppets on sticks. People set wreaths beside colorful murals. The city was the cemetery, and we watched the living pay their respects.

Father Luera tugged hard off his wine bottle, his eyes as dull as pewter. He came up next to me, still nibbling his Jesus wafers. We watched a middle-aged man lean a photograph of a toddler, no older than five, against a cinderblock wall. The man put a wooden flute next to it. And in the middle of this swarming, sidewalk memorial was Slam-a-Gamma, running, running north, fists in her hair, pushing through the crowd.

H82Live was skipping after her. Dressed for the chase, in his tracksuit.

The Aussies materialized from another bar, drunk and wobbly and squinting and watching the informal procession. They hadn't crossed over yet. The Brits were here. So were the Kiwis. The French thief, his forehead sweating, was with us too. No one had left. We were all here on the warm sidewalks, watching as though a hole had opened in the sky, funneling paradisiac light over this section of the city, where children roamed around carrying bunches of carnations.

Down the block a yellow school bus was coming, honking its horn as it rapidly approached. The bus was big and wide, wide enough to wipe someone from the map, wide and beautiful, and tempting, which was probably the reason the priest dropped his wine bottle on the cement, splashing me. A red circle spread at our feet. Even from a distance I could see the driver's white, knobby knuckles, and I thought of Rudolph, the hollow man from my childhood. One day, he was with us. Another day, he was gone. Just like that—it happened. And it happened fast. As instantaneous, it seemed, as going from a boy to landing on this wondrous day.

The mournful babbling in my head turned into the voice of that once-young boy, his singing high and true and clear, pleading with me, shouting, knocking me between the eyes, helping me feel love for these strangers, and feel great love for myself, and for Father Luera and all his magnificent sadness.

I wanted Father Luera to finish his mystery book. I hadn't wanted anything for the longest time, but I wanted this simple wish. And I wanted, for another moment more, for the sky to hold its gleaming light. And so, when the priest stepped from the curb and into the street, when he spat a wet wafer to the ground, when he assumed the stance of a linebacker, his knuckles against the asphalt, when his eyes watched the bus with a stare approaching on lust, as though he was preparing to tackle it, I ran out and yanked him back to safety. I wrapped my arms around him as the bus sped toward us.

"Not yet, Father," I said. As he struggled, I gripped him tighter. My weight held him. He wanted to drift off, wanted to become smoke, but I was here. I would not be here forever, but as long as I was, I would serve as his anchor. "I've got you," I whispered. I put my face in the priest's salty neck. "Not yet. Not yet. Please, not yet."

FULL OF DAYS

So Job died, being old and full of days.

—BOOK OF JOB 42:17

Marc Maldonado sensed the Kingdom of God within him on Sundays, driving sun-scorched trash-scattered freeways to his temple of worship, and he felt the emptiness of his own realm whenever he set the table for one, whenever he aligned his socks in the hollow dresser drawer. In this hot, high-voltage city, with its pulsing neon, with its armies of fingers slamming on video poker buttons, he felt the loving kindness, the light ache of breath in his nostrils, and he knew he was necessary.

On that day Marc drove the freeways, analyzing angles for the best possible exposure. The great desert opened to him as he cruised I-15 North-South, I-515 East-West, changing direction where the freeways intersected and formed a concrete cross.

Summer's heat was a cruel spirit upon the city. 107 degrees. 111 degrees. Heat leaked through his car window and raked his cheek. On the hood of his Honda lay a pigeon's droppings baked into the shape of an egg.

For weeks he'd been observing traffic patterns at different times of day. He was after the best coverage over the longest period of time. Vehicles moving at sixty miles per hour might only get a two-second glimpse of his billboard. He needed to capture his viewer in that brief flash. This was a twenty-four-hour city, and morning-afternoon congestion didn't necessarily apply. Las Vegas had its eyes open at all hours.

He disliked dealing with the corporations. One in particular had a near-monopoly over the city. And it was the most difficult company to deal with: sign rates were astronomical, it had restrictive guidelines and, when Marc had e-mailed the saleswoman the image he intended to use, she never called him back. Then the woman refused to accept his calls at all.

Vegas was a town of signage. Everything was advertisement: cheap buffets, pool parties, golf courses, weddings, concerts, magic shows, conventions, sporting events, discounts, skin. Marc needed a large billboard with enough surrounding space that it wouldn't be swallowed by the noise. His message had competition. New outdoor digital numbers moved and blinked and altered their commercial announcements depending on the hour.

He wanted others to see. He needed others to see, if only for an instant, the cross he bore. His message was Life. Life itself. Life everlasting. And Death.

Two words, in bold Helvetica type . . . THINK TWICE . . . would overlay the image of a second-trimester travesty: a minuscule lopped-off hand, its five tiny fingers digitally embossed upon the face of George Washington on the national quarter. A teensy hand. A significant death. The image woke you up. The image worked. The miasma of gore encircling the hand spoke the truth to him, and he approved of its lesson: All life upon the earth was precious.

+ + +

Marc occupied a corner apartment at 2202 Paradise Road. It was an L-shaped, two-story Spanish Colonial Revival building that lay in the afternoon shadow of the Stratosphere Hotel and Casino. He'd painted his door yellow to distinguish himself from neighbors.

Two days after he posted a notice in the *Review-Journal,* a man named Cameron Dunlop phoned. Cameron's speedy, grating voice brought to mind a garbage disposal. "So listen I may have something for you," he said in a quick burst. Marc listened.

Cameron had inherited a vacant lot, he went on, and the sign that stood there, which was currently unused, brought him extra income. So, yeah, was Marc interested? The billboard was located near the intersection of the Las Vegas Freeway and Sahara Avenue. When Marc heard this, he swallowed hard. He made triple exclamation points on his scratch paper. It was a prime location. Visible, with high traffic volume.

Cameron agreed to meet at 4:00 P.M.

Marc arrived early. The lot was in an industrial area, between a welding shop and a scrapyard, and it wasn't the most beautiful spot of land, but the sign was seeable and, more importantly, rentable. The white signboard rose thirty feet into the sky from behind a chain link fence. Bare, empty, and just waiting for his special hieroglyphics.

Ten minutes past the hour a massive red Ford V-10 jumped the curb and pulled alongside Marc's Honda. The truck had muddy wheels, and its owner, a hedgehog of a man, short, hairy, stooped, had to shimmy down onto a step bar to reach pavement.

Marc watched Cameron's chapped middle-aged hands fiddle with a lock on the fence. Then Cameron proudly pushed it open, as though introducing some paradise. The man squinted, staring up at the billboard's great wide empty surface. "For years we had a blonde on there with the teeniest bikini you ever saw," Cameron told Marc with a smile, thumb in his Wrangler's pocket. "You know, an advert for that place with mob ties, Crazy Horse, that titty club? The men around these yards loved it."

Marc nodded. He told Cameron he was a recent transplant and didn't know the place. Cameron stated his price, which was a bit steep. Marc hoped to nudge him down.

"Okay. Okay. Let's think," Cameron said. "Not like this sign is working for anyone right now anyway. Tell you what. Ink a six-month lease on her, and I'll give you two weeks free. And I'll knock a buck-twenty off the monthly tab."

Marc quickly calculated costs. He still needed to pay for the vinyl panels. But this was a good opportunity, the closest he'd gotten. His nose burned under the bright, burnished sky as he thought it over.

"Well?" Cameron finally said, tugging his pocket open.

Marc signed the lease inside Cameron's truck, with Al Green on the radio, the vents cooling his sweaty upper lip.

+ + +

With money from the life insurance policy, he'd arrived in the hypergraphic desert to save himself, to follow the righteous path; but there were moments, which dropped on him at night, in fits of sleeplessness, in his airless apartment, when he yearned for the Pacific coastline, the way he once fell hypnotized by the sound of waves.

He thought of the waves often. And he often thought about his last night on El Capitán Beach: his naked toes in cold sand, creeping upon the roiling in all his moonlit glory. He meant to wash himself away with the tide. Waves broke over his head, freezing and continuous, and he shook, from his knees to his lips, he shook, confused by the notion of their disappearance. Even then, some dim light refused to turn dark in him, and from memory he recalled the words he was taught in his boyhood church, suddenly reawakened to that everlasting promise, gripping to it. That night Marc lived. He lived but needed to believe they lived on as well, that he would someday join them.

It had been an El Niño winter. Heavy rains, mudslides up and down the Pacific Coast Highway. The neighbor's dog had recently ruined their Persian rug with muddy paws. Driving conditions up the canyon were slow going and treacherous on the turns, especially on that night. Puddles grew to ponds on the road's swamped shoulder as his wife and seventeen-year-old daughter, Emily, were returning from an art exhibition on Carpinteria Avenue. Marc had been at home, sitting there, had been on his time-beaten leather recliner, he would remember, he would always remember, half-happy on Cabernet, listening to the tapping rain, just sitting there, unaware of how his life would soon change.

Seven months before that night, his daughter had decided to empty a life from her belly by way of vacuum aspiration. It had been her quiet choice, hers and her mother's. The father was some surf-punk freshman from UCSB. Marc's knee buckled when his wife eventually told him—too late, and without even consulting him. After his wife's disclosure, he was struck by sudden shame, dull throbs in his throat, sunbursts of confused pain stirred around by the vague teachings of his childhood faith. He'd leaned against the kitchen counter, feeling the cool tile press into his palms, and looked at the wall calendar. Not much time had passed between the act and the hose. There hadn't been much room for gestation. After, later, his daughter started going everywhere with his wife, a puppy trailing her mother, a young woman shocked awake by life's new realities.

The police report was short, explicit, and now lived inside one of Marc's barren utensil drawers. On their return from town the car hydroplaned at fifty miles per hour and collided against a steel railing. That was all. That was everything. The impact puckered the car's hood, spun the vehicle around, and left the car facing the opposite direction, dripping fluids. There were no sparks. There was no explosion. Neither made it to the emergency room alive.

Everything soon went. Marc's job, desires. Alone, he walked wet beaches. Alone, he returned, from time to time, to the church of his youth. He journeyed east, into the desert, alone.

These days Marc's grandchild would have been seventeen months old. Probably talking. Perhaps walking. Each night, after dosing himself with ten milligrams of Ambien, he liked to imagine the beautiful round face of a baby girl on his ceiling. He imagined sharp purple veins behind translucent temples. He imagined her curious, unsteady walk. Words would be in her throat, the breath of life in her lungs.

+ + +

Danika's place was near old downtown, a lopsided single-story structure that looked as though it had been airlifted from Beirut, circa 1994, and set down in Las Vegas. It bothered Marc to the nth degree, thinking about her living in a place that brought to mind black mold and carbon monoxide.

The young woman was standing beside a retired phone booth absent a receiver, her black hair wrenched into a ponytail. She looked younger than nineteen. His belly spread and aching knees stood in sharp relief against her girl-freckles and bangs. To him, she was the image of a grown child who'd walked straight out of an Iowan cornfield.

"You need a visor if you're going to stand in the sun like that," he said, after shimmying open the car door.

"Don't have a choice," Danika said. "My roommates argue. And I don't *own* a visor."

Marc had recently begun to understand her sort, the lost lambs: squeezed into this life by irresponsible people and abandoned to its streets to learn from the gutter. It was a damn shame. Sometimes Danika said she was from Idaho. Other times she mentioned Texas. He liked to imagine Iowa. Whatever the case, some wild storm had blown hard enough to push her to this dizzying city. She fraternized with street kids and at one time lived, she'd once confessed, snickering over it, under a teepee constructed from pallets in the storm drains beneath the city.

One of Marc's THINK TWICE fliers had delivered her to him. He posted bundles of the homemade fliers throughout the valley, held in place by a single brass tack and a file folder with a pocket. He visited youth centers and supermarkets and community health clinics, offering chauffeur services to pregnant teenagers. By now he'd lost count on the number of prank calls.

"I hope you're taking the folic acid tablets I gave you," Marc said.

Danika chewed a bit of loose skin from her thumb. "Sometimes. I forget."

"And you're okay for food, all that?"

The young woman stared absentmindedly out the car's window, toward a casino, where scaffolding enfolded a wing. They passed a fenced meadow, barren except for a solo palm tree leaning north. "You ever do anything besides this?" she asked him.

"I enjoy this," Marc said.

"A real angel," she said. She sank in the seat, plunking a dirty tennie against the dashboard. "Sure. Helping young girls. Spending time with young girls. I bet you really dig this."

A tough customer, Danika. Marc braked hard at the next light.

Hormones, he told himself. It was the hormones. Her blood was boiling with them.

"I mean, don't you ever feel like doing something fun?" she asked. "I see signs everywhere. There's whitewater rafting down the Colorado. Skydiving. *Gambling.* I mean, from what I've heard, things can be great around here."

"I have plenty of fun," Marc said.

"Uh huh," she said.

Marc waited in the hot car while Danika attended her prenatal appointment. She was nearly two months in, and he'd help as long as she needed him. Sometimes he daydreamed about being at the hospital with her, being present. Perhaps he could even hold the newborn.

But Danika was the thorniest girl he'd encountered so far. Others had requested his chauffeur service, of course, and each had come with issues. Like Pam, who was in her early twenties, pain-in-the-ass Pam. She didn't own a car. She wasn't really pregnant. She wasn't even a teenager. She lied to him in order to get rides to her job. And then there was Deb, small, bird-boned, and frantic, who simply stopped showing up at the appointed street corner.

He took out his phone, sun burning his knuckles, and called the printer for an update. He was informed that everything was on schedule. Marc had to approach seven printers before finding PhantaGraphix in North Platte, Nebraska, the only large-format printer to agree on producing the weatherproof vinyl billboard panels. The company's owner, even more, e-mailed Marc a personal note: "I like your work. God bless."

Sure, the image was shocking. That was his intention. It was jarring enough as a computerized .JPEG, but it was going to be galactically disturbing when enlarged to fourteen by forty-eight feet. He was told to expect the little dead hand to appear larger than a garage door.

An hour later, Danika returned, and Marc suggested lunch. She buckled her belt without responding and fixed her eyes on the street, away from him. Again. Like a teenager. Like a brat. The girl was almost feral. In need of parents, a *father.*

"Everything tip-top?" Marc asked.

"Sure, whatever, everything's fine," she said. "He wants to see me again. Why so many appointments? I don't like that doctor."

What a surprise. Danika didn't like much. That's what happened, he supposed, when a girl her age found herself in this predicament, living in this hard bright wildland, her innocence moving further away by the week.

Instead of dropping her on the corner, Marc parked. He directed Danika to the Honda's trunk, where he had an old piece of luggage for her. And when he unzipped the bag, Danika took a cautious step back. She didn't understand such kindness, clearly. Danika was Emily's size, with Emily's slight figure. He'd kept most of it: T-shirts, jeans, sundresses. Marc remembered his daughter wearing these items, and his dry lips stung as he watched a small nervous smile appear on Danika's face. She draped an aqua-colored dress against her body. The lines around Danika's mouth softened. He watched her finger the label. Then she ran her hand over the material. Her other hand, he saw, lay still against her flat belly.

+ + +

He disliked the slogans from both camps. He didn't ascribe to the competing bumper sticker philosophies. He didn't feel the need.

PLANNED MURDER, NOT PARENTHOOD
PRO WOMAN, PRO CHOICE
AMERICA'S HOLOCAUST!
KNOWLEDGE + CHOICE = POWER

His was a singular quest to make others see—actually see—the startling image of a life taken. That one stolen life could affect another's. That life was dear. That he was here. Here he was, struggling not to plummet into a well of bitterness. That everything was grabbed from him. That he was here, laying down his footprint. That he was here, walking the earth like you and you and you and you.

Some who knew Marc thought him "off." Oh, sure, he knew people whispered, but at least he had ideas in this confusing world. As the founder of THINK TWICE, Marc was president, treasurer, and secretary. The city's denizens, anyway, needed voices like his. People needed reminders of what could be lost amid all these shiny promises of what could be gained.

He shut down the online message board on his computer. He felt irritation pouring into him. They were loonies, each one of them. He only ever visited the message board to see what people were saying. But, oh. With their anonymous handles, their annoying posts. Just faceless people screaming about which clinics to target, what state laws needed changing, the horror of allowing women The Choice. He'd come to a conclusion that rose above platitudes. Show them. Let them decide. But *show them.*

In this one life you needed conviction. And in this one life you needed action.

So Marc snatched his car keys off the end table and, like every lonely Saturday evening, he prowled the freeways.

He drove on and off The Strip. For hours he searched for wheels crossing white lines. He looked for spastic brake lights. He looked for fast drivers, slow drivers, and drivers gently drifting back and forth, technically within the lines but outside the rule of law.

At last, at 1:14 A.M., he spotted a vehicle, at Eastern and Harmon. Its left front wheel tagged a median and then overcorrected. It was quick. The vehicle was an early model blue Suzuki SUV. Marc maneuvered behind but kept his distance. A bumper sticker on the SUV said, *Lighten up!* Oh, sure. Sure, sure, sure. Lighten up.

Marc followed the Suzuki to another stoplight. He rapidly scribbled the time and the license plate number on an old receipt. He trailed, watching the SUV almost merge into another car. He hadn't seen one in weeks. Now it was his. The Suzuki turned again. Marc felt his heart thumping. His palms went clammy. He had 911 on speed dial, but he paused.

The two cars moved northeast through the warm night streets. Marc wondered where the driver was leading him, but his question was answered when the Suzuki eased into a turn lane, aiming at a satellite casino on the edge of town. Marc waited through a full stoplight cycle, but for some reason the Suzuki didn't budge. Another green flashed and disappeared into yellow. Both cars sat idling.

Marc approached the SUV's side window with care. Through the shadows he saw an elderly man asleep behind the wheel. The man's mouth was ajar, his head tipped forward into a messy beard. Marc opened the door and an alcoholic breeze swept out. Quickly he extracted the keys from the ignition. The dispatch operator answered after two rings.

+ + +

The phone woke him at dawn. Marc pulverized his pinkie toe on the refrigerator on his search for the cordless telephone. It was Cameron. Cameron said he needed to meet. At the lot. At the sign. "Immediately," Cameron said.

Marc dragged a razor over his stubble as the sun illuminated the steamy window above the shower. He took his time. A man couldn't just call another man and make sudden demands like that. Before leaving, he sipped a cup of weak coffee in the wood-paneled living room. His furniture was mostly secondhand. The room, behind thick curtains, was silent and dark most of the time. This was his chosen life now, this shell. He'd sold the house and most everything inside it, and his wife and daughter, those sutures on his heart, would be stunned to see him living like this.

Cameron was behind the wheel of his Ford V-10. Marc heard Barry White's baritone coming from the truck's speaker system. Cameron climbed down off his red beast, and the first thing he said was, "The hell you think you're doing? I didn't approve this."

Cameron was pointing at the image on the billboard. His face was red, furious.

It was up there now, above them, available for anyone with eyes, Marc's image blazing under the cheap Vegas sun. Marc was annoyed to see yellow paint splotches on the left quadrant, from those damned pneumatic paint ball guns, from some damned teenage delinquents, probably.

"It gets the message across," Marc said, prepping for confrontation. "People need to think about life."

"And looking at death will make them do that?" Cameron asked.

"Perhaps."

"You know the kind of phone calls I'm going to field for this stunt? We don't even know if this is *legal.* Take it down."

"Six-month lease," Marc said, reminding Cameron of their shared document, and then he added, "Paid in full. Up front."

"Fine. I'll remove it myself."

"Breach," Marc said.

Cameron sighed and shoved a letter at him. It was from the city. The letter, addressed to Mr. Dunlop, spoke of ordinances, proper street signage, and asked the owner of the billboard to call the following number to discuss the matter. "And you look like such a decent guy," Cameron said. "That sign is going to nuke me here."

+ + +

At St. Mary of the Valley Marc sat on a cold hard pew and remembered them. He did not pray. He rarely prayed. Prayer for him was in remembrance. Some lady, a church worker in a floral dress, was moving cardboard boxes from the altar to the sacristy. Before him, on the cross, Jesus was bloody, the bloody version—the drama of thorns, of nails.

Without meaning to, Cameron had put it succinctly: to think of death was to think of life. Across the empty nave was a small village of votive candles, lit by the living to remember their dead.

This parish priest said nothing of abortion. These days, among many church communities, the subject was becoming a topic only discussed in confidence. The church didn't want to upset anyone. The church needed to retain its dwindling membership. So the man's sermons were lessons about community, love, and forgiveness.

Marc's parents were taken by age. His sister went at thirty-six, from stage four breast cancer. Then his wife, his daughter. His family had exploded before him into molecules. Yet his feet were still part of this earth. Marc walked alone, cursed and bearing it, continuing on in the direction of another month, another year, his life a series of days.

Marc spent his days driving, hunting for another available sign, another opportunity.

He spent his days tacking fliers to community corkboards.

He spent his days with the breath of life inside him, the burden of life on him, with his hazard lights flashing, safely pulled to the freeway's shoulder, gazing up at his billboard.

He retrieved Danika from her bomb-shelter apartment and drove her through the dusty streets to the clinic. She smelled oddly feminine, which was unlike her, a faint whiff of citrus drifting through the car. He remembered how, not long ago, Emily would steal spritzes from his wife's stash. Danika was also wearing Emily's white-and-purple dress, and she looked good in it, but her whole, clean look was spoiled by what was on her lip. There was an ugly red gash on it. A cut. Marc hoped someone hadn't hit her. Marc asked about it, but Danika didn't want to talk, until she finally said, "We saw your billboard last night. A bunch of us were out driving. Totally gruesome."

"How so?"

"*How* so? Fuck, you are funny."

Danika tromped inside the clinic and Marc settled into a thick paperback thriller. He adjusted the sun visor, keeping the heat off his neck. Not fifteen pages in, the young woman returned to the car, earlier than expected.

"That's it with him," she said. She slammed the car door. "I'll be seeing a different doctor now, thank you very much. I told you I didn't like him. He asked about my lip."

"And what happened to your lip?"

"You too?" she said. Her eyes were wide. "You too?"

Danika drew her knees to her chest. The young woman looked as though she had an uneven staircase inside her. Her collarbone protruded sharply from her chest, like an instrument beneath the skin. She turned and put her cold hand on his forearm. It was the first time Marc had been touched in a long while. "I just don't know how to do this," she said to him.

He made the decision. He took her to a diner with an Australian Outback theme. Painted boomerangs decorated the walls. He ordered enough food for four, but Danika only ate three bites, not even half her plate, and not even enough nourishment for one.

+ + +

He'd acquired the high-res images from an Eastern European anti-abortion coalition for a fee. Somehow the group had access to mid- and late-term aborted fetuses inside a hospital setting. Somehow the pictures were captured. Marc didn't ask questions. The coalition hosted an online library that accepted credit cards. Initially it was difficult to look at the crushed skulls and blendered body parts, all of it backdropped by a red placental sheen.

On first arriving in Vegas, he gambled. Anger was his guide— anger, anger from loss, and the kind of survivor's guilt that required steady supplies of antacid. He threw money away on slots, on craps, on blackjack, but mostly blackjack, since that game had the best odds for a reduced man. He was nothing but a vaporous presence in the checkout line, just another dumbstruck face among the heavy-lidded eyes on downtown sidewalks. Eventually he floated, in his confusion, toward the last available light, a man broken, in need, walking the earth with little in his mind but expectancy. He returned to what he knew, to bedrock solid enough to hold his burdens. The Church, no matter where he wandered, was there.

His first act of defiance was to duct-tape photocopies of dismembered fetuses to his car doors. People looked, yes. People looked at *him.* Some even yelled. All this sin and vice, and people were aiming their sharp words at him? That was okay: as long as they looked and saw. And then, one night, he forgot to peel the photocopies off his car. That was it. By the next morning both side-view mirrors were disassembled.

Las Vegas Metro knew Marc Maldonado well. One afternoon, he stopped by headquarters on Sunrise. At the reception desk he asked for Sergeant Olsen. The Sergeant had called him in for an additional statement. The sleeping man in the suv was Marc's third drunk driver.

Sergeant Olsen, a bald man, and apparently happy to be strong, leaned back in a squeaky metal chair, paperwork spread across his desk. "Isn't there something else you'd rather be doing?" the Sergeant asked Marc.

"Well, if *you're* not doing it," Marc said.

Olsen shook his shiny head. "We *are* doing it. The best way we know how."

It was a ridiculous conversation, and Marc, bouncing on his heels, urged the officer to speed things along. Yes, Marc had seen the vehicle moving unpredictably. Yes, he'd followed the driver. Yes, he'd removed the man's keys from the ignition. Yes, he'd called the police.

Sergeant Olsen made Marc sign a form.

Marc cracked his knuckle as he pushed through the exit. The sun came down like a hammer. He cracked another knuckle in the Honda, regurgitating bits of the conversation. Marc thought of himself as protector, an Army of One, putting the streets right, doing what needed to be done. Why did it bother others when he put his foot forward?

Later, after driving around town without a destination, he stopped by the Stratosphere's concierge desk. He was powered by irritation, he was powered by faith, and to his surprise he purchased two tickets for a helicopter tour of the Grand Canyon's southern rim. Also promised in the package were views of Hoover Dam, Lake Mead, and an extinct volcano. The promotional bundle put him back a grand. So there: that would be fun. So there: it was done. He'd have some fun. *There.* He'd done it, made time for *him*, for fun, but then, shoving the receipt into the glove compartment, he reconsidered. What if some horrible hand plucked them from the sky? Young pregnant women should be resting among pillows, not whizzing through cloudwork, not blazing over desert hardpan in a glass-bubbled aircraft. Young pregnant women needed tending to by others, and young pregnant women definitely didn't need to be smoking.

"You know better than that," he said to Danika when she got in the car. She reeked. Her clothes, *his daughter's* clothes, threw off hints of half a pack—at least. The smell of cigarette smoke surrounded her like some force field. He summoned the tone he once used on Emily. "You have to start thinking about another person's life," he said.

Danika's eyes shot up, in that teenage way. "And when are you ever going to start thinking about your own life?" she said. "This? This is what you do with your time?"

He ignored her and put the car in drive.

She gave him a different address. Danika's new OB/GYN was just blocks from the hospital. He liked that. It was within the radius of safety. The office, like the last, catered to the underclass. He managed to thumb through forty-eight pages of his courtroom thriller before Danika returned to the car. She plopped her feet against the dashboard again. She was holding an appointment card.

"So, this doctor is okay? You like him?" he asked.

"Her," Danika said.

He nodded. "Okeydokey. Too late for lunch," Marc said. "An early dinner, maybe?"

Marc deduced from the way Danika held her fork that she came from an unprivileged background. A home without motivation. An old house, he imagined, with weeds spotting the yard. He sometimes wondered how such pitiful situations could produce daughters with such fierce, pretty eyes.

"I've been meaning to ask. There's this place I hit on Sundays," he said when her fettuccine arrived.

"It's called church and, no, I'm not interested," she said. "I can read you from a mile away."

"It might give you some direction. It's a community, Danika. New mothers need support. And a baby needs that too."

Danika slammed her hand on the Formica tabletop. His spoon jumped. Other patrons turned. "I am more than a baby incubator," she said firmly. "I'd rather talk about something else."

Marc's thoughts drifted to the fresh receipt in his glove compartment. He wouldn't mention it. His cheeks burned with disappointment. He considered getting a refund, scrapping the whole deal. Danika was acting like a shit. And when his own daughter would act like a shit, he'd put her to work, funnel her behavior into something constructive. But this one, this one wasn't his. This one had her own hot blood, her own way of moving in the world.

Why did He take her from him?

+ + +

Cameron and his phone calls. One voice mail, followed by another. Marc agreed to meet Cameron at the lot again. And when Cameron arrived, late, he orbited Marc's Honda several times before jerking to a stop. The guy's mud flaps were tinted in fine red dust.

"Okay, this really has to go," Cameron said.

Marc was saddened to witness it. Some joker vandal in the night had jumped the chain link fence, scaled the billboard's spine, and spray-painted a fairly decent rendition of Mickey Mouse on his billboard sign. Now the dead fetus's hand looked like it was shaking Mickey's. The sight of it nauseated him.

"We have an agreement," Marc said to Cameron.

"Agreement? Just look at that!" Cameron screamed. "Mickey Mouse on top of an abortion! Jesus. I never agreed to this."

Cameron opened the fence and they stood beneath the monstrosity. Neither man had words. But Cameron was right. With the flow of moving cars filling their ears, people were definitely seeing this, and it had to be cleaned.

First they tried the hose. Its weak spray only wet the bottom portion of the vinyl. Cameron swore and kicked at a wood pallet. At last Cameron fetched soap and a bucket from a nearby auto shop. Marc climbed the metal ladder to the narrow platform, raising the bucket with rope. Up above, he had views to the south, of Circus Circus, of the Mirage and The Venetian. Distant mountains were red, white, with rocky eroded tips. Everything else was dry desert basin, a city on top of it, a spot, perhaps, where no life should exist.

"And make sure you get all of Mickey," Cameron yelled up at him. "Jesus Christ on a stick. My granddaughter might see that."

+ + +

Weeks later Danika wasn't waiting for him on the sidewalk. And her shifty roommates didn't know where she'd gone. The pair stood side by side, framed by darkness, as though purposely blocking the mess behind them, the beer bottles and potato chip bags and one solitary mattress, which lay like a corpse on the floor. The boy, who ascribed to some tribal philosophy of rings and tattoos and indigent clothing, said to Marc, "You can try back later. I don't know where she went."

Danika had never missed an appointment.

That night he stayed up late, worrying over her well-being. That split lip, her sleazy dwelling, the tattoo on that kid's neck that looked like a lit fuse. Marc couldn't sleep. So he grabbed his keys and waited on the street outside her building, trying to isolate her silhouette behind the thin blinds. For days afterward he wondered if he should contact her doctor. But, of course, no: that relationship was privileged.

He focused on the streets, driving at night, hunting for drunk drivers. His concerns segued to landing another rentable billboard. Cameron was constantly bothering him. Always calling, begging him to take down the sign. A refund, Cameron said, a full refund: he'd give Marc his money back. No questions!

At last Marc located an empty billboard on the desert highway leading into the city. Of course: it was ideal. Visitors arriving from Los Angeles would pass it when driving into town. The opportunity lay on ranchland, private property, and he wouldn't have to worry over city ordinances. A person would need to leap a ten-foot tensile fence to get anywhere near the sign.

This sign looked like the better option, especially when it became clear that Cameron was not abiding by their agreement, which Marc saw for himself not long after. He was driving the freeway, heading toward the sign one day, in order to check on further defacement, when from the freeway he saw something off.

Up in the air, inside an industrial bucket lift, was the short man himself, dangling high above a big white truck. The stout little bastard was at the billboard, *Marc's* billboard, attempting to peel away the vinyl panels with some kind of tool.

Marc accelerated down the off-ramp, pulled several illegal turns, and skidded to a stop outside the fence.

"Breach!" Marc yelled up at Cameron. He ran underneath the bucket. "Breach!"

"It's what's right!" Cameron yelled. Marc saw the man working faster. A slight breeze carried Marc's thrown bottle cap eastward. He searched the sunbaked lot for something else to throw. He spotted the desiccated husk of a red brick. He did not want to harm Cameron. He just wanted to stop him. Cameron kept glancing over his shoulder as he worked. And soon, to Marc's horror, Cameron gained purchase on an edge, yanking the panel. Part of Marc's sign drooped.

"I want a refund!" Marc yelled.

"Too late!"

The door of the white truck was unlocked, the keys stupidly in the ignition. Marc hopped inside, put it in reverse, and began backing the vehicle away. Cameron stooped inside the bucket, his hands visible around the lip. What angered Marc more, after Cameron threw the utility knife at him, then his cowboy boot, was the belt. Cameron actually threw his belt, which bounced off the windshield as Marc reversed the vehicle, easing it forward and onto the street, sailing the lift, with Cameron inside it, through the oven-like air.

The following afternoon a phone call roused him from a nap. Marc's mouth tasted metallic, and he didn't recognize the incoming number. He thought it might be a lawyer. He'd phoned several to inquire about his breached contract.

"Mr. Maldonado?" asked a woman.

Marc said, who wanted to know?

"I'm calling on behalf of Danika Hooper," she began.

The air left his lungs. Marc listened. To tamp the heat inside his chest, to control his fury, he scribbled zeros on a piece of scratch paper, listening to the nurse, writing down her major points, namely one word. *Procedure,* she kept saying, Danika's *procedure.*

Marc already knew the address, and when he hung up he hurled the phone against the wall. His elderly neighbor, Mr. Timmerman, would ask about that. He didn't care. He considered leaving her there, abandoning her to wallow in post-sedation. And then he thought of leaving this forsaken place, with its endless strip malls and promises of instant wealth and carnal release.

In the car he grabbed the wheel and shook it with all the violence he could summon. His jaw ached. Why was he so cursed, why so many curses on one man? Marc Maldonado was a man alone, and the world around him kept departing.

It was a standard office, tight-woven, wall-to-wall carpet with women's magazines beside houseplants. Air-conditioning bit into his sinuses.

The nurse, a woman younger than her phone voice, was expecting him. "She's been here for hours," the woman said. "Office policy is to bring your own ride. She lied. She told us you were outside."

Farther in, through the door, the office was more hospitalized: steel trays and shiny instruments and glass containers with cotton balls. He wondered where they'd taken what was left, wondered if there had been a prayer over it.

Danika was in a mechanical bed at the end of the hall, wearing Emily's dress from Sausalito, that foggy weekend, clams for dinner, a day's hike down Mount Tam. Sunlight dropped through the blinds and painted her young face in stripes.

The sight of her in bed turned his lungs cold, but the hardness usually in her eyes had vanished. She looked exactly like what she was, a lost young woman. He went to her. When she reached for his arm his legs nearly gave.

"Sorry your billboard didn't work on me," she said.

The nurse stood in the doorway, pursing her lips in a tight smile, holding her hands in a bunch.

Marc escorted the girl from the room, down a stairwell, into the car. Danika told him she felt wobbly, but, really, okay. It was not what she'd expected. "In fact I don't even feel—"

"Let's not talk about it, Danika. Please."

There was nowhere decent for her in this town. Her apartment was not safe for a young woman in recovery. That was nowhere for anyone. It hurt him that there was nowhere she could convalesce, including his own dark pathetic two-bedroom. This was no place to live. As far as he was concerned, every grain of desert sand could liquefy and swallow the whole business.

A worry gained hold inside him. When he was gone, when he was absorbed into creation's great energy, who would step forward to act as redeemer? He grew furious at Cameron, at the all-around street signage. Nothing spoke of the proper messages. On busses, taxis, walls, on kiosks and as vehicle wraps, not one of them calling for compassion, not one of them recognizing his great, ongoing grief.

He struck his fist on the dashboard. Danika jumped. She looked at him with a lifetime in her eyes. He caught himself turning where he should have kept driving. Then he accelerated, crossing two lanes at a time.

"What are you doing?" Danika asked.

The father in him, after such prolonged silence, struggled to reappear, and he knew he could no longer have his feet on this earth, on this hot concrete, not at this time.

"Marc? Where are you taking me?"

He drove south on Las Vegas Boulevard, past tourists parading in drunken groups and New York, New York and Mandalay Bay and that black freak-show pyramid. He wanted his one life to mean something. And if he couldn't find answers for himself, he hoped he could help Danika find hers. And he needed, he *needed,* he suddenly understood, he needed an animal, a companion, yes: a cat.

He stopped beside the airport's executive terminals. The sign on the building was far more professional than his rinky-dink attempt at signage. Two other cars occupied the lot.

"You're serious?" Danika said.

"If you're game," he said. "Check the glove compartment."

Danika removed the folded receipt.

"Depends if they have room for two more," he said.

The helicopter was climate controlled and allowed passengers 180-degree views. Donning a big black headset, Danika looked tiny, tiny but well and embodying this one decisive day. Soon the rotors began and Marc felt his heart shake as the steel beast hummed to life. Adrenaline flooded into him. And they lifted, smoothly. The pilot pulled away from the earth. Marc clenched onto a handle, momentarily disoriented. The city's ugliness diminished as they ascended, their perception of the world sliding into a new kind of knowing. The Strip, and its ridiculous buildings, soon looked like mere child's toys. They climbed upward, thousands of feet in the air, and he watched Danika's mouth play into a smile and disappear. She would love, and be loved, and she would one day come to understand the magnitude of her verdict. Marc released his grip on the handle, urging himself to let go, and they went, momentarily untethered from the world and into the day's pale light.

TODOS SANTOS

A wave jumped at the reef, and crested, and peeled off, misting Tom's salty dreads. Only Luis had decided to join him in the lineup this morning. Luis was good like that, usually game for a session. Despite the early hour Luis already looked blunted-up. His red eyes searched for the next perfect set. Tom paddled away from his friend, away from the light rip, feeling calmed by the water. It was the same sort of tranquility he thought Luis probably got from smoke. Nevertheless, there were times when he was out alone in it, brief, contained moments when dark, hulky shadows swam underneath his naked toes. But Tom, long ago, had learned how to avoid thinking about shadows.

There was a lull, and the water flattened. Soon another set approached. Tom picked a roiling, aqua slug. It hit from behind. A whisper of shoreline wind glassed out the face as he trimmed a tight line. He jumped aboard several more lefties before he saw Linda waving her yellow bandanna at him from the beach.

All morning he'd watched rental jeeps stirring dust on the desert road that led down to their cove. Business at his hut was picking up, but the tourists bled him of patience. Tourists often trashed his beach and clogged the lineup with dreams of catching a clean, Baja wave. Tourists over the years had changed the vibe of his backwater seaside rancho, but he couldn't turn down eighty dollars a head. That's what people paid him to learn how to paddle on the sand like a bunch of high-centered turtles. Tom watched Linda ascend the sloped beach, drawing pleasure from her long,

tan, scissoring legs. She passed beneath his hand-painted sign—
Tom's Office.

At the hut, Linda was leaning on an old foam board that doubled as the counter. He quivered his board and overheard her explaining the standard waiver to a family of three. Another family
was in line behind them. He knew Linda got annoyed with him
whenever she worked while he was in the water, and this time was
no different. She caught his elbow and dug her nails when he tried
sidestepping on his way to the hammock in the palapa. His arms
were noodled, and he felt in line for a nap.

"Doesn't this kid need to be a little bigger for waves this size?"
she asked him.

Tom considered the blond boy. Then he looked out at the
breaking chin-highs. The waves would reach the boy's forehead.
"When he falls," Tom said to the kid's father, "it'll clean his sinuses.
So just keep him in the soup, okay?" The father nodded, smiled,
and mussed the boy's hair.

While the kid's parents looked over their forms, Linda surprised him by reaching for the drawstring on his shorts, and tugging. "Another letter from your mother arrived," she said with
some coziness easing into her green eyes. From a wood cubby she
pulled an envelope and tapped it against his wet chest. "Ever going
to open them?" He plucked the envelope from her fingers.

Three other letters were on his desk in the storage room. Tom
closed the door and unfolded the most recent, expecting to read
about his mother's boring church potlucks, but the heaviness of
her opening line whipped up the past like a gale. Even from a distance of 6,000 miles, Tom could hear his mother's Long Island
voice vibrating off her tight, strangulated cursive. The boy was
now eighteen, she wrote. Tom's legs softened and he felt behind
him for the steel chair, and sat. The boy's mother had reached out
to his mother. The boy now wanted to meet him.

+ + +

How it happened wasn't a mystery. He fell in love with a thing, he
followed the thing, and before long the thing had its hooks in him

and it was the only thing he knew. He was a surfer, but he resented the stereotypes.

Every so often he paid a visit to the church on the zócolo. The church was probably the only part of him not to fully unglue from his mother's ways. Plus, Tom liked the town padre, a man with tiny, busy hands who sat in the plaza on Saturdays and handed out free mangoes from his orchard. Tom never attended Mass, but he visited the padre because the man's judgments were light, and in the small, transient town, with its ebb and flow of tourists and snowbirds, the church seemed to him the only rooted ground.

Early morning Tom parked on Avenida Hildago. The sun buffed the edges of his jeep's rearview and bougainvillea perfumed the air. He tugged on his dreads, and with two rubber bands he wrapped the salty ropes as tight as a bundle of sage. He spotted Rainy dragging a sawhorse out of her photography studio. She waved. He returned it. A few other expats were on a bench blowing steam off coffee cups. His gal Linda, when she'd arrived with her backpack, with her dog-eared Mexico guidebook, took fast advantage of the new yoga studios in town. Tom liked her type, the roll-around kind, who after sessions in bed would blow in his ear about Dharma.

Even though he didn't like to admit it, the high, hollow nave of the Iglesia de Nuestra Señora de La Paz tickled him in the same way the water did. He knew a thing, and over time the thing just snagged with its hooks. He felt a crazy sense of childhood wonder as he walked through the church's tall doors. He dipped four fingers in the holy water font and spritzed his eyes. Then he waited in a pew at the back. A sliver of blue light fell from a stained glass window and caressed his knuckles. Throughout his boyhood his mother had been a strict Sunday worshipper, and she'd dragged him along until he'd finally gagged down the confirmation wafer. His mother still worshipped, energetically. She even kept his father in an oak box on her mantel alongside all her other holy curios, as though it were her shrine.

At last, Tom saw the padre pad across the sanctuary toward

the confessionals. He waited for three elderly campesinas to enter, and say their peace, before his turn came.

The padre's window slid sideways. The man's chubby face was braided by black lattice. "Ave Maria Purisima," the padre said to him.

"Sin pecado concebida," Tom said. "Padre, tengo catorce meses sin confesarme."

It had been about fourteen months. Tom listened for the sound of footsteps outside the confessional. He didn't want one of his neighbors to overhear him. He heard the padre's raspy breathing, and he rolled his confesión into English, since he didn't want the padre to understand him either. He never knew whether or not the man could understand him. "Yeah, well, so my son doesn't know me," Tom whispered. "Because I wasn't around."

Tom held in his stomach. Uttering those words drenched him in a weird kind of guilt. He disliked the feeling. He tried to shake it off.

There was silence. "Sí, sí," the padre eventually said, as the man always said, and Tom awaited his benevolent sentencing. "Dale gracias a Dios porque es bueno. Reza un Ave Maria, hijo."

Together they went through the Acto de contrición, which Tom read off a Xeroxed photocopy tacked to the confessional's wall, and then he breezily made the sign of the cross and entered a wood pew to blow through his small penance. He pressed knees to the kneeler and held his hands in that way. Through the high yellow walls he heard gulls crooning outside. All around was the image of the Holy Mother, but what intrigued him now was the symbol of her suffering Son, those thorns, that ridiculous body of tendons, which always struck him as contrived. Tom sat back, rubbing his shoulders into the hard pew. He could never really get into believing, but going through the motions, participating in the ritual, helped him feel weighted down. The ritual anchored the buoyancy in his chest. Over the years, whenever thoughts about his son happened, Tom had drowned them by quickly turning his attention elsewhere, anywhere—the sky, the sea, the brine of a woman's neck. The mental exertion required to keep his son from his mind was exhausting, and it had left him as empty as a cup, had left him feeling that his toes might one day detach from the soil, and off he'd float.

He knew his mother had the idea that he'd been sleeping in the dirt all these years with a leaf as his blanket. But things had never been that way. It was more like keeping a baker's hours: rising before dawn, listening for the locomotive sound of breakers exploding outside the bamboo walls of a beachside cabana. Surfing had been an easy transition into something that filled him with a satisfaction he'd never known in her tacky, six-bedroom mansion-ette. The pull started early, during a teenage vacation in Puerto Rico that became, wondrously, his life.

Water grabbed hold, and he coasted with the tides. After Puerto Rico came Huntington Beach. After Huntington Beach, Hawaii. A phone call from an acquaintance would wake him in the middle of the night: Hanalei or Honolua Bay were throwing out heavy righties, and soon after he'd stagger off the plane, dis-oriented, gunk in his eyes, trying to remember if he had landed on Maui or Kauai. He followed new friends with complicated weather maps and knowledge of buoy readings, and then there were newer friends, and sometimes no friends, until eventually he was alone with the seasons.

Florida, a beach in Florida, was where he met Ali. Sweet, sugary Ali, who had small teeth in her gummy smile and bright, caffein-ated eyes. She had been a young woman, Tom remembered from time to time, who knew how to wear tight jeans.

But her jeans weren't nearly as tight as the conversation that remained a distinct memory in his mind: Ali, in her small studio apartment, leaning against a green pastel wall and playing with her cuticles and delivering the news. He remembered Florida sun bursting through the blinds. He remembered sitting down—he believed he sat down—and listening to her nervous chatter, not knowing how to respond, but eventually he set a sweaty beer bottle on a women's magazine and asked, "How far along?" Before Ali went to the bathroom, she bent to peck his temple, and he pan-icked. He went for the door. He went for the road. He went.

+ + +

Tom bought an international calling card from the mercado. He phoned his mother to ask if she'd received his reply. He listened to her crimped voice.

"Don't screw this up for us," she said to him. "All this time and I finally get to be a grandmother. At least I still have a few years left."

"Oh, Jesus Christ. Stop it, Mom."

"Language," she said.

When he heard back from her with the date, with the flight confirmation, Tom couldn't sleep for days. Concentrating was impossible. His surf lessons were uninspired, half-assed attempts, and one customer demanded a refund. He felt off as the days counted down to his son's visit. He felt uneasy. He felt nervous. He felt an odd tight weight center inside him, which gave him backaches. He tried to right himself by following waves up and down the coast, ripping along reef breaks and beach breaks. The waves at San Pedrito, at least, were leavening into pretty tubes. One morning Luis sat beside him at the hut, the stench of weed just thrumming off his T-shirt. Luis patted Tom's shoulder and said, "Qué onda compa? Listen, let me take your spots on the chalkboard. Only two families want lessons today." Tom blamed his absentmindedness on allergies, on the changing seasons, on getting older.

He did not swallow the Eucharist, but more and more, before driving to the hut, he spent mornings in the cool calm quiet of the Iglesia. Unlike before, he considered the cross with renewed focus, trying to get somewhere with it, but goddamn, he couldn't.

There were lightning veins in the sky on the morning he told Linda. How could he keep it from her? It was inevitable. She'd find out soon enough. They were at the hut, both of them watching broad, sallow clouds hovering over the eastern cliffs and shouldering out the sun. It was a washy surf day, nothing out there but closeouts. Wind belted across the beach and threw sand in the faces of beachgoers. Tourists dumped sand from shoes and brushed their arms and ran to the line of jeeps. The wind brought a chill. Soon rain came. Sheets of water jumped off the thatched eaves, and Linda held herself in a hug and leaned against him. Her hair smelled of lemons. He liked when she used the lemon peel shampoo.

"My son's coming to visit," he said into her ear.

Linda detached from his shoulder, straightened herself, and turned to look him in the eyes. She was such a pretty creature. "You never told me you had a son."

"I didn't know how serious we were," he said.

"Jesus, Tom." Her eyes hardened. "I've been here for six months. I've been with *you* for six months. How could you keep something like this from me?"

"I didn't know how long you'd be around," he said. "People pass through. It's that kind of town." He hadn't meant to turn their conversation into a state of the union, but here it was. "I don't usually tell people," he said.

"What? That you have a kid? Why not?" she asked.

"I don't know."

"Why don't you know?"

"I don't want to think about it," he said. "I try not to think about him."

"And why's that? He's your *son*."

"I know," he said. "But thinking about him—it just hurts. So I try not to."

"Jesus, Tom," she said. "Jesus."

"His name's Simon," he said. "I don't know a thing about him."

Linda stared at him in a new way. She pressed him for more details. The mother, Tom explained, had returned sun-kissed and pregnant to North Carolina a long, a very long time ago. As his eyes wandered up Linda's twenty-eight-year-old thighs, her muscles clutching beneath goose-pimpled skin, he told her what he knew of Ali's family, how they were religious, how the issue wasn't taken care of, and that during those ten months he couldn't remember where he'd even been—El Salvador? Costa Rica?—odd-jobbing to pay for flights and enough room for his feet and his board. Eighteen years was a long time. He struggled to remember how it all happened.

"About a year after his birth, a summons arrived at my mom's place," Tom told her. "From this stupid, junked pay phone on this filthy Nicaraguan street—you wouldn't have believed this pay phone, Linda, just a ball of wire—I told my mom to ignore the summons. Maybe that was a mistake."

"Maybe that was a mistake?" Linda said.

"Another summons came. Ignored that too. Ali got sole custody."

"And you haven't ever visited him?"

"There were so many guys at Cocoa Beach that summer," Tom said. "Everyone was sharing towels and showers and beds. I didn't know if I was the one."

"Are you?"

"Yeah, I guess."

"How do you know?"

"I knew Ali. I knew the kind of girl she was."

"Okay, okay," Linda said, fidgeting with a chipped nail. "I'm trying to understand this." She paced. She sat. She stood. She bit off a piece of her nail.

A week later Linda left on a charter bus headed for La Paz. She was angry, she said. He'd kept too large of a secret, she said. But even in her anger she was kind to him, never yelling. Her anger manifested as rolling away from him in bed. As it happened, Linda volunteered to leave during his son's visit. She needed time to think, she said. She had to take time and mull over this new information. Linda, anyway, he figured, had only brought along a backpack and a book, and she took those items with her to La Paz. Whether or not she ever returned was her decision. He hoped she would.

He knew before long that something along these lines was bound to happen. In the past, during two rare moments of weakness, he'd told two previous lovers about his son, about not knowing him. Those women didn't stay long after the disclosure. So he'd made a silent pact to keep it to himself. But he had to tell Linda his son was visiting. He didn't have a choice. Whatever happened with Linda would happen. And anyway, he knew another hippie surfer would eventually arrive in town, and the townspeople would point their fingers down the road to his hut, and he would give her a job. And she would need a pillow, and the waves would roll and roll, and he would lie next to her, distant and uncapturable and thinking of wet swells.

+ + +

He awoke early on the day. Outside, the sky was shot through with spectral colors. He was surprised by how it electrified him, the troposphere organizing light and dust into beauty and stretching it upon the backs of pillowy clouds. Tom stood at the window and watched the length of that magical minute, when magenta darkened in increments and turned ruby. Another minute passed, and then it was not the same, never again to be repeated—gone, as though nothing had happened.

All morning, a weird, buzzing excitement shifted through his chest, and it felt right to him. It felt good. He was nervous, sure, but even that felt good. Until now his days and weeks and years had been spent inside particles and elements, his liquidy footsteps no more able to leave an imprint than a soft breeze. But somehow, without much effort, without *any* effort, he had left an imprint. He had a son.

He'd told his mother to tell the kid's mother to tell the kid to meet him on the marina's breezeway in Cabo, which was equidistant from his town and the airport. Tom found it odd how he couldn't wait to see the kid's face. For one thing, it would cut out the middle people. He was a man, and this was his boy, and he wore a red scrunchie in his dreads so that Simon would recognize him. He'd chosen the marina because it was a public place, and the shuttle bus from Los Cabos Airport let off nearby; and because, in the event his son cried or something, Tom wanted it to happen within the tourist zone, where the only ones watching would be college tequila crews and fat Texans in Bermuda shorts, and nobody cared about them.

In Cabo, he strolled into Greenberg's and ordered a Tecate from the bartender. As soon as the beer hit his coaster, Tom saw the kid outside, standing decent and strong under sunlight. It had to be him. The kid was early. He was pulling a plastic roller suitcase. He also humped around a backpack firmed at the shoulders. Tom felt the strangest, most pleasurable pain swim through his legs.

He left the beer after one sip and walked over. "Simon?"

The kid turned. He was a good-looking boy. Tom held out his hand, and his son's violent grip startled him. Tom quickly pulled his hand away and scratched his neck. "So," Tom said to the boy, "three days. What do you want to do?"

Simon, staring into his eyes, said, "I—I don't know."

He looked at his son, as he was sure his son looked at him, scanning for similarities. Simon was compact. Brown hair, same eye color, a bit shorter than him, but with the strong shoulders of a waterman. A stranger hustled toward them from the public restrooms. The man pulled the same kind of roller suitcase Simon had. He waved over and yelled, "Simon! Simon! Wait for me!"

Simon said, "That's my dad."

"Oh," Tom said and took a step back.

Introductions were short. The stranger's name was Paul. Tom knew nothing about Paul, not even a whiff, and for a moment he imagined flying to Long Island and wringing his mother's neck. All the phone calls, all the back and forth letters, and she'd never once mentioned to him anyone named Paul.

"We finally meet the famous ne'er-do-well," Paul said in a low, booming voice. It was a voice that originated deep in the man's lungs and bothered Tom's eardrums.

"So, you ended up with Ali," Tom said.

Paul squinted. "She goes by Alison now."

The man was a bit older, soft thighs, polo golf shirt, with parted hair and angular canines the shape and color of bronze bullets. And the guy stood, Tom noticed, too close to his son. The pair dragged their identical suitcases as Tom led the trek to the parking lot. At his jeep, Tom insisted on lifting his son's suitcase—he knew his jeep and knew where to cram things—but Simon struggled with him over the plastic shell until, finally, the boy put his hands up and backed away.

Simon said little as they drove up the cape. But Simon's

stepfather liked to talk. The man laughed at his own jokes. Tom played with the idea of depositing Paul on the side of the desert highway. Paul worked as a certified public accountant, and that information struck Tom as just about right. Paul stated his occupation with a blend of pride and derision, as though Tom was supposed to feel daunted and shamed, but what Tom said, and what made his son snicker, was, "So you count beans."

Tom watched his son in the mirror. The sun dropped and the dying light painted Simon's cheeks gold. His son's gaze migrated across the ocean and to the hills. It was incredible how just looking at Simon lifted a wind in him. His son, Simon. Simon, his son. He could get used to it.

He stopped the jeep at the requested spot. The Hotel California. He knew of better boutiques in town but people liked this one for the song. In the lobby he waited near the couches while Paul got everything squared away at reception. His son stood beside his stepfather and extracted a foot from his flip-flop to scratch his well-formed calf with a toe.

"So. All ready for dinner?" Tom said after they'd checked in. "I already picked a place." He scratched his chin, feeling the bright expectancy of a first kiss, but the boy, his boy, Simon said, "Nah, it was a long flight."

"We ate at Dallas/Fort Worth," Paul said. "Three hour layover. Plus, this guy needs ten hours at least."

The wind from before left him. Only three days. He had three days. Still, they agreed on a time for the next morning. Tom said he'd like to head into the water for a session with his son, and Simon paused before saying, sure, okay, that sounded fine. Before he left them in the lobby, Simon dropped his backpack on the ground, unzipped it, and removed a large book. It was a massive, overstuffed photo album. Simon heaved it at him.

"Hey, this is for you," Simon said. He watched Paul set a hand on his boy's shoulder. "My mom made me put it together. It's about my life."

+ + +

A tight, hot ache gripped his chest with each new photograph. Later that night, Tom sat in bed, flipping through page after page after page of photos. The photos showed a boy's happy life. Soccer teams. Cub Scouts. Birthday parties. A waddling baby. A wise-ass teenager. Tom came across the same infant photo his mother had pegged to her fridge with a crucifix magnet.

Paul's face began appearing in the photos when his son had been a toddler. In the pictures Paul had a bushier helmet of hair. When Tom had time, he'd scissor the man out. He turned another page. It was like looking at etchings from a distant century. He tried to do the easy math, tried to triangulate where in the world he'd been when Simon—who looked, he couldn't tell, seven?—visited the Washington Monument.

It was too much information to ingest in one sitting. Thinking about Simon out there during the years left him exhausted, a body-wide exhaustion, like after sunburn.

He put the album on the floor and hitched up the blinds for a clean shot of sky. The bedroom in his small, whitewashed casita had excellent views with limitless access to long stretches of nothing, and he drew comfort from looking out into it. He got up and wandered through the rooms. He listened to the ocean echoing off the hills, and for a moment he began to miss Linda. She had left little reminders around the house. A potted barrel cactus, Tibetan prayer flags in the patio. There were a lot of similar tokens around his place, each deposited by the women who'd passed through. Over time he'd hardly had to decorate his casita at all. And already, already he missed brushing his thumb inside Linda's bra strap, and the way she'd swat at his hand. The way she played with the hair at her temple. And that thing she did in bed with her crook'd knees.

He fell into bed again. Buttressed against the headboard, he watched airplanes and satellites and dead stars sparkle and blink inside the warm, black night. Then he grabbed the photo album from the floor and started at the beginning, thinking of his own boyhood photos, where the face of his father was absent.

+ + +

In the morning Tom parked along the zócolo and was irritated to see Paul puttering around the shops. Paul was wearing white linen and looked like some holy monk. From the jeep Tom watched the guy cup his hand over his eyes and peek into several artist galleries. Before long, and to Tom's surprise, Paul strolled right into the Iglesia de Nuestra Señora de La Paz—as though he owned the place.

Tom followed him inside. From the vestibule he saw Paul kneeling in the front pew. Tom watched the man cross himself in the same serious way his mother did. To know Paul carried the faith put him on edge. By the way Paul tipped his head, by the way he held his hands in a tight ball, the man looked like he actually believed. Tom walked out. He waited in the plaza.

People paid Tom to help them douse their chins in spray. Often they bought T-shirts from his hut to commemorate the day. Few popped up on the first try, but his son, he popped, as though he'd inherited the stoke, and it was a gnarly thing to witness. Even if it was only soup, his son surfed it, laughing and hooting, and Tom followed closely behind with his knees on his board, holding Simon's tail to help him stay balanced.

When Simon had surfed too far in, Tom yelled at him to sit down. And Simon sat, gripping the board with his thighs, and the wave passed. His son's smile could have lit up the entire coastline. They paddled through the breakers again, as Tom had shown his son, duck-diving through the cool coming water until their shared struggle delivered them like saints to the lineup. Then Simon conquered a few more clean waves. Tom couldn't believe it. He could clearly see seams bursting inside his son, the instinct emerging, and as he watched Simon falling for a thing, his lungs heavier than they'd been in years, he thought he might be falling for a thing too. It was a beautiful morning. Down the beach Tom saw Luis having a hell of a time with a beefy kook in the water. The dude was refusing to bend his knees and kept leaning too far and nosing into the waves.

His son paddled over and grabbed the tip of his board. "This is pretty amazing," Simon said. "I didn't think I'd like it, but I do." Water leaked from the boy's nose. For a moment Tom studied Simon's hands, his knees and shoulders, none of it familiar, but every part of him somehow significant: even the wet tips of Simon's bangs, which looked like the teeth from a comb. "Good to be taught by someone who knows what he's doing," he said.

"Not just someone," Tom said.

"I guess I mean you," Simon said.

"Just remember," Tom said, "keep your board aimed out to sea. And don't get behind anyone on a wave. A wave comes and you fall off, and it could thrust your board into someone's spine."

"Yeah, I remember," Simon said. "And keep my back arched when I paddle."

"And never take off on someone else's wave."

"I know, I know. I got it," Simon said.

"And try to take off mid-wave, at an angle."

"I said I got it."

"Okay. I'm sorry."

"Wow," Simon said. "I can't believe the man said it."

Tom laughed, uncomfortably. So much missing time stood between them that his son's comment was entirely too heavy and complicated to unpack, and Tom quickly turned his gaze on a seagull caught by a breeze and moving sideways across the sapphire sky. Soon he noticed Simon looking toward the beach, where Paul was sitting in the sand like a black speck, his forearms draped over his knees. Tom was glad for the momentary distance from that man.

After a while Simon's arms began to shiver.

"Let's ride in," Tom said.

Simon carried his longboard one-armed up the beach, like a pro, and Tom walked alongside, sand gathering around his ankles. Tom said, "You did it." He tried slinging an arm over his son's shoulders, but Simon moved away from him.

Paul was holding three brown lunch bags as though showing off newly won trophies. The man had made them a cutesy little picnic spread on a beach towel.

"That's something out there," Simon said and dropped the board on the sand.

"I'd go out with you, but my hip," Paul said.

"You do need solid hips," Tom said.

During lunch Paul sat between him and his son. The wind had sculpted Paul's brown hair into a geeky upwarp, and Tom was irked by how the man tended to his lunch bag, how he counted everything inside, how he commented on every item he'd ordered. Paul even computed the number of mayonnaise packets. Paul's sandwich accidentally got a scoop of toe sand when Tom crossed his legs. Then Paul started in with questions, as though the man was scavenging for something in Tom's life that wasn't his to know.

"It's sort of a hidden cove," Paul said and bit into a pickle. "Is it hard to attract business down here?"

"The hut carries me," Tom said.

"Kind of an isolated town, too," Paul went on. "Is it hard to meet new people?"

"Yeah, like girls," Simon added, and smiled.

"You'd be surprised," Tom said.

"Oh yeah, how's that?" Paul asked.

"Women arrive here seasonally," Tom said. "Like fruit."

Paul squinted and nodded, as though he wanted him to say more.

"You should have seen the last one," Tom said and shaped his hands into twin cones and held them at his chest. "Let's just say she had big lungs."

"Keep on going," Paul said.

But Tom stopped himself when he noticed his son's balled fists. Maybe he shouldn't have said that. Maybe he went too far, got carried away. He was trying too hard to impress the kid. Whenever he got nervous, Tom sometimes had a problem with talking without thinking.

His son's eyes were darting and landing everywhere but on him. Paul's questions stopped, and the man popped the rest of the pickle in his mouth, smiling and chewing it open-mouthed. Almost proudly. Tom ate one bite of Paul's store-bought sandwich before shoving it back inside the paper bag, before depositing the bag in a trash can.

Paul said he wanted some time in the afternoon to read, and Simon offered the same lame excuse and tumbled out the jeep when Tom stopped at the hotel. The sun was dissolving into the Pacific and, without Linda around, his casita would be dark and silent. Tom wanted the boy to like him, but there was so little time. And what was that business, anyway, he wondered, with the mayonnaise packets? Paul even kept the ones he didn't use.

Later, at dinner, at a seafood restaurant, the waiter sat Paul and Simon directly in front of a lit aquarium. Tom took the chair opposite, but it bothered him when, every so often, tropical fish as bright as lollipops swam into his son's ear and out the other.

"We saw a donkey on the streets earlier. The thing wandered right into the hotel," Simon said.

"The housekeeper swatted it back outside," Paul said.

They laughed. Tom was peeved to hear how Simon's laugh sounded like Paul's.

"Sure, sure, cute funny town," Tom said. "But what did you think about today? The water?"

Simon took a moment before responding. "I thought those waves were kind of small."

"Good waves to learn on. Three feet. Waist high," Tom said.

Simon crossed his arms, and leaned back, as though he remained unimpressed.

"Okay, you want bigger?" Tom said. "There's a spot down the highway, but only veterans surf that wave."

"Might as well tell me about it, then," Simon said. "Since I'm sitting here."

The wave he told Simon about was not for him. Beyond some fairly manageable beach breaking waves was an outer reef, which was bordered by rocks that rose fifteen feet from the waterline. Situated between those ocean boulders was the wave. "It's something you only attempt after twenty years in the water," he said.

"Gee, golly, trippy," Simon said.

Yes, yes. His son was getting it.

"Exactly," Tom said, "trippy." And he believed he caught a brilliant gleam in his son's eyes, and only after a day—and often it only took a day to catch the bug. He was getting excited thinking about it. Tom had once known the reaction, a sort of chemical blossoming that Luis compared to a soulful acid hit.

Tom outlined the wave's personality for them, told them about its dangers, the rock and urchin bottom, the scar on his chin from a wipeout, and more than once Tom caught his son's eyes wandering to the ceiling, as though he was mentally conjuring the wave's dimensions. Paul tapped on his chin and turned his ear to hear him better. Tom's talk of the wave segued into talk of Hawaiian north shore tubes. Simon asked few questions. His son seemed too taken to respond, which created another full wind in him. And so he told his son about Australia. "That was probably when you were about two," Tom said. And he told Simon about Indonesia, and his year in Belize. "Oh, you should have seen it. You must have been eight years old by then, or something," Tom said. And he told Simon of those long, cold months surfing gray water on the Washington and Oregon coasts—when Simon was maybe ten?—but as he kept rolling out the stories he noticed Simon leaning back in his chair, his cheeks turning red, until Simon set down his glass of water and firmly grabbed his bicep and said, "Okay, enough. Please stop. I don't need to be reminded."

+ + +

They were waiting for him in the lobby holding different editions of the same paperback book. Like they were a two-man book club. A mystery novel, or something. Tom didn't ask. Paul was wearing linen again, and Tom could still feel his son's handprint on his arm from the night before, as though a hot iron had grazed him.

On their drive down the coast the expat radio announcer said to watch for precipitation in the next forty-eight hours, and when it hit, her voice said, keep a lookout for flash floods. Dry afternoons could quickly turn tidal, Tom knew, accompanied by thunder-and-lightning orchestras. He hoped it wouldn't be a stormy day. At the moment the sky was nothing but beauty. Sun was cresting the purple hills, rimming them in an otherworldly, pristine light. And his son sat up front, right beside him.

Tom pulled from the highway onto a dirt road. The jeep rattled along ruts. In the mirror he watched Paul's jowls jiggle. He glanced at Simon, who was quietly applying sunscreen to his forehead and had, as far as Tom could tell, a look of rested determination. Simon had agreed to try the water again. And Tom wanted another chance to win him over by showing off the wave.

On the other side of a palm grove they encountered a small encampment of tourists on the beach. Tom almost spat. He hated to see it. "Those goddamn know-it-all guidebooks are ruining everything," Tom said as he parked. "Used to be this place was for locals. Used to be you'd have the beach to yourself."

Campers were here, and several suntanning families. They watched peddlers scamper across the beach, skittering blanket to blanket, hawking straw vaquero hats and lemon tree vases. At the far end of the sandy, crescent cove, Tom saw a local shuttle bus parked under a palm tree. Its driver was standing in the blue shade, smoking.

"Well, I'll give it to you," Simon said, unfastening his seatbelt. "That is a bigger wave. Don't you think, Dad?"

By "Dad" Simon meant Paul, which Tom couldn't get used to. But anyway, the outer reef wave was indeed much bigger. Tom wanted his son to see it. The curling beauty off in the distance didn't appear too heavy from shore, but Tom knew that when you put your nose at the waterline it felt like a mountain coming at you. The power it created was awesome. Tom saw a nice barrel forming between the rocks. Any amateur kook could surf the inner shore break, but the outer break was dangerous. He'd keep his son near the shore.

Tom pulled the boards from the jeep. Few people were in the water. Signs in Spanish warned of an occasional rip, but Tom still spotted several bodyboarding speed bumps out there. They'd only get in the way.

While Simon wandered off across the beach, presumably to get a better view of that outer wave, Tom built two beds of sand, set down the boards, and unwrapped his wax from a sandwich baggie. Paul announced he needed to find a tree—as if Tom cared. He was relieved the moment the man walked away. Soon a young woman jogged over from the shoreline to interrupt his waxing.

"Are you Tom?" the young woman asked. Thin lines of water were running from her black bikini and down her legs. Her stomach was a firm pouch specked with translucent blonde hairs. Sunlight, from behind, haloed her face.

He told her, sure, yeah, he was Tom.

"Good. That lady at the grocery store in town said to find you," she said. "She told me to look for the battered red jeep. Everyone told me to look for your jeep. And here you are."

"Here I am," he said.

Her name was Katie, and she was hunting for a job. Tom told her to drop by his hut in a few days. Then he decided, as he watched her backside sway toward a white pickup truck, she had just earned the position. The bed of her truck was down, and he noticed a folded sleeping bag and camping gear.

Paul returned from his pee break to stand over him, annoying Tom with his fat calves, gazing down as though Tom was his captive. More and more Tom disliked the man. Disliked the man's square hairdo, his know-it-all grin, and his sausage fingers. Tom only had one more day with his son, only one more day of Paul. He looked around for Simon and located him on the cliff that overlooked the water. The kid was sitting on a rock. Tom noticed Paul's gaze align with his.

"He's a nice kid," Tom said.

"The best," Paul said.

"Ali did good work."

"We did," Paul said, "and we know."

Tom looked up at him. The muscles in Paul's jaw tightened as he put his hands on his hips and pushed them forward in a stretch. When Paul's back arched, he noticed a silvery cross appear in his chest hair. "It would be nice if you asked the boy a question every once in a while," Paul said. "He's going through a lot. Meeting you."

Tom was silent for a moment. "You think I'm not asking questions?" he asked.

"And I find it interesting how you decided to settle in Mexico," Paul said.

"Great climate, consistent waves."

"Sure, that," Paul said. "And North Carolina courts couldn't long-arm you into financial support."

Tom returned to his work, rubbing bumps of wax into his son's deck. He didn't look up again. He knew Paul was looking down. "He's eighteen," Tom said. "And anyway, I didn't have much to give."

"I can see that."

Oh, God. Paul sounded like his mother. "Listen," Tom said, growing annoyed. "I'm trying to show my boy something here."

My boy. That seemed to irk Paul, because he said, "You wouldn't know it by looking at me, but back in the day, when I was around Simon's age, I played in a ska band. Sure, I had my fun. And the only little reminder I have of that time is this indentation in my earlobe. You know, it's good to know when to say goodbye to something, and also when you shouldn't."

Paul was finished, thankfully. His shins turned into his calves, and Tom heard the man heading back toward the jeep. He watched Paul pull out a long umbrella borrowed from the hotel and pop the thing into a daisy. Then Paul organized a place in the sand and sat down without a towel.

His son was so unlike Paul. God, he disliked the man. There was nothing fat or flimsy about Simon, and he admired that. The kid had good reflexes, solid arms. Firm knots of muscle padded his hips, while that stepfather of his harbored a soft koala gut. A ska band? Oh, please.

Paddling into the mid-tide waves looked like easy business for Simon. They made it to the simpler, inner beach break, and Tom taught his son how to turtle roll his longboard to breach the belly of a wave. Simon tried surfing, caught one, tumbled several times, and then fell off more than Tom would have liked. Either the kid was jet-lagged or he was losing his hunger for the attack.

So they sat on their boards, drifting. Tom watched dust billow from the looming desert cliffs. Sunlight sifted through thin cloud canopies and threw light over half the beach while the other half was under shadow. He kept noticing Simon's interest roving to the towering rocks, to the bigger wave a hundred yards away. If his son kept at it, he'd someday get there.

"Does your mom still have that dimple?" Tom asked his son.

"What? I don't know," Simon said. "Yeah, sure, I guess."

Tom searched himself for another question. "I saw in the photo album that you visited Waikiki. What did you think?"

Simon raised his chin and squinted. "My dad had some kind of work conference," he said. "So he took me along."

"Oh," Tom said.

"We've gone a bunch of places. Including here. He likes having me along."

That guy, that uppity Catholic accountant on the beach, sitting safe and sound under an umbrella as though he might wilt. Tom zeroed in on him. He hoped a wind would come and knock the umbrella over. Tom stroked the water once, and said, "Paul," and he said to his son, "he can sometimes act like kind of a chode, don't you think?"

"A chode?"

"You know, a dick." Tom felt a kind of pressure shoot from his son's eyes and into his chest. "Oh, come on," he said. "I'm only joking. You know I'm joking. Right?"

Simon lay on his board, drifting for a while, his toes hanging off the tail, neither paddling closer to the lineup nor attempting to enter a wave. Tom felt the sun on his knees as he waited out the lengthening silence. He tried to think of something that might score his son's attention.

"Um, I've thought about you," Tom finally said. Simon tipped his head, suddenly looking soft, looking like a ground squirrel peering from a hole, but out of the corner of his eye he saw a gorgeous wave amassing. "Oh, shit. I need to grab this one," he said. He paddled hasty tugs and felt the lift and skimmed the face down into the trough, riding the wave for ten seconds before cutting back and falling on the board.

Simon was still bobbing in the water. Tom waved. He hoped Simon had seen his abilities. But for some reason Simon turned with three solid strokes. He aimed his board at the outer wave between the rocks. Tom watched for a half moment in disbelief. He was the stronger paddler, but there was something fierce and animalistic about his son's splashing. He couldn't believe it. Simon was heading directly for the monster wave. He yelled for Simon to stop, to turn around. His forearms burned as he tried to catch up. Simon was really moving, and getting closer to the impact zone. "Simon! Simon, stop!"

Spray hit, then the sound of watery thunder. Even on a good day Tom had trouble out here. He watched Simon paddle straight into the dissipating boil, not equipped with the tricks, the knowledge. Spume from a broken wave kicked the tip of his son's board, carrying him back. Still, he saw his son's strong arms work. Tom paddled harder, trying to get close enough to grab his son's foot. There was a brief lull, and then he saw a green hump unify and hit the reef, shaping into a double overhead behemoth, and his son turned his board parallel to shore, unzipped the Velcro ankle leash, and dropped like a stone in the water.

The wave came, and the abandoned longboard burst toward him. Tom dove late, without taking a breath, and the fin nicked his temple. He was under, in froth and blue darkness. The undercurrent caught his board, yanking his leash and his leg. His back raked across rocks. When he climbed the leash, breaking the water with a gasp, he saw Simon was already halfway to shore, swimming in a desperate freestyle. Simon's board thrashed in the chop, hopping around the water like a shot duck.

Tom tracked down the longboard through the waves and set it on top of his. His shoulder blade ached, his gash stung. He skimmed onto the beach on his knees. He saw Simon punching apart the fabric and spokes of the umbrella while Paul stood silent with elbows in the air and hands behind his neck. Tom felt blood oozing down his temple. His shoulder was spattered in pink. He threw the two boards down, and sat.

There had been good days on that Florida beach with his son's mother. They had shared laughter. They had shared hot skin. His reaction, after he'd found out, was to head into the surf and clear his mind at a distant break. An acquaintance later told him that Ali had walked up and down their beach, until the sun fell, searching for him, and now he saw his son walking away on another beach, stomping off in the direction of the shuttle bus. Paul was hurrying behind Simon, dragging the ruined umbrella.

Tom called out, "Simon, we have another day!"

Simon turned. "You've shown me enough!"

But Tom had shown him so little. He watched his son walk away, his strides steady, Paul's arm easing across his sunburned shoulders. Beyond them, in the distance, the young woman was sitting on her truck bed, swinging her naked easy feet.

A warm wind washed his neck. Tom shivered. For a moment he was struck by how fast and short the years were, and how impossibly big, and how rapidly the past could overtake the present. After all these years he could still remember Ali's delicate neckline. That was nearly all he had of her in his memory.

Tom gripped fistfuls of hot, wet sand, trying not to lift off, trying to contain the abundance of seeing his son before emptiness reclaimed its known place. He watched Paul's shadow mingle with his son's, and his son's shadow blend with the crowd gathering by the bus. And once more, Tom opened his hands and let go. He watched until his son became just another kid, until Paul was any other stranger, until their faces were indistinguishable from others, until fullness left with a breath, until they were nothing— gone, like so many sunrises, and again he was on a wide, pretty beach, the waves his companions, and everything was as it should be on the sand and in the cool water.

ACKNOWLEDGMENTS

I owe great thanks to the editors who first published these stories: David Lynn, Stephen Corey, Robert Fogarty, Laura Cogan, Oscar Villalon, Mitch Wieland, Jennifer Cranfill, and Alison Weaver. Thank you to my friends and teachers for your friendship, humor, advice, and guidance: Josh Benke, Ireri Rivas, Scott Benke, Caleb Cage, Ben Fountain, Julian Rubinstein, Aaron Gilbreath, Jesse Lichtenstein, Clifton Spargo, Antonya Nelson, Robert Boswell, Willy Vlautin, Pauls Toutonghi, Don Lee, Blake Nelson, Josh Weil, Mario Zambrano, Sam Moulton, Dan Engber, Andrés Carlstein, J.T. Gurzi, Dennis Cooper, Pardiss Kebriaei, Ann Townsend, Jillian Weise, Justin Tussing, Rus Bradburd, Sam Chang, Ethan Canin, Marilynne Robinson, and Andy Greer. For the tremendous gift of time and space I want to give big thanks to Martha Jessup and Douglas Humble at the Lannan Foundation. It's a great pleasure to work with the University of Nevada Press again, and I'm immensely grateful to Justin Race, Eric L. Miller, and Luke Torn. Huge thanks, naturally, to my agent, Maria Massie. Thanks to my mom, my stepdad, and my entire family for their love and support. As always, thank you Robin Romm, the world's greatest partner in crime: xoxo.

ABOUT THE AUTHOR

Don Waters is the author of *Sunland,* a novel, and the story collection *Desert Gothic,* which won the Iowa Short Fiction Award. His fiction has been widely published and anthologized in the *Pushcart Prize, Best of the West,* and *New Stories from the Southwest.*

His journalism has appeared in the *San Francisco Chronicle,* the *New York Times Book Review, Outside, The Believer,* and *Slate,* among other publications. Waters is a graduate of the Iowa Writers' Workshop and currently teaches at Lewis & Clark College.

Originally from Reno, Nevada, he lives in Portland, Oregon with his partner, Robin Romm, and their daughter.